# SUMMER PROMISE

D1453382

WITHDRAWN

**LARGE PRINT**
**MAINE STATE LIBRARY**
**STATION 64**
**AUGUSTA, ME 04333**

# SUMMER PROMISE

A collection of stories to suit every mood
...tender, funny, romantic, ironic, bitter-
sweet, nostalgic...

The couple in *Summer Promise* are placed
in an appalling situation, but nevertheless
in the warmth of southern France their relationship develops in an unexpected way. *The
Meeting* describes the ten-yearly reunion of
a group of friends which, dwindles each
time...and the two members most closely involved come to a decision that was, perhaps,
inevitable. *Model of Beauty* is set in a painting class, where the temporary illness of the
generously endowed model brings about
surprising consequences....

# Summer Promise

*by*
Elvi Rhodes

**MAGNA PRINT BOOKS**
Long Preston, North Yorkshire,
England.

JUN 0 7 1994

British Library Cataloguing in Publication Data.

Rhodes, Elvi
  Summer promise.

  A catalogue record for this book is
  available from the British Library

  ISBN 0 7505 0209 6

First Published in Great Britain by Transworld Publishers Ltd.,
1990.

Copyright © 1990 by Elvi Rhodes.

The right of Elvi Rhodes to be identified as the author of this work
has been asserted by her in accordance with the Copyrights, Designs
and Patents Act, 1988.

Published in Large Print 1992 by arrangement with Transworld
Publishers Ltd., London.

All rights reserved. No part of this publication may be reproduced,
stored in a retrieval system, or transmitted in any form or by any
means, electronic, mechanical, photocopying, recording or otherwise, without the prior permission of the Copyright owner.

Printed and bound in Great Britain by
T.J. Press (Padstow) Ltd., Cornwall, PL28 8RW.

All of the characters in this book
are fictitious, and any resemblance
to actual persons, living or dead,
is purely coincidental.

# Contents

# Summer Promise

'Are we nearly there, Mummy?' Nicola asked me.

'I hope so. According to the map it's not much further.'

'How will you know which house it is?'

'I'll find it, darling,' I said. 'Don't worry.'

I hoped I sounded more confident than I felt. Nora had been vague about the last bit of the journey.'

'Of course I've not actually been there,' she confessed. 'But Fiona says it's a super place.'

Fiona was the owner of the house. Through Nora she'd agreed that I could rent it for two weeks in the school holidays at a price which I could just about afford.

I had no business, I thought, to be splashing out on a holiday in France. But the last two years had been the low point of my life, at times almost more than I could bear. The divorce. Jim, whom I still missed so much, emigrating to Australia with his new wife, so that even the children were deprived of him. The move from our lovely house to a smaller one which was

11

cheaper to run.

And then the long cold winter. Grief, I believe, can be harder to bear in an unkind climate. Both can eat into your heart.

It was on a bitter Saturday, the ground hard with frost, the wind sharp and cutting from the east, that I met Nora in the High Street.

'It's awful, isn't it?' she said. 'But thank goodness we've just booked our summer holidays. Spain again.' It was obvious that she could already feel the hot sun.

'Why don't you go abroad, Linda? Take the children. You could all do with a change.' That's the stupid kind of thing Nora says. 'You could rent a house or something.' Perhaps not so stupid.

Later she remembered Fiona, and made all the arrangements. My bank let me make out a cheque for the rent in advance, and from then on I started to dream. And plan, and save, and brush up my French. And nurture my elderly Mini.

So here I was, driving along this narrow, twisting road in the south-west of France. Nicola and James in the back of the car. Not sure where I was, and any minute now it would be dark. But I'd find the house, and then our holiday would really begin. Two glorious weeks. Sun, warmth, freedom. Country air, good food.

My daughter looked in need of a holiday. She's a seven-year-old edition of me. Fair hair, pale skin, slender or downright skinny according to how you look at it. It can all add up too quickly to an air of fatigue. James is dark and sturdier, and at four years old absurdly like his father, so that sometimes it hurts just to look at him.

'Why don't you be like James and have a sleep?' I said.

'I don't want to,' Nicola answered. 'I want to be awake when we get to the house.'

I pulled into the side of the road and looked at Nora's scribbled instructions. It seemed that if I took the left turn after the bridge, followed the road by the river and then turned right up the hill, I couldn't miss it.

On the river road the overhanging trees completed the darkness. I put my headlights on full and braked to avoid a fox caught in the strong beam. Turning away from the river the country opened up, and at the top of the hill I could see a house silhouetted against the sky.

'This should be it,' I said. My heart beat faster with excitement.

And then a light came on in one of the downstairs windows, so I thought it couldn't be the house I was looking for. Even so, I'd stop and ask for directions. I hoped I'd be able to understand them.

We reached the house. 'Wait in the car,' I said to Nicola.

There was no bell or knocker. I rapped hard with my knuckles on the heavy door. All the windows on this side of the house were shuttered. The one from which I had seen the light was round the other side.

Eventually the door was opened by a man. He was tall, dark-haired, and I judged him to be in his late twenties. He waited for me to speak.

'*Excusez-moi,*' I said. '*Je cherche Les Champignons, s'il vous plaît.*'

He didn't answer immediately, which I put down to my faulty French.

'*Excusez-moi...*'

'Don't bother,' he said. 'I'm English.'

'Thank heaven! I think we're lost. I'm looking for a house called '*Les Champignons.*'

'This is *Les Champignons,*' he said. 'What do you want?' He sounded surprised.

'Oh, marvellous! We're staying here for the next two weeks. I've rented it from the owner.' He was probably the local agent, I thought, come to see that everything was in order.

'I'll get the children in first,' I said. 'If you could give me a hand with the suitcases

I'd be grateful.'

'Children?'

'In the car.'

'You say you've rented this house from the owner?' He sounded as though he didn't believe me.

'Yes. Actually I have a key. I hadn't expected to find you here, but I'd glad you are. Perhaps before you leave you'll show me where things are kept.'

He continued to block the doorway and I began to feel impatient. It had been a long drive and we were tired. Food was our first need, and as quickly as possible after that, bed.

James and Nicola got out of the car and came and stood beside me on the doorstep.

'May we come in, please?' I asked.

He looked at the three of us.

'You can come in for a minute,' he said slowly. 'But you can't stay here. *I'm* the owner and I'm living here.'

I stared at him, not believing what I heard.

'You can't be. I've got the key. I've got my receipt for the rent!'

'I assure you I am. And as you see, I'm living here.'

'If you're a squatter,' I said, 'it's no go. I shall call the police.'

James started to cry. Nicola clung to my hand.

'Mummy, I want to go home,' she said. 'I don't like it here.'

'I am not a squatter,' the man said. 'I *am* the owner and I'm living here with my son. Since you're here you'd better come in and we'll sort this thing out.'

We followed him through the porch into a large living-room. There were comfortable easy chairs and a large sofa. Two or three lamps threw pools of light on to the pale stone walls. It was everything I'd hoped for. A small boy, about Nicola's age, sat at a family-sized table doing a jigsaw puzzle.

'Please sit down,' the man said. 'Mike, fetch some lemonade and some biscuits for these children.'

'Now,' he went on, turning to me. 'I'm Graham Harker. I assure you that I own this house and I'm here with my son for the summer. What about you?'

'Then I can only think,' I answered, 'that I've come to the wrong house. There must be another house of the same name.'

'There isn't,' he said. 'Not around here. There are very few houses and I know them all.'

It occurred to me as I was speaking that

I had no proof that he was who he said he was. But I had proof of my rights. I fished in my handbag and brought out the key, and the scrap of paper which was all Nora's friend Fiona had sent me in the way of a receipt.

'Here's the key,' I said. 'I'm Linda Preston and here's my receipt for the rent. If my key fits, then I'd like some proof of *your* identity. I'm sure you understand.'

He looked at me in astonishment, and then burst into a loud laugh. He was really amused.

'It's not funny!'

'Forgive me! But from my point of view... A complete stranger arrives after dark, comes into my house and asks me for proof of my identity!'

He leaned across and took the key, a large, heavy affair. 'That's the key all right,' he agreed. He held out his hand for the receipt. As he studied it I watched his face flush. When he looked at me his eyes were hard, angry. I felt a little afraid.

'Fiona!' he said. 'I might have known. What the hell does she think she's up to now?' There was a world of bitterness in his voice; more than my affair merited.

The boy came back into the room with the lemonade as his father was speaking.

'Is Mummy coming *here?*' he asked.

'No.'

Graham Harker turned to me. 'It's obvious what's happened, Mrs Preston. Fiona is my ex-wife. She and I bought this house together, but she never stayed here. She prefers places like New York, Athens, Rome. I've just completed buying her out. So you see, she'd no right to let it to you.'

'But it was last January,' I protested. 'I paid the rent. Why didn't she let me know.'

'That's Fiona. She wouldn't mean any harm to you. Little things just never stay in her mind.'

'Little things! Do you realize...'

'Equally likely,' he said, 'if she did remember, she'd leave the problem to me.'

I thought I would faint. The man in his red pullover, the green-upholstered chair in which he was sitting, the lamp behind him, blurred and began to spin. I gripped my handbag, willing myself not to keel over. Then the room steadied.

All those months of scraping and saving; of going without. The clothes I'd made for the children. The food I'd hoarded over the months and brought with us to save money in France. But above all, the sorrows and unhappiness and frustrations of the last two years which were all to have been healed by

18

these two wonderful weeks. It was not to be borne. I had no words to say. Nicola and James, sensing my feelings, came and stood beside me.

'I'm sorry,' Graham Harker said. 'I'm truly sorry, but you can't stay here.'

'But where are we to go? What are we to do?' I was utterly bewildered.

'I suggest an hotel,' he said.

'An hotel? That's impossible. If you knew what a struggle it's been to save enough money even to get here, you wouldn't talk about hotels.'

'I meant for tonight.'

Go back home tomorrow, he meant. Turn the car around and drive four hundred miles back to Dieppe.

'I shall get in touch with your ex-wife,' I was shouting now. 'She's responsible. She'll have to do something.'

'I quite agree. I hope you know where to get in touch with her. I seldom do.'

I didn't. I would have to contact Nora, and that I couldn't do until morning. I knew this house wasn't on the telephone.

'I didn't think you could be a friend of Fiona's,' he said. 'You're not the type.'

Not sophisticated, he meant. Provincial, gullible; defenceless. Well, I was all of those.

19

'I'm sorry,' I said.

'I'm not. I can't stand Fiona's friends.' I thought he warmed a little towards me for that very reason.

'Could we get back to the subject of what I'm going to do?' I asked him. 'Even if I could afford an hotel, I don't think we'd get one tonight, not this late. And we've already slept one night in the car. The children are desperately tired.'

I heard myself pleading, asking to be allowed to stay the night under his roof.

He sighed. 'It's very inconvenient, I don't...'

'I have loads of food in the car,' I interrupted.

'I have work to do. I'm working to a deadline on a set of plans. I can't do with people around.'

'But just for tonight? We'd go to bed quite soon.'

He looked at us. The children stared at him silently.

'Very well,' he said, 'but only for tonight. You'll all three have to share a bedroom, but it's big and there are two beds. I expect you've brought sheets and things?'

Suddenly I was shivering, unable to keep a limb still. I felt sick.

'Wait a minute,' he said. 'You look all in.

20

I'm going to pour you a glass of wine, and when you've had that we'll get your things in from the car.'

Lying in bed a couple of hours later I tried to sort out what we'd do, and faced the fact that we might have to turn around and go back home. I also wondered how safe we were, sharing a house hundreds of miles from home with a man we didn't know. But I was glad to be there, and too tired to care about anything else. And in his own way he'd been quite kind to us. I slept soundly until morning.

When I wakened the bed which Nicola and James had shared was empty. For a second I panicked, and then I heard their voices through the open window; light, clear, laughing. I got up and looked out of the window. There was a stretch of land on this side of the house which someone was trying to turn into a garden. My children were standing with Graham Harker and his son, carefully examining two or three fresh molehills in a flowerbed. Nicola and James were dressed in the clean tee-shirts and jeans I'd put out for them last night. I must have slept heavily not to have heard them get up.

'Hello there,' I called.

'Good morning,' the man said. 'We thought

we'd let you sleep.'

He looked older in the clear daylight; probably he was in his thirties. His hair was red-brown in the sunlight.

'Is it very late? My watch has stopped.'

One of the features of the holiday was to have been a total disregard for time. As a teacher I must always pay strict attention to a timetable. My life is ruled by the school bell.

'I'll be right down,' I called.

'There's hot water if you want a shower,' he said.

I felt better after a shower and a hairwash: more able to face things. Hot coffee and some fresh bread added to my well-being. Of course I knew it couldn't last.

When Nicola and James went outside again after breakfast Graham Harker remained at the table. He poured another cup of coffee and then said:

'I'm sorry, Mrs Preston, but I shall have to ask you to make other arrangements from today. I really do have work to do. Also, Mike and I aren't geared for company.' Mike, I thought, would have been pleased for us to stay. He seemed glad of the children's company. He was probably a lonely child.

But I was helpless. This man was, after all, in possession. If there was to be any solution it must come through his wife.

'I understand,' I said. 'We'll go to the village right away and I'll telephone my friend; ask her to get in touch with your wife.'

'Ex-wife,' he corrected.

'...whatever. She *must* do something. I hold her responsible. One more favour—could I leave our things here until I've telephoned? I'll come back and pack later.'

He hesitated and then said. 'Very well.'

'I shan't trouble you,' I assured him. 'I promise I'll move out this afternoon.'

Where to, I didn't know. I thought it was essential to stay in the area for a day or two, to give Nora or Fiona time to come up with something. It looked as though what money I had would have to be spent on hotel accommodation and then if there was nothing forthcoming from Fiona we'd have to go home.

I wished I'd never left there. Or I wished I'd simply taken the children to the seaside. They'd have enjoyed that, perhaps more than the long journey through France. I realized now that in choosing this holiday I'd been thinking of myself: my need to put a distance between myself and all my troubles.

It took three attempts, spread over an hour, to get through to Nora. Even then I wasn't sure that she'd heard or understood me.

'The very least your friend Fiona can do is put us up in an hotel for a fortnight,' I shouted. Before she could reply the line went dead.

We came out of the post office into the hot sunshine. I was grateful for its warmth on my shoulders, which were stiff from yesterday's long drive.

'I'm thirsty,' James said.

'Can we have a drink?' Nicola asked.

'Soon. First of all we must book into an hotel for the night. Then we'll have a long, cool drink.'

There were two hotels in the village. Both were full.

'It will be the same everywhere,' the *patron* said. 'It is the season.'

'I'm thirsty,' James persisted. 'And hot. Also my head aches.'

I laid my hand on his forehead. It was dry and burning.

'And I feel sick,' he said.

We went into a bar and I ordered cold drinks. It was cool and shady in there and Nicola and I felt better for it. Not so James. He drank avidly but his cheeks remained red, his eyes too bright. Without a doubt he had a temperature. He walked around the table and

24

leaned against me, whimpering a little. *Now what was I to do?*

I'd have to look further for an hotel, but just supposing there weren't any vacancies? The thought of starting back for home with James ill in the back of the car was not to be endured.

'Why can't we stay with Mr Harker?' Nicola asked. 'It's nice there. And we like Mike. Don't you like Mr Harker?'

In other circumstances, I thought, I would have. Right now he was a great big stumbling-block.

'Unfortunately,' I said. 'Mr Harker doesn't like us that much. Certainly not enough to have us stay.'

I couldn't, simply could not, ask him if we might stay another night. His attitude that morning, though polite, had made it plain that if asked he would refuse.

'I want to go to bed,' James pleaded. 'Can I go to bed, Mummy?'

'He must feel *awful* to want to go to bed,' Nicola sympathized.

'We'll go back to the house,' I said. 'You can lie down on the bed while I pack. After that I'll make up a nice bed in the back of the car while we look for somewhere to stay.'

When we got back to the house Graham Harker and Mike were nowhere to be seen and Graham's Renault was missing. I laid James on the bed, sponged his face with cold water, gave him another drink. He was hotter than ever, turning his head from side to side, unable to find comfort. I closed the shutters to cool down the room. Then I stripped the other bed, collected the garments I'd washed in the morning and which had been drying in the hot sun, packed the case and carried it to the car.

When I came back to collect James he had fallen asleep. I stood beside the bed looking at him, touching his forehead. His skin was still hot but asleep he looked more comfortable. I decided to let him lie until the last possible moment. As long as Graham Harker was out of the house he couldn't object to us being there, and the urgency of finding an hotel would have to take second place to my son's present need.

I felt utterly weary now, as though I had no strength left in me to make even one more decision. I lay down on the spare bed and the tears, refusing to be held back any longer, ran down my cheeks. Nicola came and lay quietly beside me, holding my hand.

'I've made a very special wish, Mummy,' she confided. 'I can't tell you what it is because if you do they don't come true. But I made it.'

She gripped my hand tightly and then we must both have fallen asleep.

When I wakened Graham Harker was standing in the bedroom doorway. The sight of him brought back my troubles and I closed my eyes to shut him out—but it didn't.

'We were just going,' I said, getting up. 'I'm all packed. Only James isn't well and I didn't want to move him until I had to.'

'Did you find an hotel?' he asked.

'No. Everything's full. I must start looking again now.'

Nicola was standing by James's bed.

'He's very red, Mummy,' she said. 'Come and look.'

His face was covered with spots. I lifted his tee-shirt and saw the spots on his chest. Chickenpox!

'Hell,' Graham Harker said. 'Damnation!'

Then he ran downstairs and I heard the front door slam as he went out. A minute or two later he came in again and I went downstairs to meet him.

'You win,' he said tersely. 'You can stay.'

'I'm sorry,' I said. 'I didn't want it this way. It gives me no pleasure.'

He didn't answer. He simply walked into the living-room and began taking books and files from the shelves.

'What are you doing?' I asked.

'Packing. I shall leave with Mike in the morning. We'll find somewhere. We'll be back Friday week.'

'We'll be gone then,' I said.

'I figured that. And if you ever get in touch with that goddam wife of mine you can tell her what I think of her!'

He hates us, I thought. He really hates us. I felt as if I wanted to creep away and hide. And then suddenly I was angry. Why should *I* feel guilty? What had *I* done wrong?

'You can do that for yourself,' I flared. 'I shall be too busy on my own behalf. Do you think I want to be in this position? I don't want your charity. I want the house I paid for in good solid cash. *I'm* the one who's been cheated. I'm the one whose holiday's been ruined.'

I was shrieking at him now. Nicola and Mike ran into the room, Nicola to me, Mike to his father. I became conscious of James's whimper from the bedroom.

'We've been cheated,' Graham Harker said. 'But that's typical of Fiona. I paid good money to have this house to myself. I have drawings and plans to complete which must be submitted to my client in ten day's time. How do you think I can concentrate with all this going on?'

'I don't know. I don't know and I don't

care!' I screamed. 'I've got problems of my own. And just about more than I can cope with!'

I heard myself screaming like a fishwife and I knew it had all gone too far.

'I'm sorry,' I said.

'That's quite all right, Mrs Preston.'

Nicola tugged at my hand. 'Mummy, James is calling,' she said.

Next morning James was much better. Although he was still covered with spots, his temperature was down. I smiled at him as he sat up in bed, his dark hair lying damply on his forehead.

'Oh James my darling, why did you have to have chickenpox? You *have* complicated things!'

When I went downstairs Mike was already in the car. He had wound down the window so that he could talk to Nicola, who was standing beside the car. In fact, they were not talking; simply being together. Mike's father was packing the boot.

'Good morning,' he said, not looking up.

'Good morning. Is there anything special you want me to do in the house while you're away? What about your post, or any messages?' I asked.

'No one knows I'm here.'

'Very well then. And thank you again,' I said. 'We'll leave everything in order when we go.'

He got into the car, slammed the door, switched on the engine. Nicola and I watched them disappear from sight round the bend of the road.

'I didn't want them to go,' she said. 'It was fun with Mike.'

'Never mind. We'll have fun,' I promised. 'James will soon be better and then we can *really* start our lovely holiday.'

As we turned to go into the house I saw the postman cycling along the road towards us. He waved an arm and shouted.

*'Un télégramme!'* He dismounted and gave it to me.

'For Monsieur Harker and Madame Preston,' he said.

'For both of us?'

*'Mais oui!'*

'Monsieur Harker has just left,' I told him.

'I know. I saw him. I waved the telegram but he did not stop.'

I opened it and read it. In the circumstances, it was no help at all. It had come too late.

'Come along, Nicola,' I said. 'Let's have some breakfast.'

It was while I was pouring the first cup of coffee that the Renault screamed to a stop outside the house and Graham Harker marched in.

'Forgot a notebook,' he said. 'Can't work without it.'

Mike ran into the house after him. 'We saw the postman,' he said. 'We saw the telegram.'

His father looked confused, caught out. I handed him the telegram.

'It's for both of us,' I said. 'I opened it.'

'*Both* of us?'

'From Fiona.'

He read it, a frown creasing his face. I watched him, waiting for his verdict. I knew what it would be.

'Hm!' he said. 'Sometimes Fiona has the most irritating way of saying the sensible thing. It was a habit I disliked in her.'

It seemed I might be wrong.

'Is it *really* possible?' he said. 'Do *you* think it's possible?'

'It was you who was against it. You didn't want to be disturbed. But in fact it could work out well. I could look after Mike while you got on with your job. That way you'd be through in no time.'

'I was hasty,' he said. 'And rather rude, I'm afraid. I suppose you could be right. Shall we give it a try, then? For the sake of the

31

children, I mean.'

'For the sake of the children, of course!' I agreed.

'I haven't ever read a telegram,' Nicola said. 'Can I see it?'

'Sure.' I handed it to her and she read it out loud, stumbling over the unfamiliar words.

'TEN THOUSAND APOLOGIES. CAN ONLY SUGGEST SHARING. HAPPY HOLIDAY TO ALL. FIONA.'

Graham sat down at the table, poured himself coffee. I knew from that moment that the holiday was going to be everything I'd hoped for. Perhaps even better than I'd hoped for.

# The Centre of Attraction

She marches rhythmically into the square, like an invading army. Clomp-clomp; clomp-clomp. As my old grandmother would have put it, 'All on her own she marches four abreast.' Her bounteous bosom, unconfined beneath cotton tee-shirt, bobs jubilantly up and down with every stride. Her hair—thick, white, tied with a red bow into a far-too-youthful ponytail—bounces in unison.

Of course, she has ruined my painting. She just does not fit into the composition. The washed-out pink of the buildings, the far background of sand-coloured cliffs, the faded terracotta of the pavement—everything calls out for the muted palette I have arranged. Ochre, gamboge, the siennas.

Walking purposefully towards the table which was to have been the focal point of my picture, she unharnesses herself from the large rucksack, inserts her ample blue-clad behind into the fragile white chair. Her face, glistening with sweat, is a rich shade of tomato, only a little less brilliant than her scarlet shirt.

Her sturdy, suntanned legs culminate in emerald green socks and heavy boots.

We are the only people in the square, she and I. The only signs of life except for the mongrel dog asleep under a table, and the fly which torments it. The Minorcan siesta is not to be taken lightly, and only middle-aged foreigners, who think they know better, ignore it. The reason for my foolishness is that I am a man who likes to paint empty spaces. In the morning I am too lazy to get up. In the evening all is bustle. So, although I do not like the intensity of the midday light, I am too indolent to change my ways. I compromise by wearing a pair of slightly tinted spectacles which tone down my surroundings. And when I feel guilty about not painting the truth, I remind myself of the theory that the Impressionists would not have painted as they did had they not been shortsighted. My sunglasses seem to do no harm to my potboilers. They sell with pleasing regularity, and at prices which please both the owner and myself, at the small art gallery near to the west door of the church.

My spectacles, however, are powerless to dim this intruder into my picture. She stands out from the background as vividly as a humming-bird against a bush—but larger. She looks around expectantly and, since she is one of those women born to rule, without so much a a lift of the finger on her part, the waiter emerges from the dark cavern of his bar.

'*Buenos dias.*' Her voice is clear, loud, with an accent common among my English friends. Spanish was not on her school curriculum.

'*Buenas tardes*' the waiter corrects her. '*Buenos dias,* good morning; *buenas tardes,* good afternoon.'

These little niceties of Alonzo's, and the smile which, even for the plainest women, accompanies them, earn him a small fortune in tips over the summer months.

'*Buenos tardes,*' she repeats. '*Gracias.*'

While waiting for her drink she looks across at me, not attempting to hide her curiosity. Since I am dark-haired and have been a year in the sun of southern Europe, no doubt she thinks I am a native. There is nothing against staring at natives. Besides, I have an easel set up, and a collection of brushes in my hand. Anybody, anywhere, may look at a painter. They may stand behind him, watch him work, praise or criticize him to their heart's content, and always as if he were not there, or was stone-deaf. If I were a writer, would they peer over my shoulder and say, 'I like the way he describes her hat'? But a painter is different.

Sure enough, here she comes.

*'Buenas tardes, senor.'*

'Good afternoon, madam.'

She is ever so slightly disconcerted to hear that I too, am English-spoken. But no matter. It will make it easier to discuss my work.

'Bertha Conway.' She stretches out her hand and her grip is every bit as vigorous as I expect it to be. She backs to a position a yard or two behind my easel, head on one side, eyes narrowed, evaluating my work. I move aside because I do not like people breathing down my neck. Also, I can study her while she looks at my painting.

I suppose, before she was covered by too much flesh in the wrong places, she must have been an attractive woman. There are still signs of it. Dark, widely-spaced eyes, broad forehead. Finely-chiselled ears cluttered with large pearl clips. Real pearls.

She makes no comment on my painting; simply nods her head once or twice. In fact I have only blocked in the shapes—everything else is still to come—so I am pleased she does not make some clever-sounding remark.

Alonzo places a jug of sangria on her table, its ruby colour glowing through the glass. I hope she knows it is well-laced with brandy.

'Will you join me, Mr...?'

'Salter. Mel Salter. If you don't mind, I

won't. I want to get on.'

'As you wish.'

She returns to her table. But how can I get on while she sits there in her confusion of colour? Her size, too, obscures the pink-flowered bush (I still do not know its name) which I wish to include.

She pours the sangria into her glass and drinks it greedily as if it were no more than orange squash. Ah well! She will soon know. She raises her hand, summoning Alonzo. Great God! She cannot be ordering more. Drat the woman! I must go and warn her. It is I who will have to pick her up when she slumps to the ground.

'Then, since it is already ordered, you must do me the kindness of sharing it with me.' Her eyes are already brighter than they were. Alonzo, bringing the new jug of liquor, looks at me and lowers one eyelid almost imperceptibly. From a well-filled wallet she extracts a five-hundred peseta note. Then she pours me a generous glass of sangria, and herself a third one.

'It's quite potent, you know. You don't feel it at first, but later you do,' I warn her.

'It's delicious, Mr Salter. Quite delicious!' (Do I already detect a trace of difficulty in her enunciation?) 'I like it! I like this place. A pretty village. I think I shall stay here a day or two. We'll have another little drink and then you can show me the hotel.'

'There's no hotel in the village. Across the bay there's a big one, owned by the tour company. Very comfortable, I believe, but atrocious food. The folks come across here in the evening to buy steak sandwiches.'

'Then I must find a house nearby. Someone, I'm sure, will be able to put me up.' She speaks with the confidence of one who has seldom had doors closed against her. 'I shall ask the waiter. A dear man! He'll have a cousin or someone who'll give me a bed. My wants are quite simple. The food of the people. And this pleasant fruit juice they drink.'

I have noticed that people who expect to be lucky usually are. Bertha Conway is no exception. Alonzo is sure that his brother's wife will have a room and will be pleased to have the lady. Not to worry, he will see to everything. She tips him in acknowledgement of his good intentions.

All is finally arranged as Alonzo has promised. His brother's wife is very happy to offer the lady a room—from which I am quite certain four small children have been temporarily evacuated. Eventually Bertha Conway is escorted out of the plaza by the sister-in-law, like a ship in full sail accompanied by a tugboat.

I wipe my brushes, clean my palette, fold up my easel. So much for today's work. Better luck tomorrow.

But luck is not on my side. Tomorrow is here, and so am I. It is siesta time again and I have just begun to paint the deserted plaza when Madam Bertha walks once more into the middle of my scene. She waves a hand. Today she wears a shiny bright blue blouse, with yellow trousers straining over her behind. A green chiffon scarf adorns her hair and she has changed her pearl earrings for ruby-coloured danglers. She carries a large tapestry tote bag.

Why, you ask, can I not paint another angle of the plaza, excluding the lady? Well, to start with, the plaza is quite small, and since she sits in the middle there is no viewpoint which will exclude her. In any case, I was here first, and the siesta period is my time for painting. Why can she not lie down on her bed for an hour or two? Or, if she must exercise, go for a stroll along the beach?

Alonzo hurries across to her, jug of liquor in hand. It is obvious from their manner that their friendship progresses. He is all attention, adjusting the sunshade over her table, moving her chair.

She beckons me to join her but I am damned

if I will. I make signs to indicate that I must get on with my painting. She smiles happily and takes an embroidery frame and a heap of coloured thread from her bag. I am surprised by the dexterous way she handles her needle, her unusually small hands moving back and forth like butterflies over a cabbage patch. No doubt she is making some hideous piece of nonsense for the church bazaar. Some poor soul will win it in a raffle.

It is no use. I cannot paint. She dominates the scene. I sit down and close my eyes. As I cannot work I might as well rest. But because I am angry with her, she also dominates my thoughts. Blast the woman! I glare at her and she waves back. My fury mounts. I must speak with her, find out how long this state of affairs is to continue.

But I must be cautious. Perhaps I can persuade her to move on, to leave this scene to me. I shall say something flattering about her needlework. I cannot resist the temptation to stand behind her, viewing her work as she did mine. She continues deftly pushing the needle through the canvas, drawing it back again.

I am astonished by what I see. The design is abstract, original; not the tortured crinolined ladies and hollyhocks I had expected. More than that, the colours are exquisite. Soft greys, mauves, smudgy greens. No, she is not working to someone else's instructions, painting by numbers, as it were. Where she has not worked, the linen is bare. She holds some hanks of cotton against it, judging the colours, making an unerring choice.

'It's beautiful! Quite beautiful!'

'I'm glad you like it. I hope you've come to join me for a drink.'

Even so, I remind myself, what about my work?

'I like this place. I think I shall stay here quite a while. Alonzo's sister has made me very welcome and the children are darlings. Yes, I shall be very happy here for a month or two.'

A month or two! But that will be the summer gone, and most of the autumn! What is to happen to my painting? Curse the woman!

'You look quite flushed, Mr Salter. Ought you to be out in this heat?'

'I was about to ask you the same question, Miss Conway. Is it wise? Should you not rest quietly indoors in the middle of the day?'

If only she will absent herself for two hours, just two hours each day, all will be well.

'Please call me Bertha. No, I like the heat. I can stand any amount of it. I was born in India, you know.'

41

There is simply no hope for me then. No hope at all.

The days go by. Each day, promptly at the same hour, she sits with her embroidery and her jug of sangria, at the table in the middle of the square. Each day Alonzo teaches her a little more Spanish and grows richer on the tips she gives him. And each day I paint a little less.

There are painters—good ones—who can make notes, draw sketches, and complete the painting in the studio. I am not one of them. I must put it down on canvas while it lives in front of me; otherwise it is no good. Yes, I know also that there are other places than this small plaza. All over the island there is beauty in abundance.

But it is this scene which draws me, and draws me still. There have always been artists who painted the same scene over and over again. In addition, I am obstinate.

In the end, like the athlete who must exercise if he is to retain his skill, I have decided I must paint my picture whether Madam Bertha sits there or not. I shall, as it were, paint through her, to what I know lies behind. The flowering bush; the small stone fountain. With a stroke of my brush I shall wipe her out, obviate her presence.

The decision made, I am immediately more excited than I have been since the day she moved in. I squeeze the colours out on to my palette—great generous blobs of paint. I work quickly, with wide brush strokes. She sits there, sewing, oblivious of me. It has never gone so well. Never. Two hours later, perspiring, exhausted, realizing that the square is now full of people, I put down my brushes and stand back to look at what I have done.

There, in the middle of my canvas, is Madam Bertha in all her glory. Red shirt, blue trousers, green socks and all. I know instinctively that this is good. It is the best thing I have ever done. I did not know I had it in me, this depth and quality of painting.

Back home, I set up the canvas in the middle of the living room. I dart about, viewing it from every angle; now from halfway down the stairs, now glimpsing it from the kitchen doorway, now full on: like a woman seeing herself from all sides in a triple mirror. From every viewpoint it is good. Naturally, there is still a lot to be done to it. I look forward to the next day's work.

Were it not that the light would be all wrong, I would plan to start early in the day. As it is, after a night in which ambitions, hopes, plans for the future take over from sleep, I waken late in the morning. I leap out of bed and rush downstairs to look at it, my beautiful painting, flinging back the shutters to let in the daylight. It is still as vivid, still as powerful. I can see where I must work on it next.

A quick swallow of coffee, my gear packed, I hurry to the plaza. I shall need at least four more sittings. At least. It is to be a work of perfection: the turning point of my career. Thank God I didn't persuade her to leave.

She is not yet at her table, but I am earlier than usual.

Alonzo brings me my drink.

'Where is Madam?' I ask, setting out my palette. No muted colours this time. Reds, yellows, blues. God, I hope she will be wearing the same outfit; I should have had the sense to warn her!

He shrugs. 'Who can say, *Senor?* With the pack on her back, as burdened as my father's old mule on market day, she left us. My brother's wife was sorry to see her go, but the little ones are glad to have their room back.'

# Meet The New Caroline Pritchard

If you have just looked in the mirror and you're thinking of taking some treatment which promises to make a new woman of you, think about it carefully. Do you realize what you're letting yourself in for? Could you cope with the New You?

You know the kind of thing I mean. You've read it in the magazines; there was even a programme on the telly. They take you as you are, warts and all, on a particularly black Monday; photograph you in close-up, being careful to reveal all your worst points—your lank, shapeless hair, a cold sore in full bloom right under your nostrils, figure like a hippopotamus.

All that, and more, they did to me. But I can't complain. I brought it on myself. I wanted to do it for Richard. If only I *looked* better—different—I thought, maybe everything would be all right between us again.

So nobody pushed me. I wasn't even asked.

I invited myself right after I'd seen that show on the box.

Perhaps you remember it? They'd brought these two women from different parts of the country—and they transformed them. A complete overhaul. After which they supplied them with new outfits, top to elegant toe, and wined and dined them at the Talk of the Town with two dishy DJs.

Richard had just stormed out of my flat, furious because I wouldn't go with him to a local football match.

'Six months ago,' I yelled through my sobs, 'you wouldn't have left me even for the Cup Final!'

'Six months ago,' he shouted, just before he slammed the door, 'you'd have come with me anywhere!'

I could tell he was going off me. It wasn't only football. He'd joined the local darts team (mixed) and was also threatening to take up snooker. I did not see myself as a 'Pot Black' addict.

Much more serious was Richard's recent reluctance to linger in front of furniture shop windows. And, at twenty, a well-brought-up girl like me begins to think of settling down. Marriage, children, a front-loader washing machine and a tumble drier.

46

Richard has the true bachelor's attachment to the launderette.

So when he left the flat I switched on the telly for company and was confronted by these two women, waiting to be made beautiful. They looked like I felt, so I went into the kitchen to make a consoling cup of coffee. By the time I came back they'd been replaced by two raving beauties.

Well, not actually replaced. It was just that I didn't recognize them, and no wonder.

One now had a mass of blonde, corkscrew curls while the other girl had a cap of jet-black, gleaming hair, decorated with diamante stars. Someone had also waved a magic wand over their torsos and they were now as slender as daffodil stems and clad in tight garments, which revealed totally unexpected beauty of leg and bosom.

Which was when I remembered our local department store's promotion stunt. They were offering the full beauty treatment to the woman whose letter impressed them most.

*What can you do for me?* I wrote. *I have all the problems you could wish for: split ends, broken nails, spare tyre.* I made the list as long as possible, inventing a few things like dry skin and flat fleet to encourage them.

*I am willing to submit to any publicity,* I concluded, *and ask only for a New, Better Me—plus the usual perks.*

*Yours sincerely,*

*Caroline Pritchard.*

I also enclosed a photograph. I have a fair selection of awful photographs since Richard is not at his best with a camera. This was one of me leaving the cross-Channel ferry at Newhaven after a rough crossing. I am a bad sailor.

Petronella—she is head of the shop's Beauty Department—told me afterwards that my letter had arrived at exactly the right moment.

'So many of the letters and photos were from ordinary-looking women. One glance at your photograph and I knew we couldn't lose!'

Let me tell you all about it...

It began early one Monday.

I'd managed to get a few days off work. For starters they took me to this photographer's studio, which was a cross between a deserted garage and a derelict barn.

The man's name was Jake. He was tall and brooding and about twenty-five. He snapped away like mad and produced masses of instant prints which, as horror photographs, were in a class by themselves. They were terrifying!

48

'Could it be you always wanted to work for Hammer Films?' I asked him.

'Don't talk,' he said sharply. 'I'm starting on the real stuff now. I want this lot deadpan. And stick out your stomach! Let it go!'

He danced around me, viewing me from every worst angle.

'Head down,' he ordered. 'Shoulders rounded. We're trying for a double chin. And now think of something that makes you really sick!

I thought of Richard with that blonde who throws a nifty dart.

'Not murderous,' Jake said. 'Just sick-making.'

Richard, by the way, had suddenly been sent on a two week course in Luton, taking the place of a colleague who had gone down with shingles. Or so he said.

Still, if it was true, it suited me. Through all the trials ahead I would fortify myself with the thought of the vision he'd behold on his return.

Everyone except me was delighted with the photographs.

'Fantastic!' Petronella drooled over them. 'You look absolutely revolting, Caroline darling! We'll have a good display of them in the window and then we'll come up with the New Year You next week.

'No,' she added thoughtfully. 'Say two

weeks. It's got to be believable.'

'Here's hoping we get as good a set of Afters,' Jake said, squinting at me through narrowed eyes. I scowled at him.

From then on, life was one mad whirl of hairdressers, massage parlours, beauty salons, dress shops. Petronella accompanied me everywhere, as if she were taking a pet poodle for clipping. She was enjoying it, but as far as I was concerned it was hard work.

I should have gone on a survival course first, come to think of it. Perhaps then I could have learned to live without breathing for when they bunged up my nostrils with the face pack, to stay silent when my hair was practically pulled out by the roots, to stand immobile while some sadistic seamstress stuck pins into me on the pretext of fitting a dress.

'The trouble is,' Petronella said, 'Brightbourne isn't London. We have to make do with what's available.'

The other trouble was Petronella's flair for 'discovering' people: hairdressers experimenting with new theories, little dressmakers seeking experience.

'Originality,' she enthused. 'That's what we're after!'

It was not what I was after, but it was too late to back out.

50

The hairdressers, Mervyn and Clive, worked as a team. Mervyn did the styling, Clive commented on it when it was too late.

'It'll all have to come off, ducky,' Mervyn said. He lifted a strand for inspection, holding it gingerly by his fingertips as if I had the plague.

*'All come off?'* I didn't recognize the high squeak of my voice.

'Marvellous!' Petronella gushed. 'We're in your hands, Mervyn!'

She meant *I* was in his hands. She'd confided in me that she always took the quickest route to Knightsbridge when her hair needed cutting.

Snip, snip. Snip, snip. I'd been growing it since I was fourteen and now it was lying in heaps on the floor. Tears filled my eyes as a small female slave swept it up and threw it in the litter bin as if it were so much fluff from under the bed.

'The colour's no good,' Mervyn said.

'I conceive...' he said, looking in the mirror as if seeing a vision (which he was), '...I conceive the warm, red glow of a New England maple leaf in the fall!'

While muttering spells he mixed a concoction which looked like an old-fashioned remedy for indigestion. He caked my hair with it and then baked my head in a little oven. Petronella

51

sat in a comfortable chair, reading a magazine.

'What you've given birth to,' Clive said acidly, when it was finished, 'is the cold, rough red of grated carrot in a winter salad, and about the same texture!'

He was right. I wondered if Richard would mind me wearing a headscarf permanently for the next two years.

The Facial. Since Petronella didn't know any half-trained, failed beauticians I was taken to Madame Rochelle, the store's own expert.

This time Petronella left me while she went to the pub to meet a friend. At first I thought I might enjoy this bit. Everything smelled so fantastic. Then Madame got enthusiastic with red-hot wet towels. She slapped them on my face in an attempt to suffocate me.

'Let me out!' I yelled. 'I'm done to a turn!'

But too late, she had gone for her morning coffee, leaving me to cool down. She took a long break, so that by the time she returned, rivulets of icy water were coursing down my neck.

'Splendid!' she cried. 'That's really opened up the pores! But now, *what* am I going to do about your eyebrows? Tell me that!'

'Couldn't we just leave them?' I begged.

'My dear child...!' Words failed her.

That little chore brought out her worst instincts. She went to work as if uprooting trees for the Forestry Commission. Then, when she'd got rid of *my* eyebrows, she drew in new ones, more to her liking.

'Well,' she said doubtfully, when my face was finished, 'I *think* we've made an improvement.'

'And now your dress!' Petronella said, when she came back to collect me. 'I know the most splendid little woman. Doreen. She's just finished a course of evening classes and now she's starting up on her own.'

'You're slimmer than I thought from the photographs Petronella showed me,' Doreen said later. 'I'd have said a plump fourteen. You're no more than a ten.'

'Ah, but we've been working on her!' Petronella said.

'I was *always* a size ten!' I protested. By this time I felt the need for something to cling to.

'But differently distributed, darling,' Petronella said. 'A good bra is a work of real engineering.'

It has never occurred to me before that my 34A bust needed the attention of an Isambard Kingdom Brunel.

'Anyway, we can rely on Doreen to come up

with something different,' Petronella said.

It certainly was different. I doubt if its like had ever been seen in Brightbourne. It was a sort of deep purple balloon gathered in below the knees. I look like an animated aubergine from *The Muppet Show.*

'And now for the photographs!' Petronella said. 'I wonder what Jake will say when he sees you.'

'Crikey!' was what Jake said. And then 'Well, well!'

'You wouldn't have known her, would you, darling?' Petronella asked.

'I wouldn't have known her,' he agreed.

But, oddly enough, the photographs turned out well and I looked well—all right. Petronella was thrilled by them. It just proved what a camera in the right hands can do.

'And last, but not least, your little reward for the job,' Petronella said kindly. 'In addition to the hairdo and the dress, of course. Jake has been chosen to take you out to dinner at Lorenzo's Italian Restaurant.'

'Sorry we couldn't get Terry Wogan,' Jake said. 'Also, it'll have to wait for a week or so. I'll call you. First thing tomorrow I have to go to the Middle East to photograph a disaster.

'That's his more usual line of work,' Petronella explained. 'We were lucky to get him for you.'

'Don't worry about me,' I said to Jake.

Surely he didn't think a little thing like a meal out mattered to me? My main worry was whether Richard would approve of the New Me.

Well, he did approve. Of course it was a shock when he first saw me, and he turned pale and had to be given a stiff drink, but after that he seemed to quite like the New Me.

'Stimulating' was the word he used. He didn't enjoy Luton, and for some reason he'd gone right off darts. But he was definitely not off me.

Has it worked out for the best? Well, that's another matter. But yes, I think it has. You see *I've* gone off Richard. Don't know what I ever saw in him.

I knew it for certain when I went to Lorenzo's with Jake.

'Do you know what I like about you?' he said, leaning across the table, holding my hand.

'Tell me!' I whispered.

Could it be my red hair? My eyebrows? Was he fond of aubergines?

'What I like,' he said, 'is that underneath all this razzamatazz—' with the hand not holding mine he indicated my appearance '—is the real you. The one I saw that Monday morning.'

He grinned. 'It was the hardest assignment I ever had, trying to make you look awful. I know the real you is in there, waiting to get out. I want to be around when she does.'

'You will be,' I promised him.

# A Gull Named Helen

Daniel followed the woman up the narrow, spiralling staircase of the lighthouse. Behind him came Miriam, the children's Group Leader. 'And now I'll show you your room,' the woman said. 'As you're the youngest in the party, I thought you'd like this one. It's the smallest room in the lighthouse.'

It was tiny. The narrow bed took up most of the space, leaving room only for a small wooden table, no bigger than a stool, beside it. The window was narrow too, and like all the windows in the lighthouse, thickly glazed and curved to the shape of the outside wall.

'Of course, if you'd rather be with the other children, we could manage that,' the woman said.

'I like this best,' Daniel said quickly.

He didn't want to be with the other children. Besides, their rooms were in the basement, not up here in the real part of the lighthouse.

'I think it's a dear little room,' Miriam said. 'And mine is just a little farther up the staircase if you should want me.'

'Supper downstairs in fifteen minutes,' the woman said. 'I ring a bell for all the meals. You'll hear it wherever you are.'

'Thank you, Mrs Porter,' Miriam said. 'That will give me time to unpack.' She turned to Daniel. 'Shall you be all right, Daniel?' she asked. He said nothing, and smiling, she left.

People were always asking him if he was all right; looking at him to see if he was enjoying things; waiting for him to smile or laugh. 'He never was one for laughing,' he'd heard his mother tell Miriam, when she'd left him with her. 'Always was a quiet little boy. But since his grandma passed away he hasn't had a word for the cat.'

What did they mean, 'passed away'? he wondered. Did it mean she'd gone away and would come back? When he'd returned to school he'd found out about it. 'Your gran was knocked down on the crossing and killed,' a boy had told him.

They had thought that a holiday with these other children would cheer him up. 'Take him out of himself,' his mother had said. It was a kind thought, but stupid. How could ten strange children take the place of his grandma? They were nothing like her.

Some of the children had never been to the

coast before, but he had been on a day trip to Brighton with his grandma. He remembered everything about it. They had walked on the Palace Pier and at first he'd been afraid at the glimpse of the dark sea far beneath the floor-boards. Supposing he slipped through? His grandma had laughed at this and he'd stopped being afraid.

He had put money in most of the slot machines in the amusement arcade, and after that they had had fish and chips in a restaurant. Then, on the long hill up to the station, he'd stopped and bought a coloured glass seagull as a present for his mother.

Later on, after his grandma had died, his mother had said he could have the seagull back. He had brought it with him to the lighthouse. He unpacked it carefully and set it on the table. Next he climbed on to the foot of the bed and looked out of the window.

This seaside was nothing like Brighton. He looked out over the grassy cliff top to where the sun shone on the face of the white cliffs, turning them to silver and gold.

To the right, for a very long way, until it met with the sky, was the sea. It was a pale, shining blue and almost, but not quite, flat. Bumpy, like the frosted glass in the bathroom window at home. He wondered how it was possible to see so far from such a small window.

Nearer to the lighthouse the seagulls flew around, swooping and diving, soaring in the air, inter-weaving patterns against the blue sky. They chattered and cried as they flew, uttering harsh, melancholy sounds which sank without an echo into the sea.

At the edge of the cliff on which the lighthouse was built a solitary bird, as still as if it were carved from chalk, gazed out to sea. It was much bigger than he had expected a seagull to be: almost as big as a hen. It shone in the sunlight, shining white, with a pale grey back, pink legs and a great golden-yellow beak.

It perched motionless on the edge of the cliff while Daniel, equally still, watched from the window. Suddenly it spread its great, black-tipped wings and flew away. At the same time a distant bell rang for supper, echoing up the stone staircase.

Supper was good. They had fish fingers, tinned peaches and fruit cake.

'I was naïve about the food bit when I started having children here,' Mrs Porter said to Miriam. 'I thought they'd appreciate fresh vegetables, fruit, honey, local fish. Not so! Only the gulls grow fat on that diet. I had to learn that fish comes in bread-crumbed oblongs and peas in tins!'

After supper Miriam told them the rules. They were to make their own beds, and everyone must help in turn with the washing-up.

They were not to go into the village or on to the beach without permission, and no one was to go beyond the wire which ran about two yards in from the edge of the cliff. They were always, Miriam said, to keep away from the edge of the cliffs, whether in the lighthouse grounds or anywhere else.

'There's a drop of more than three hundred feet to the beach below here,' she warned them. 'If you were to drop a stone it would take seven seconds to hit the beach. That's how steep the cliffs are.'

'Also,' Mrs Porter interrupted, 'the edges of the cliffs are sometimes unsafe and a bit of the ground collapses. This lighthouse used to be nearly a mile from the cliff edge, instead of fifty yards as it is now.'

'Do you think it might fall into the sea, Mrs Porter?' a boy asked.

Mrs Porter smiled. 'They reckon it might— in another four hundred years. So I'm sure you're safe for the next week or so.'

It was dark by the time Daniel went up to bed. Miriam came with him and together they looked out of the window. Everywhere was black: no street lamps, no lights from the houses. And then as they watched, a long beam of light lit up the sky in the distance.

'That's the beam from the new lighthouse,' Miriam said. 'It flashes all through the hours of darkness to warn the ships off the rocks.'

'Did this lighthouse once do that?' Daniel asked.

'Yes. But there was very often a mist at this point on the cliffs, so they built another lighthouse in a better place. I think you should go to sleep now.'

When she had gone, he lay on his back under the thick, blue-checked rug and watched the light sweeping the sky. Last of all, he thought about his grandma. Each night he thought about the different things they had done together. She would have liked the lighthouse.

Early next morning, he was wakened by the sound of the gulls. He scrambled to the bottom of the bed and looked out of the window. There was a cloud of them flying around a short distance away, screaming and crying, sometimes sounding angry, sometimes as if they were laughing. Closer to, on the same bit of grass, was the solitary gull he had seen yesterday. His gull.

He pulled on his jeans and sweater and

hurried down the stairs. A door led to the kitchen and another to the garden.

Mrs Porter, already at work preparing the children's breakfast, called out to him. 'Where are you going, Daniel?'

'To watch the gulls.'

'They'll like you better if you offer them something to eat.' She cut and handed him a thick crust of bread.

'Break it into pieces,' she said. 'Herring gulls are greedy birds. And here's a slice for yourself. I expect you're hungry.'

He walked out on to the short, springy grass. It was still early in the day and the sun had not dried the dew. It sparkled on the ground like scattered diamonds. He stood on the wide stone terrace and watched the birds, wondering just what to do.

His bird was still where he had last seen her from the bedroom. The others crowded the air a little distance away. He would like, if he could, to feed only her. Also, it might be frightening if all the others flew down to him when they saw the bread.

He said the words to himself. 'Herring gull. Herring, herring, herring.' It was a funny word. In a way, it was a little bit like his Grandma's name, which was Helen. 'Herring, Helen; Helen Herring,' he said softly, trying it out.

The bird ignored him at first, but he kept calling out the name. He was sure she had seen him by the glint in the bright yellow ringed eye that was facing him. There was a slight nervous flutter of wings, but otherwise she remained still.

Presently the other birds, finding something more interesting, wheeled as a flock and moved further away. Now was his chance.

Carefully, Daniel broke off a piece of bread and threw it towards the bird. She leapt quickly, with a slight movement of her wings, and seized it in her strong beak. He threw another piece, which she took at once, and then he threw one much nearer. The bird hesitated, walking a little from side to side, turning her head away, but not coming nearer.

'Come on!' he coaxed. 'Helen Herring, come on!' He gave a short, low whistle and flung another piece of bread.

She answered his whistle with a quick, low cry. 'Quark,' she said.

He felt pleasure run over him like warm rain. He whistled again and spoke the name he had now decided to give her.

'Quark,' she replied. Stepping nearer, she took the piece of bread and at once retreated.

'There's another piece,' he said.

'Quark,' she said, stepping forward to take it.

After that he broke the rest of the bread, including the slice which Mrs Porter had given him for himself, a piece at a time until it was all finished. Each time the bird took it; each time she uttered the same cry. When she had eaten the last piece she spread her wings and flew out of sight below the edge of the cliff. Daniel went back into the lighthouse.

Mrs Porter was measuring tea into a pot. 'I expect you gave them your own slice as well,' she remarked. 'Do you want another?'

'Yes, please,' Daniel said. He was sharply hungry. 'I gave mine to Helen.'

'Helen?'

'That's the seagull's name.'

'Oh. Does she know, then?'

'Yes,' Daniel said. 'She answers when I call her.'

'Funny,' Mrs Porter said, handing him a slice of thickly-buttered bread. 'I've always thought of her as "Fred".'

'I think she'd prefer "Helen",' Daniel said.

'If you say so. Do you know anyone else called Helen?'

'Not now. My grandma was called Helen?'

'I see.' She poured tea into two mugs, and handed one to Daniel. 'Tell me what your grandma was like,' she said.

Daniel thought about it. It was difficult to

65

describe her, You didn't always look at people carefully. They were just there.

'She had a white jumper,' he said. 'She was a little lady, nice and fat. When she washed her hair she put it in blue rollers. She had holes in her ears, and gold earrings.'

'I see. She sounds nice.'

Each day after that he fed the gull. Mrs Porter let him have the scraps after all the meals. He waited until all the others had flown so that he could give his bird all the food and she, in turn, was always waiting for him.

Each day she came a little nearer, and on the fourth day she took a piece of bread from his outstretched hand. He was a little frightened by that because her beak was so large, but he managed not to flinch as he felt it knock against the palm of his hand, and it was gentler than he expected.

They talked together a lot. Mostly she said 'Quark', but sometimes it meant one thing, sometimes another. He always knew. He told her several things about himself. Once he told her about his grandma.

She reminded him, in a funny sort of way, of his grandma. There was something about her bright eyes, her round white chest, and the way she waddled slightly from side to side when she walked. Also, her legs were thin and pink under her big body.

On the Thursday, in the middle of the night, there was a tremendous storm. The wind screamed and howled round the lighthouse and large hailstones beat against the window until he was afraid they might break it. All through the storm the beam from the new lighthouse swept intermittently across the black sky.

Once, he thought he heard a bird's cry out there on the cliff, but when he looked out of the window it was impossible to see anything for the thick curtain of rain. He crept back under the covers. It was a long time before he fell asleep again.

Next morning he woke up late. The rain had stopped and the sky was clear. From his room, there was no sign of Helen. He dressed quickly and ran downstairs.

'She's not there,' he said. 'Helen's not there, Mrs Porter.'

'You're a bit late,' Mrs Porter said. 'Birds are creatures of habit. They nearly always come to be fed at the same time every day. I expect she's been and gone away again.'

'What shall I do if she's gone?' Daniel said. 'What shall I do?'

He ran outside and called to her but she did

not come. There were no gulls anywhere.

'She'll come back,' Mrs Porter said. 'After a storm the gulls sometimes go up the coast a little way to the harbour. The boats put in there and there's food to be had. I expect that's where she's gone?'

He was not convinced. He was more sure than ever that he had heard a cry in the night. Supposing she had fallen down the cliff and was lying there at the bottom? It was possible. He had to know.

After breakfast he went out again. It was forbidden to go beyond the wire to the cliff edge, but unless he did so it would be impossible to see over. Lying flat on his stomach, he squeezed under the wire and inched his way to the edge of the cliff, making for a point where it curved inwards. Holding on tightly to the tufts of grass, he looked down to the beach.

Cautiously, he stretched out his right hand towards a stone, which he dropped over the edge. They were right. He counted up to seven before he heard it hit the beach. There was neither sight nor sound of the bird.

He lay there, watching and listening, until he heard a voice frantically calling his name. He turned his head and saw Miriam shouting and waving back at the lighthouse. Carefully, he crawled backwards to safety.

Miriam was angry. He explained about the bird, but she seemed not to understand and forbade him to go beyond the terrace for the rest of the morning. He sat there with the basin of bread in his hands, calling out Helen's name. She did not come.

After lunch the minibus was to take all of them, except Mrs Porter, into Easton. He felt it impossible that he could go while he didn't know what had happened to Helen. She might still be on the beach. She might even be dead. But he had to know. Therefore he made his plans.

At lunchtime he said he didn't feel well and couldn't eat anything, which was a pity because it was bacon and chips, his favourite meal.

'My stomach aches,' he said. 'And I feel sick. I don't think I can go on the bus. I'd like to go to bed.'

'I suppose you'd better,' Miriam said anxiously. 'I hope you're not sickening for something.'

'He'll be all right,' Mrs Porter said. 'I'll look after him. Off you go, and tell that driver to take care. There's a mist coming in with the tide.'

Daniel had to undress and go to bed, but as soon as the minibus left he got up again. Mrs Porter wouldn't hear him because she was

69

already busy with the vacuum in the basement. Also, she had the radio on loud.

He wrapped the food scraps in a paper bag and left the lighthouse by the side gate. His aim was to get on to the beach and to walk back to the spot underneath the lighthouse cliff.

He closed the gate behind him and set off along the cliff path. Somewhere, he had heard, there were steps leading down to the sea. It was a rough path. Also there was a strong wind blowing from the land. Sometimes it was difficult to stand upright, or to get his breath.

In the end, when he thought he must have missed them and could go no further, he found the steps. In fact, it was no more than an old wooden ladder going down the cliff side. He was worried to see that the rungs were rather far apart. He hoped his legs would not be too short.

Carefully feeling for each rung before he put his weight on it, and not looking down because it made him go dizzy, he reached the bottom of the ladder. It didn't quite reach to the ground and he had to jump the last few feet. He rolled over and grazed his knees, but apart from that he was all right. Now he had to walk back along the beach in the direction from which he'd come, back towards the lighthouse.

He had never seen a beach like this before. There were large rocks, covered with slippery green seaweed and, in the hollow of the rocks, pools of sea water. There were not many people about. He passed two women looking into the rock pools, but they took no notice of him.

Before long his sandals were soaking, but he was glad to be wearing them because in between the rocks the beach was rough and pebbly.

The going was slow. Everywhere he had to pick his way. It was no longer windy down on the beach, which was good, but he was a little worried about the sea. He knew that the tide went in and out but he was not sure about the times. All the same he must go on. If Helen was there he had to find her.

His legs ached. Also his knees were now bleeding again from scrambling over the rocks. He was not sure how he would recognize the lighthouse cliff. He had thought that it would be possible to see the lighthouse from the beach, but because the cliffs went straight up, and overhung at the top, he could see nothing of the land.

In the end he knew he must rest for a while. He had come a long way. There was no sign of Helen. Could she be there? He would make up his mind when he had rested.

He wondered if Helen would mind, since he had had no lunch, if he used some of her food. He sat down against a rock, and ate some of the stale bread.

Afterwards he didn't remember falling asleep, but he must have done so or he would have seen Mrs Porter walking towards him along the beach. As it was, when he wakened she was shaking his shoulder. Her face was white and he knew she was frightened.

'Daniel! Wake up!' She took his hand and started walking quickly back along the beach.

'We must hurry,' she said. 'The tide's coming in faster now, and the mist with it.'

It was not as difficult walking back along the beach because Mrs Porter helped him over the difficult places. Also she knew some proper steps a little further along, so that they didn't have to use the wooden ladder.

'How did you know where I was?' he asked.

'I guessed. And I met two women who'd seen you. Don't bother to talk. Save your breath for the climb. We'll have the explanation later.'

On top of the cliff the mist swirled around, so that sometimes it was clear for a minute and then quite thick again. He held on to Mrs Porter's hand and they kept to the path.

When they reached the lighthouse she made him change his clothes and put on dry shoes, while she made a pot of tea and buttered some currant teacakes. While they ate he told her his thoughts about the seagull, and about how he had thought that the gull named Helen was a little like his grandma Helen.

Mrs Porter eyed the sad-faced little boy. What a dim view he must be getting of life. First, his grandmother whom he had adored suddenly gone from him, and now the gull, which the child regarded as particularly his, had vanished too.

'It's very sad,' she said presently. 'Would it have been better if you'd never known her?'

Daniel looked at her in surprise. 'Of course not,' he said. 'She was my friend.'

Mrs Porter poured another cup of tea and fetched some coconut buns from the tin. 'I never had a grandma,' she said. 'She died when I was a baby.'

'I wasn't talking about my grandma then, I meant the gull.'

'I know. But it's a bit the same isn't it? You were so sad when your grandma died, but wasn't it lovely to have known her and been friends with her.'

He silently took in what she said. He saved a bit of his coconut bun, just in case. The bird was particularly fond of coconut buns. After they had finished the tea and buns he went out on to the terrace. Now the sea was completely hidden. The seagulls were back. He could hear them everywhere, and from time to time he saw them as they swooped through the mist. There was no sign of Helen. He whistled, and held out his hand with the coconut bun on it. He was not very hopeful.

Suddenly, the gull dropped down through the mist on to the terrace. She took the piece of bun from his hand.

'Quark!' she said.

# A Summer Remembered

Laura held her fingers under the running tap. 'Enough is enough!' she cried. She had burnt her hand, though not seriously, because Christopher had barged into the kitchen, knocking into her at the very moment she was taking the mince pies out of the oven.

'Thank goodness it only comes once a year!'

'I want some paper for Daddy's present,' Christopher said. 'Don't you *like* Christmas, Mum?'

Laura dried her hands and climbed up to a high cupboard, searching for the wrapping paper she could have sworn she had put there.

'Just at the moment,' she said, 'I don't think I do. I liked it when I was your age. Well, there's no paper here. Look in the cupboard in the dining room, and *don't* leave everything strewn on the floor!'

As Christopher left the kitchen, Milly entered.

'Ooh!' she said, 'what a lovely smell! Can I have a mince pie, Mum?'

'No. How many did you have out of the last batch?'

'Four.'

'You'll be sick,' Laura threatened. 'And you'll get fat!' But she couldn't imagine her eight-year-old daughter being fat.

'I'm never sick,' Milly said complacently. 'There's one here which is a funny shape. I could eat it up for you.'

'Get out!' Laura said. 'Get out or I'll set you on to the washing-up. Go and help Christopher to find some wrapping paper.'

Milly was gone in a flash. She was not domesticated and bully for her, Laura thought. But I really am a bad-tempered so-and-so. Talk about goodwill towards men—I can't even manage it towards my own children. She was filled with remorse. It evaporated in a flash as she surveyed the kitchen.

It looked like a disaster area. The duck, which was a tradition with them (heaven knew why) for Christmas Eve, lay there accusingly, waiting to be dealt with. The table had to be set, there was a mountain of dirty saucepans, the children must be put to bed, and Dick was not yet home.

She suspected he was buying her present—at the last minute as usual. If he gave her another lacy nightdress, or a large bottle of scent of a brand she didn't like, she'd scream. It was too bad that he wasn't here to lend her a hand. Other men, she felt sure, didn't work so late on Christmas Eve.

At the same time, she didn't want him back too soon, because he was picking up Aunt Hesther. She would hate her neat little aunt, who had spent every Christmas with them since her husband died, to see the state she was in.

Also, she now realized, catching her misty reflection in the kitchen mirror, she must have been mad to have cancelled her hair appointment.

Why was she so disorganized? You'd think after ten years of marriage everything would run like clockwork. Still, if it did, would that be even more boring?

The raspberries were thawing nicely. Or was it too soon? When it was time for the pudding, would they be a soggy mess? She picked one, crimson-red and juicy, out of the basin, and ate it—and was at once transported back to the July day when she'd gathered them. That had been fun.

She'd taken the children to the fruit farm. They'd picked for most of the afternoon, Christopher small enough to find the biggest and best fruit underneath the lower branches, Milly eating as many as she picked.

Between the three of them they'd filled two

great baskets, and she'd been jamming and freezing until after midnight. Now, as she ate another raspberry, and another, she remembered the delicious sweet smell which had pervaded the house.

But, standing in the kitchen on Christmas Eve, thoughts of the day of the raspberry picking could only lead on to the memories of the golden days which had followed so soon after. It was times like this, when life was getting her down, that she remembered them most clearly.

Where might she have been this Christmas, if she and Martin had followed the dictates of their own hearts? (In another kitchen, cooking a similar meal, common sense whispered; but she was not interested in common sense.)

She and Dick and the children had gone to Normandy for their holiday, renting a cottage which stood high on the cliff above the beach where they spent most of each day. She had never been to Normandy before and she fell in love with it at once—and, almost at once, with Martin.

She put the dish of raspberries in the fridge and began to stuff the duck. She wished she had not been reminded of the holiday. It only made things worse.

She pushed the duck away, poured herself a large glass of cooking sherry, picked up a mince pie—not the one with the funny shape but, deliberately, the most perfect she could find—and walked out of the kitchen, closing the door firmly behind her.

Then she immediately turned around again, went back into the kitchen, collected the bottle of sherry and two more mince pies and took them on a tray into the sitting room.

'To hell with Christmas!' she said, emptying the first glass and pouring another. 'To hell with Christmas pudding, useless presents, the rain beating on the window and tree lights which have gone on the blink! To hell with Cousin Maud and old Mrs Battye, who have sent me cards when I haven't sent to them, which is because *they* didn't send to *me* last year.

'To hell with stuffing ducks and to hell with the fact that three mince pies will make me fat and two glasses of sherry (or maybe more?) will make me squiffy! Why do we have to have Christmas? Why can't it always be summer?'

Why, she thought miserably, can't it be Normandy? A sheltered beach, the sea so warm that they'd been in and out all day. In a summer not renowned for good weather they had picked a fortnight of hot sun and blue skies, broken only by starlit nights.

From the moment their children had found

each other—Martin and Tessa's two were the same ages as Christopher and Milly—she had been attracted to Martin. So tall, looking down at her with appreciative eyes as she lay on the beach; so bronzed, so fair, so—oh, everything!

And he had been immediately attracted to her, he told her a day or two later when Dick and Tessa were swimming and she and Martin were sitting in the sun, oiling each other's backs.

'You have the most perfect skin,' he said. 'In fact, Laura, my love, you are perfect in every way! If only...!'

'If only what?' she said, knowing the answer, wanting to hear it said.

'If only we had met sooner, you and I!'

'If only!' she sighed.

But it would have been unlikely since at the crucial time, just before she married Dick, she had been reading English at a northern university while Martin was beavering away in Bristol. Fate was very, very cruel.

For two weeks they had held hands surreptitiously, played footsie under the table in the dark little restaurant where the four of them dined each evening, uttered (when possible) sweet words and sighs and, once or twice, held each other close in a local dance hall. It was delicious, and very, very frustrating.

'You know I couldn't do anything to hurt Tessa or the children,' he said in a stolen moment on the last night. 'You understand, my love?'

'Oh, I do!' she murmured. 'I could not love thee Dear so much, lov'd I not honour more.'

'How beautifully you put it!' he said admiringly, poetry obviously not being his strong point.

Martin and Tessa came here every year, they said. Had done for ages. They liked the beach and the restaurant, baby-sitters were easy to come by, and somehow they always met another couple they could get on with. People like you, they said. They'd be back next year, Tessa said, so why not make it a foursome? An eightsome, really, including the kids, though they were so occupied one hardly knew one had them.

'Fabulous?' Laura said.

'Great!' Dick said.

Martin said nothing and Laura knew that it was because he was too full for words.

'Oh, Martin!' Laura said out loud, tears running down her face and mingling with the third mince pie as she raised it to her lips.

Christopher came running in with what must surely be the last cards for this Christmas. One was obviously from her old school friend, Mavis.

The writing on the other was strange to her. She opened it first: a fat robin on a holly bush. Inside it said: 'Thinking of you. Martin and Tessa.'

'Why are you crying, Mum?' Christopher asked. 'Don't you like the card?'

'I like it,' she said, sniffing. 'I'm crying because I have to stuff the duck and do the potatoes and decorate a cake and give you two a bath. And because I've had two glasses of sherry and three mince pies!'

'I'll do without a bath,' Christopher offered.

Miraculously, it was all done by the time Dick arrived with Aunt Hesther. He carried a large, heavy parcel about which Laura tactfully asked no questions. It couldn't possibly be either underwear or scent. She hoped it wasn't something useful for the kitchen.

'Off with your coat, Aunt Hesther, and let me give you a nice glass of sherry,' Dick said.

'Do that, dear,' Laura said. 'No, not for me, thank you.'

The duck was delicious. With it they drank a bottle of expensive claret they had brought back from France and saved for the occasion.

'And the raspberries!' Aunt Hesther cried. 'They're like a taste of summer! So clever of you!'

Why did I not look forward to her coming? Laura wondered. Aunt Hesther had admired the decorations, gone into raptures about the tree, declared the children to be perfect darlings, and had even admired Laura's hair. 'Not too set,' she said approvingly.

'There's a card from Martin and Tessa,' Laura said to Dick when they were getting ready for bed. 'If we're going to team up with them next summer we should write to them fairly soon.' She hoped she sounded more nonchalant than she felt.

'We'll see,' said Dick.

On Christmas Day the children had their presents in the morning but the adults always waited until the afternoon.

'It was the way your mother always did it,' Aunt Hester said. 'So much more enjoyable when the rush of Christmas dinner is over. I like to open my presents slowly.'

She did so, gasping with delight at the calendar Milly had made for her and at the crayon drawing of an elephant which was Christopher's gift.

'Exactly what I wanted!' she said. 'What clever children you are!'

Dick handed Laura a very small parcel. So where was the big one?

'Open it,' he said. 'Stop trying to guess what's inside and find out!'

It was a small brooch in the shape of a flower, the centre of the flower an amethyst and each petal a fiery opal.

'Oh, Dick it's perfectly beautiful! It really is beautiful!' Laura cried.

'I'm glad you like it,' he said. 'But it's not your main present. Hang on while I fetch that.'

He came back into the room carrying the big parcel, only now it was wrapped in flowered paper and tied with a ribbon bow. Laura suspected Aunt Hesther's hand there.

'Don't try to guess this one,' Dick said, 'because you never will.'

Unwrapping the paper, she found a huge pile of holiday brochures.

'This is your real present,' he told her. 'Though you can't take delivery of it until the summer. Pick any holiday you like. And just the two of us. Aunt Hesther's going to look after the children for us.'

'Oh, Dick. I don't know what to say!' How could she tell him that she wanted nothing so much as to go back to Normandy, to the same beach, the same restaurant, the same people?

'Don't say anything until you've looked at

them. And remember—anything! And just this once, money no object.'

'But *why?*' Laura asked.

Dick shrugged. 'Just something I wanted to do. I didn't think you'd had the best of holidays last summer. Oh, it wasn't bad—but I had the feeling you were a bit fraught...'

'Well...perhaps I was a little,' Laura said slowly, her mind racing. Did he know? Had he known all along?'

She turned over the glossy pages of the brochures and began to read out loud. ' "Scintillating night-life, blue skies, gorgeous scenery." "A country whose magic captures the imagination". "Sip an aperitif and watch the world go by." I wonder who writes these?' she said. 'They're out of this world.'

'That's what holidays should be,' Aunt Hesther chipped in. 'One of the best things about them is that they're unreal. Everything you thought you wanted, packed into a couple of weeks! I remember once in Scarborough, it was only a couple of years after we were married, I met this man...oh, my goodness!' She closed her eyes and leaned back in her chair.

'Aunt Hesther,' Dick said. 'I don't believe you!'

'Oh, but it's true! You're not a woman, you see, so it's hard for you to understand. We had to part, of course, because there was Donald. But do you know what this man said to me? He said "Forever wilt thou love and she be fair"!'

'Keats,' Laura murmured, reading about Greek islands.

'Keats, was it? Well he knew what he was talking about. Whenever I think about William —that was the man's name—he's tall and sleek and charming, with a small black moustache. He could be bald and fat and bad-tempered now—but never in my memory. And then there was Henry,' she mused, 'I met Henry on a cruise the following year...'

'Aunt Hesther!' Laura cried. 'You shock me, you terrible woman! You don't mean to tell me...'

'And George, and Ferdinand—he was a waiter in the hotel—and Waldorf...I think his name was Waldorf but sometimes I get them a bit mixed up. But such happy memories!'

'You amaze me,' Laura said.

Aunt Hesther looked at her niece, her bright blue eyes meeting Laura's.

'Oh, but it was never serious. We pretended it was, you have to do that, but we knew we were pretending. It was just part of the holiday. Your Uncle Donald was the love of my life. He was worth twenty of anyone else I ever met.'

The two women continued to look at each other, challenge in their eyes. I don't know that I believe a word of it, Laura thought. Dick leaned forward and touched her hand.

'I want whatever makes you happy,' he said quietly. 'If you would prefer to join up with Martin and Tessa, then that's what we'll do. We'll write to them tomorrow to arrange it.'

Laura concentrated fiercely on the brochures. She must not, she must not cry she thought, flipping through the brightly coloured pages. 'Golden beaches', 'Idyllic setting', 'Distant, snowy peaks', 'Dance the night away'. When at last she thought she could control her voice, she looked up.

'Oh no, darling,' she said. 'I'd much rather just the two of us. There's a cruise here. "Sail away to happiness on moonlit nights at sea." How does that sound?'

'Wonderful?' Aunt Hesther said dreamily. 'And you never know *who* you'll meet on a cruise!'

# Children On The Shore

Until I saw the two small boys playing on the beach on that Sunday morning I had not realized that the decision I must make would be such a difficult one. It was not going to be only between me and James. That was only one side of it. On the other side—literally, since they were three thousand miles across the Atlantic—were my daughter and my small grandson.

Sharp tears stung my eyes as I glared angrily at the blue-green sea which separated me from all the family I had.

It was a brilliantly sunny day, so that coming out of the hotel I'd had to put on my sunglasses, but here by the water's edge there was a sharper wind. I turned up the collar of my jacket and pulled my cap further down over my ears. It would have been more sensible to have stayed behind the plate glass windows of the hotel verandah, a cushion at my back, a pot of coffee and the Sunday papers on the table.

I wasn't feeling sensible this morning. I was

happy, fulfilled, confused, and sad—all at the same time. I needed time to think and I had to be on my own.

James found this difficult to understand. He'd followed me to the bedroom when I'd gone to get my jacket.

'Darling Claire, please don't go! Or let me come with you,' he begged. 'I can't bear you out of my sight! And we've so little time.'

I looked in the mirror and tidied my hair. It would be so easy to stay. Part of me wanted to; to lie on the bed and let James make love to me, in the middle of the morning, bathed in the light which streamed through the tall window. If he takes me in his arms, I thought, if he were to give me one gentle push on to the bed...I wouldn't be able to help myself. But that wasn't his way.

I'd explained that it was always like this when something moved me deeply—and last night it had been pure joy—that I had to get away on my own, to sort things out.

'It's one of the things you have to learn about me,' I told him. 'There's so much we have to learn about each other.'

'I'm eager to,' he said.

I kissed him lightly, and left him.

'I won't be gone more than an hour.'

Leaving the hotel I climbed down the steep

path to the undercliff promenade where it was sheltered from the wind. I turned my face to the sun and walked, my body growing warmer with the exercise. There were very few people about and it was good to have the world to myself.

Seadean had been James's choice. I'd been with my parents when I was small, and later, the year before we were married, with Martin. I hadn't mentioned this to James since he was so set on the hotel he'd recommended.

This was the first weekend we'd been away together—really together—though we'd known each other for several months now. We'd had lots of days out. Sunday mornings at the zoo, where I always wanted to spend my time watching those glorious pink flamingoes while James could hardly be dragged away from the polar bears. Saturdays we'd go walking in the hills: evenings we'd spent at his flat or mine, listening to music. But never a night together. Never anything like this.

James is a radiologist at the city hospital. I'd met him there when I'd gone as a temporary secretary to Outpatients. That day I'd had a difficult morning. Case papers had gone astray and Staff Nurse had been sharp and sarcastic. I was sitting at a table in the staff restaurant when James approached with his piled-high tray and asked if he might join me.

'Please do,' I said. I hoped he wouldn't chatter. I wasn't in the mood.

'I haven't seen you around until today,' he said. 'I noticed you in Outpatients when I came to see Staff Nurse.'

'Then you'll have heard all about the incompetent temp who lost a patient's case history?'

He laughed. Until then I hadn't really bothered to look at him, but at the sound of his deep musical chuckle I looked up. His whole face was alive with humour. One corner of his mouth curled up more than the other and laughter lines were deeply etched around his eyes. He looked older than his voice had promised, his hair changing from black to grey where it sprang from his broad forehead. Well, at forty-two I had a few grey hairs myself.

'So that was you?' he said. 'Don't worry, you're not the first to lose a file. They always turn up, usually on the consultant's desk!'

'It did,' I said. 'But not before Mr Gardner *and* Staff Nurse had been hopping mad with me at the delay.'

He reached for the pepper and scattered it liberally over his spaghetti.

'What's your name?'
'Claire Moffat. Yours?'

'James Parker.'

I remained at the hospital for six weeks and I shared a table with James on several occasions. From time to time I had to go to his department to pick up X-ray plates. Sometimes he brought a batch to Outpatients.

'Since when have heads of departments done their own fetching and carrying?' Staff Nurse asked him.

'I like old James,' she said when he'd left. 'I've known him a long time.'

'*Old* James?'

'Well, maybe not. He's forty-five. But he's been on his own a long time and it's aged him.'

His marriage, she told me, had ended in divorce. There were no children. It had been a deeply unhappy period for him and ever since, though he was pleasant enough with everyone, he'd held back from relationships. Staff Nurse wasn't one for gossip. I think she told me because she thought I ought to know.

By the time my hospital stint was ended James and I were seeing each other regularly. I had not had such a friend since Martin's death, in an accident, several years ago. We were not lovers, but when a man and woman have a close relationship such as ours there comes a time when the light kisses on greeting become warmer; the parting kisses hold words which have not been said; the touch becomes more intimate.

It was James who suggested the weekend together, but by this time, I thought, he must have been sure of my answer.

James had picked me up at my flat and we'd driven towards the coast. It was a long journey from the city, but James drove his small car fast and we arrived at the hotel in good time. Before dinner, sipping our drinks on the little balcony outside our bedroom, we watched a small cargo ship, black-silhouetted in the red path of the sun across the sea. The whole scene—the ship, the darkening sea, the two of us—was held fast, suspended in a moment of time.

The night which followed was no less perfect. Widowed now for many years, I had learned to live without sexual love, until in the end I'd thought it was beyond me. That part of my life, I believed, was over. Oh yes! Any presentable widow, even in her early forties, will tell you that the world is full of men who think you'll be grateful of their attentions. But casual affairs are not my line. What I had with James, that which had been developing in our lives since the morning I'd first met him, was no trivial growth. Last night it had flowered: magnificent, delicate, flamboyant, sturdy—for a flower can be all these things.

We had been apprehensive; as shy with each other as if we were young, inexperienced lovers. But it was all right. Everything was all right. It was like...coming home.

It was partly because it had been so perfect that I now had to be for a little while on my own.

'Don't change!' James called out just before I closed the door. He spoke with a sudden anxiety.

I walked for a while, filling my lungs with the sharp air, tasting the salt on my lips. After a while, almost lightheaded with the strong air, I stopped and leaned against the sea wall. The beach was several feet below, to be reached by worn stone steps, covered in seaweed. The receding tide had left shallow rock pools, the rocks covered with varieties of seaweed and encrusted with barnacles.

Two small boys, carrying fishing nets and jam jars with string handles, hopped precariously between the pools. Their voices, clear and high, were carried towards me on the wind as if from another country. The words were indistinct but the excitement was there. They came together and crouched down, utterly absorbed in whatever it was they had found in the pool. Close by, a black mongrel dog without an owner frisked in and out of the water.

Suddenly I wanted to be down there with them, barefoot on the wet rocks. I wanted to feel the sand under the soles of my feet, to dabble my toes in the cold sea water. I always seemed to be on the edge, on dry land: a spectator, afraid of getting my feet wet, of spoiling my high-heeled fashion boots.

Soon, I thought, watching the boys, David will be as old as they are. A few quick years—and then a few more years and he'll be grown up. And I shall have missed it all. I shall never have splashed in pools or walked on a beach with him; flown a kite or taken him to the fair. I will be his grandmother in England, who sends him letters and presents and birthday cards. I will be the woman in the photograph on the mantelpiece.

Frustration rose in me, and on a sudden impulse I took off my boots, rolled up the legs of my trousers and stuffed my socks into my pocket. Holding the boots in one hand, and with the other balancing myself against the slippery wall at the side of the steps, I descended to the beach. Picking my way across the shore, I went towards the children.

They were watching a crab in the water, trying to entice it out of its corner. It was about five inches across, larger than they had expected. Including me at once in their conversation they said: 'If you touch it or it sees you, it will scuttle away.'

Like some people, I thought.

I parked my boots on a spit of dry land and crouched down. The pool was dark, mysterious. Small creatures darted about in the water. Weeds made curtains for them to hide behind.

'Look! By the stone!' I said. 'There's a sea anemone.'

'It's like a flower,' one of the boys said.

'Yes, but watch when I touch it.'

I found a piece of driftwood and gently prodded the anemone. Swiftly, it drew in its feelers and was at once camouflaged with a coating of minute shells and pebbles.

For a few minutes we watched the underwater world of the small pool, then: 'What's the time, miss?' one of them asked.

'Eleven o'clock.' I was sorry to be reminded that time existed.

'We'll have to go.'

They picked up their jars and nets and ran swiftly along the shore, leaping across the rocks, racing up the steps, disappearing from sight along the promenade. The dog had long since vanished. I was alone again. My feet were coated with wet sand and, unnoticed until now, the sea had soaked the bottom of my trouser legs.

Without warning, the day turned dull. Gulls screamed overhead. The tide turned, bringing in the rain clouds. I picked up my boots and started to walk back.

Along the promenade there was a coffee stall. I was cold now, and glad of a hot drink. While I drank I watched the sea, racing in before the wind. The blue, which earlier in the day it had borrowed from the sky, was gone. The waves were steely grey and threatening. I thought about my family from which it divided me.

I suppose because my husband had been killed before Alison was a year old, she and I had a particularly close relationship as she grew. I'd had to earn a living but I managed to get jobs which left me free to spend the holidays with her. We'd had such good times. I could have remarried, but no one had measured up to Martin or been what I wanted for Alison, so I'd tried to be mother and father to her.

I think it worked. I'd never been possessive with her. I'd been contented for her to leave me to go to university at the other end of the country, and when, in her first year, she'd met and wanted to marry Nicholas it hadn't occurred to me to stand in her way. I'd married at eighteen and my only regret had been at the brevity of my marriage.

I liked my new son-in-law, though I was a little shaken when he was offered, and accepted, a two-year post-doctoral position in Toronto. But we were excited, and smiled, and told each other that two years would soon pass. I would have preferred Alison to stay in England to have her baby but she wanted to be with Nicholas.

I'd visited them soon after David was born. He was a darling, my grandson. He was walking now, Alison wrote, and saying one or two words.

I took his photograph out of my handbag. Round, chubby face. Hair which stood up in an unruly tuft on the top of his head, exactly like Alison when she was a baby. I fished around for Alison's recent letter. She wrote in a generous scrawl, sheets and sheets on thin blue paper. There was no need to read it, I knew it by heart.

Nicholas had been offered a permanent position in the university and the promise of a bright future if he stayed there. Neither he nor Alison had any hesitation in accepting. They liked Canada. They enjoyed the kind of life they led there. They thought it was a good country for their children—Alison was pregnant again.

I was their only worry. They wanted me to join them, not for a visit but permanently.

'We want you around when our children are growing up,' Alison wrote. Nicholas had added a postcript. 'I agree with everything Alison says.'

I'd be so welcome. I knew that for certain. And I wanted so much to be near to them. My own flesh and blood.

Why did I have to think about all this now? James was waiting for me. It was to be a new beginning for the two of us; a new life together.

I realized now, replacing Alison's letter in my handbag, taking another look at David's photograph, that at the back of my mind I'd always thought that one day I'd emigrate, join my daughter and my grandchildren; be part of a warm, loving family.

I thought of the little boys by the rock pool.

'Why, oh why did you have to be on the beach this morning?' I shouted out loud.

James and I drove home that afternoon in near silence. The rain which had threatened with the incoming tide had settled down into a heavy downpour. It beat on the roof of the car and ran in rivers down the windscreen. The traffic was heavy, as if everyone was in a hurry to get home and close the doors against the day. James concentrated on his driving, and I was glad because I didn't want to talk. I had too much to think about.

It would have been easier for me if things could have drifted for a little while, if I could put off my decision; but James, having reached his, was impatient. He'd been waiting on the hot verandah when I'd returned from my walk, anxiously watching for me. He had a martini in front of him and ordered one for me and another one for himself.

'You're driving me to drink!' he joked.

Even before the fresh drinks arrived he started to talk.

'You know I love you,' he said. 'I'd do anything in the world to make you happy. Please, Claire, please marry me!'

I wanted to say yes and I couldn't. Nor could I explain why. I didn't know whether it was the thought of Alison and her family which held me back, or whether it was marriage itself which frightened me. It was so long since I'd known it. I knew that sexually we'd be all right, but there was more to it than that. I'd grown out of living with another person. I had my own ways. One can grow selfish, living alone. I tried to say some of this to James, not mentioning Alison.

'I understand all that,' he said. 'It's the same for me, you know.'

I felt anguished that I couldn't give him an answer, either a straight yes or no. He didn't deserve to be kept in suspense.

'Let's not talk about it just now,' I said. 'Let's not spoil the weekend with discussions.' I wanted to keep the perfect time we'd had the previous night unspoiled; but of course, and we both knew it, the weekend was already spoiled by the time I'd returned from my walk on the beach.

When James stopped the car outside my block of flats I made excuses not to invite him in.

'I'm dreadfully tired,' I said. 'And I have to get things ready for morning.'

'Where are you working tomorrow?' he asked. 'Let me know, and I'll pick you up afterwards.'

'I don't know, but I'll call you.'

'Claire!' He took my hands, then kissed me very gently on the lips. 'I love you very much. Remember that!'

'I will. And I love you.'

I didn't sleep much that night. My body

longed for James's. I guessed that he would have the same longings.

Next day my agency asked me if I would take a job out of town. I was to type, and do a certain amount of research, for an author who, after years of travel, was writing his auto-biography. There were facts and dates and all manner of records to be verified, as well as typing the manuscript. It would take several weeks, he told the agency; and because his place was so inaccessible there was a cottage nearby which I was required to occupy if I took the job. For a month or two I would be free to go home only at weekends.

It sounded the kind of job I'd like, and I was all too ready to jump at the chance to be away from familiar surroundings. I needed time.

I telephoned James at the hospital, told him about the job and that I'd decided to take it, starting next day. He wasn't best pleased, but there was no time to talk and we arranged to meet when I returned on the following Friday.

By the second post there was a letter from Alison.

'I know you must be finding the decision difficult,' she said, 'but we do so want you to come. I'd like you to be here before David's sister arrives.' (She was quite certain she was having a girl.) Nicholas had added his usual postscript.

'Come on, Ma! Start packing!'

I had to leave that afternoon to start my new job next day. *That* packing was done through a curtain of tears, and most of the time I didn't know who I was crying for—James, myself, or my loved ones in Canada.

Nevertheless, I made one decision. I sat down and wrote to Canada House for information about emigration. That much wouldn't commit me to anything.

My new employer was waiting for me at the station. He walked towards me, hand out-stretched.

'You must be Mrs Foster. You fit the description. Five feet five, blonde hair, green suit. I'm Robert Eastern.'

He looked older than the photographs I'd seen on his book jackets.

'I know what you're thinking,' he said. 'They *will* use photographs fifteen years old.' Nevertheless he was still handsome.

His car was a stately old Rolls which he drove as though it was a small sports car. He took me to his house, gave me tea, outlined the job, and then showed me the cottage where I'd live. I liked it. I liked the man; I liked the sound of the job.

He drove me hard that week, no nine-to-five nonsense, but every minute was interesting. He'd been everywhere, done everything. Only with the greatest difficulty had his publishers persuaded him to stay on the ground long enough to write his memoirs. The moment it was done, he planned to take off again.

'There's a great deal more to see and do,' he said. 'One is never too old to start something.'

'People will tell you it's important to *finish* things,' he went on. 'Poppycock! It's the starting that counts. I'm so long in the tooth that I might never finish the next thing, but as long as I start it...When you're afraid to begin, then you *are* old! You might as well shut up shop.'

The week flew by. On Friday afternoon I tidied my desk and left.

'You've done very well,' he said. 'See you Monday.'

I'd telephoned James and asked him to supper. I knew now what I was going to say to him. I wanted everything to be right. I took a lot of trouble with the meal, chose the wine carefully.

When I answered the door to James he stepped inside quickly and took me in his arms.

'I've missed you so much, Claire.'

'I've missed you too, James. Such a lot.'

We kept the talk light during supper. I told him about my new job, he filled me in on the hospital gossip. The meal was good.

'You're a super cook!' he said.

I went into the kitchen to make the coffee. James followed me.

'We've got to talk, Claire. You know that, don't you?'

He carried the tray into the living room and I poured. I crossed the room and picked up a photograph of Alison from the desk, then put it down again.

'Stop fidgeting,' James said. 'Come and sit down.' He patted the sofa beside him but I went and sat in the armchair.

'Claire, I'm asking you again,' he said. 'Will you marry me? I love you with all my heart. There's nothing I wouldn't do to make you happy.'

I looked at him. He was the nicest man I knew, and the dearest man in the world to me; the only man I'd ever met who could take Martin's place. It was hard for me to say what I did.

'Then, James, you must let me go. Perhaps not for always. I don't know. Certainly for a time. I'm not ready to marry you—or anyone.'

I tried to explain to him. I had learned a

lot in the last week. If I were to marry James now it would be because I was running for shelter, warmth, security. Because I was afraid of the cold winds, afraid of getting my feet wet.

'It was to have been a happy ending for us,' James said.

'I know. But there's so much I haven't begun.'

He took my hand, kissed my fingers.

'Will you come back to me, Claire?'

'I might. I think I might well. But I don't know.'

Next day I wrote to Alison.

'...And so, though I long be with you all, and though I miss you very much, I know that it's too soon for me to settle down yet.'

It was difficult for me to express what I wanted to tell her: that although a week ago I'd believed I had a choice between two ways of life, now I learned that the world was full of choices for me to make. My own life stretched before me, full of new and exciting beginnings. I was free to choose anything, go anywhere.

'I daresay I shall visit you all next spring,' I wrote.

But I wasn't sure, even of that. Who knew where I would be next spring?

## Be Your Age, Dear

Leaving the office, I remembered that I must break my journey home and drop in on my daughter. She'd promised to collect my long skirt from the cleaners; also I had this message from the *Evening Argus*. And it would give me an opportunity of ten minutes with my beautiful granddaughter. At fourteen months, Sara was the most enchanting baby in the world.

As soon as I walked in I could see that Diana was in a bad mood. Well, I knew how to deal with her. I flopped on the sofa.

'I'm dead! It's been one of those days. Could we have a cup of coffee, love?'

She didn't answer: just walked away into the kitchen.

'Where's my darling Sara?' I called out.

'In bed.'

'So early? You knew I was coming.' I couldn't keep the disappointment out of my voice.

'She hasn't slept all day. She was worn out.'

'So that's it? That's why you look a bit peaked?'

'No, it is not! I'm quite capable of looking after a fourteen-month-old baby.'

'Sorry!'

She really was touchy. She'd been like this once or twice lately.

'Had a row with Richard?' I asked sympathetically. Richard is a dear, but anyone can have a row.

'No, I have not had a row with Richard! Why do you always assume it's other people?'

'Other people? What do you mean?'

'I mean it's you. Your behaviour. In particular your behaviour at the party last night. Not that that was the only time!'

'My behaviour?' Now I was really puzzled. Had I...? I couldn't have...

'You're not telling me I drank too much? Did something I can't remember? Stood on my head or recited?' Only the look on her face stopped me from giggling.

'No, I'm not. I daresay you were stone cold sober, which makes it worse.'

*'What did I do?'*

I thought it had been a good party. I hadn't enjoyed myself so much for a long time. But clearly I'd somehow disgraced myself.

'I don't understand,' I said.

'Oh yes you do! Heaven knows, you always chase the men, but this...this *exhibition*...and with Richard's brother...'

'Exhibition? With Martin?'

'The Charleston was bad enough...everybody standing around and clapping...but that sexy dancing afterwards...! Everybody noticed. And then going off into the garden for hours!'

'To cool off. And about a quarter of an hour, actually. It was perishing cold after that. As far as I'm concerned, I behaved quite naturally.'

'Yes, I suppose it was natural for you!'

'Then how do you want me to behave?'

'Just be your age, that's all,' Diana shouted. 'That's all I ask. Stop going after young men. You're my mother and Sara's grandmother. I wish you'd remember that and behave accordingly.'

I took a deep breath. Keep calm. Play it cool.

'I'm aware I'm your mother,' I said. 'Have been for twenty years. And for sixteen of those years your father as well. I've done my best...'

'I'm not denying that. I just wish...'

'Wait a minute, Diana. Let me finish. It's also one of the greatest pleasures of my life to be Sara's grandmother. But I'm also myself, Chloe Patterson. I'm a woman, and lots of the time I feel like a woman. Do you think because I'm now a grandmother I should opt out of life?'

'You could at least try behaving like a grandmother. Not go after men half your age.'

'Martin is exactly ten years younger than I am. As I recall it, he went after me. He's a nice fellow: I enjoy his company. That's all there is to it, but if there were more I don't need permission from you. And I'll behave like a grandmother, whatever that means, to Sara, and to no one else. I'm not the world's grandmother!'

We were shouting at each other like fishwives so that we didn't hear Richard's key in the lock.

'Whoops!' he said. 'Mistimed! I'll go out and come in again.'

'Don't bother,' I snapped. 'I'm going. And please don't bother to kiss me or I'll be accused of seducing you.'

'*That* I'd enjoy,' he said, putting an arm around me.

'You're saying all the wrong things,' I warned him.

'Funny,' he said. 'I thought that would have been a right thing to say. Most women seem...'

'Well, it's just been pointed out to me that I'm not so much a woman as a mother and grandmother. And I've got to learn to behave accordingly.'

'Don't you dare! And sit down, both of you. I'm going to pour you each a gin and tonic, with lots of ice to cool you down.'

We calmed down. Richard has that effect.

'All the same, I really can't stay,' I said eventually. 'I came partly to discuss this thing from the *Argus*, and now I'll have to go and see Gran about it.'

My mother was to be sixty on the following Friday and the *Argus* wanted to take a photograph of the four generations of us; my mother, me, Diana, Sara—and of course to interview my mother.

Not that sixty is a great age, but ever since my mother said something outrageous when taking part in a television panel game, she's been something of a personality. Her opinion is sought (and freely given) on a variety of subjects about which she knows little or nothing. The Middle East, the Pill, the state of the economy. She attracts publicity like a flower attracts bees.

'Heaven knows what she'll say in the interview,' I said. 'You know what she's like.'

'*Formidable,*' Richard said, pronouncing it in French, which seemed to give it extra meaning.

'Why don't you mind about *her?*' I asked Diana. 'She's always up to something. She's far more outrageous than I'll ever be. Remember that Spanish waiter!'

113

There was a thoughtful silence while we all remembered.

'What a woman!' Richard sighed. 'The strain gets weaker with succeeding generations. I'm afraid Sara might be quite conventional.'

'It's not the same,' Diana said. 'Gran's old. She's simply eccentric.'

At what age, I wondered, does unacceptable social behaviour become lovable eccentricity?

By the time I stood up to go Diana seemed to be back to normal. And I remembered that a pregnant woman—which Diana was—can be over-emotional, and made allowances.

But as I drove away everything Diana had said rang in my ears. I tried to push it away, to concentrate on my driving, but it was far from easy.

Curiously, it was the fact of Diana being settled with Richard and the baby which had allowed me to start being a person again. I'd known for some time now that I was waking up, wanting something more from life than I was getting. But I didn't know what I wanted. My job was safe, but dull. I had a bit of money in the bank. And I never went anywhere or did anything exciting. Was that why I'd gone a bit mad at the party?

I parked the car in front of the block of flats where my mother lived. When my father was alive they'd had a largish house in a village. My mother's doings—she had always been unconventional—had kept the village interested for years and they were disappointed when after my father's death she decided to leave.

My father was a senior civil servant of fixed habits. She must have driven him almost mad. But he gave no sign of it, ever, and he adored her till the day he died. He was never as embarrassed by her goings-on as I was.

Mother waved a newspaper at me as I entered.

'Look at this!' she cried. 'Sex is Good For Pensioners, says doctor. Of course it is! Everyone knows that. I could have told them if they'd asked me.'

'They will,' I said. 'Sooner or later.'

'Do you think so?'

'I won't have a drink,' I said, 'I've just had one with Diana and Richard, and I have to drive back.'

'You're so conscientious, Chloe darling.'

She poured a neat vodka which she tossed down her throat in Continental fashion. She made conscientiousness sound a dull virtue.

'And how are my granddaughter and great-granddaughter?' she asked.

'Diana's a bit jumpy.'

I felt the need to tell her about the quarrel.

So I did. In spite of her frivolity, my mother often sees things clearly.

'Have you ever noticed, darling, how *elderly* the young can be?' she said thoughtfully. 'They take life so seriously. I've noticed it in you many times. Thank Heaven you're growing out of it. Or I hope you are. Is he nice, this young man? Can I meet him?'

'Oh Gran!' I protested. 'Do stop it! I've told you, there's nothing in it.'

'Do you mind,' she said, 'not calling me "Gran"? I am not your grandmother. I often wish I'd made you call me "Ellen" from the beginning. But your father wouldn't have of it. He was all for rôles.'

'Well, Diana takes after him,' I said.

'Chloe, darling, I think you ought to find yourself a nice man,' she urged. 'Not necessarily to *marry*. One likes a change. You're far too settled. It's not healthy. I don't intend to settle down for a long time yet.'

'If ever,' I said. 'Let me tell you about the *Argus*.'

I explained that we'd all come round on Friday morning and the reporter would take a picture of the four of us together. And then he'd ask her for a few reminiscences, and so on.

'You don't have to do it,' I told her.

She gave me a sharp look. 'You know perfectly well I shall enjoy it!'

I was afraid of that. 'Do be careful what you say to him,' I begged her. 'Remember, it's family this time.'

'Oh, they'll just want a few pearls of wisdom,' she said airly. 'But actually I'm not sure...'

'What?'

'I'm not sure that I'll have time for an interview.'

'Not have time? What do you mean?'

'I've got lots to do,' she said. 'Lots of irons in the fire.'

'Oh, you mean preparing for the party. But that's all taken care of. Diana and I are going to do that. I told you, I'm taking the day off. There's no need for you to do a thing. You can just sit with your feet up.'

When I left she was deciding what to wear for the photograph, choosing between a clinging velvet dress and some tight red linen trousers, both more suitable for a woman half her age. But since she's a size twelve, she can get away with it.

By the time I reached home I was in a turmoil. My daughter thought my behaviour too young; my mother was sure I was prematurely old. I loved them both, cared what they thought. But what about me? Will the real Chloe Patterson please stand up?

I didn't see my family for the rest of that week. We were busy in the office on the annual budgets and I had to work long and late. They weren't completed until late Thursday night.

In fact, I was glad that working late had prevented me from seeing anyone. I was sorting myself out, and until I'd finished I preferred to be alone. By the time Friday arrived, I'd come to terms with myself. I knew what I was going to do.

When I got to my mother's flat Diana and the baby, and the photographer, were standing on the mat.

'We've been ringing for ages,' Diana said anxiously. 'I do hope everything's all right. Have you got a key?'

'Yes. It will be,' I assured her. 'You know how unpunctual Mother is.'

We went in. The shelf over the mantelpiece, and the sideboard, were covered with birthday cards. In the middle of the table was a white envelope addressed to me, and a similar one addressed to 'The Reporter, *Evening Argus*'. I read mine out loud.

'Darlings,' it said. 'Forgive me for not being with you on my birthday. This lovely chance came to go to Tunisia. I couldn't refuse it, could I? Have a fabulous party and drink my health. PS. The sausage rolls are in the freezer.'

Irons in the fire indeed!

'What does yours say?' I asked the reporter.

'Much the same,' he said. 'Except that my PS says "You're only young once". I say, this is fantastic!'

'Fantastic? If you mean unbelievable, I assure you it isn't.'

'What a headline!' he enthused. 'Can't you just see it? GREAT-GRANDMOTHER ELOPES!'

'Hey, we don't know she's eloped,' I protested. 'Also she wouldn't like the way you put it. Not Great-Grandmother. Just Ellen.'

'How about Great-Grandmother Ellen?' he said. 'What do you think? Yes, perhaps I could have your views on the situation generally. What are *your* plans now that your mother has...er...left?'

'My plans? Do you mean what am I going to do about my mother? Actually, nothing at all. I have plans of my own. I intend, the minute this party is over—if it ever takes place at all—to go off on a cruise. I fly to Venice on the night plane to join the ship. I have the tickets. Venice by moonlight. The blue Adriatic. The warm breezes of the Greek Islands.'

119

'Mother! Mother, stop it!' Diana exclaimed. 'What do you mean? What are you talking about? What about your job?'

'I gave it up at nine o'clock last night. Ten years, seven months and eighteen days is long enough on one job, especially one as boring as that.'

'Super!' the reporter said, rapidly writing in his shorthand notebook. 'Can I ask if you'll be accompanied on this cruise? You know what I mean?'

'I do. The answer is, not to begin with. But the brochure is full of promise.'

'Fantastic,' he said, struggling to get it down. GREAT-GRANDMOTHER ELOPES! GRAND-MOTHER RENOUNCES ALL FOR ROMANCE!'

'Grandmother!' I said. 'I give up!'

'And what about *you?*' he asked Diana. 'What news can you give me? My goodness, what a family!'

'None,' Diana said firmly. 'Absolutely none. I'm happily married and I'm going to stay put and soon I'll have my second baby in peace. That's all I ask now.' She turned to me. 'Well, I just hope you know what you're doing, Mother!'

'Oh, I do.' I assured her.

'And I just hope you'll be happy, that's all.'

'Thank you, darling. That's nice of you. Of course, I'll be back for my new grandchild, and I'll send you all lots of lovely postcards.'

'Young wife gets pregnant,' the reporter said thoughtfully. 'I think you're right. It's not really news, is it?'

# A Trip To The Park

I'm walking in Central Park, New York, on a Sunday afternoon, although I've been strictly forbidden to do so. The last thing Richard said before he took the plane for Cincinnati was 'Don't go wandering around on your own, Cassie, darling. New York isn't Twickenham. And there's plenty to amuse you in the apartment.'

He'd waved his hand towards the books and records, neatly stacked in precise order on the purpose-built shelves.

'But be careful with the record player,' he'd warned. 'It's quite precious.'

'I will,' I promised.

'And I'll be back Monday morning—early.'

I tried to stay in the apartment. I read, played some music, listened to the radio. I'd have done some chores but the apartment was pin neat; nothing to be done. So when I couldn't bear another minute of the sun streaming into the apartment, I switched off the record player, put my book back in its correct place on the shelf, and walked out. If you walk in a straight line from Richard's apartment in East Eighty-fourth Street down to Fifth Avenue, the park's right there in front of you.

It looks as though everyone else has had the same idea. It's crowded, at least it is in the bit where I am. It's as busy as the High Street on a Saturday, only people look happy, and no one is hurrying. In spite of Richard's warning about being mugged, or conned, or worse, I'm sure I'm going to be all right.

There are all nationalities here and everyone is out for enjoyment. Ice-cream, pretzels, novelty toys, cold drinks. Parents, children, grandmothers in Sunday hats. Over there a group is playing old-fashioned jazz: the New Orleans stuff. People are tapping their feet, clicking their fingers. One or two are starting to dance.

Now I'm edging into a crowd; quite a thick one. I'm not tall enough to see what's happening, but I wriggle through to the front. We're watching a young man, a boy really, with dead-white make-up, like a sad clown, doing a miming act. With no props except his own body—and no words—he tells a long story. Sad, romantic, comic. He's marvellous. I understand everything his mobile hands say.

Suddenly there's a cry of agony behind me. I

turn around and see this guy grimacing with pain.

'You're surely quite a weight for a little one,' he says. 'Felt like all of one hundred and forty pounds on my foot!'

'Eight stones exactly,' I say. 'I'm very sorry. I didn't realize I'd moved. Have I really hurt you?'

'Crippled me for life, I shouldn't wonder!'

Then everybody around us is saying 'Sssh!' and 'Keep quiet, can't you?' So I do.

Presently, the performance ends. We all clap like mad, and then start to move away. A few, a very few, toss a few cents into a dish in front of the performer. I turn around to apologize to this man I've trodden on.

'It's nothing,' he says. 'A broken toe. A bruised metatarsal. Nothing that time won't heal.'

'Well, I *am* sorry!'

'You're forgiven.' He smiles. He has a nice smile. His skin is brown and his eyes are dark. He could be Italian, but his voice is very American.

'He's good, isn't he? The performer, I mean.' I haven't any intention of getting into conversation with him, but when you've practically lamed a man, you owe him something.

'Sure is,' he agreed. 'I've seen him before.

125

He's often here on a Sunday.'

'You live in New York?'

One minute we're standing there, about to go different ways. Next minute we're strolling in the same direction.

'Yes. My folks live in Wisconsin, but I have a job here.'

'You're not limping,' I accuse him. 'I can't have *crippled* you.'

'It comes and goes,' he says, and breaks into an exaggerated limp, so that passers-by stare.

'What are *you* doing in Central Park on a Sunday afternoon,' he asks. 'Your voice doesn't belong here.'

I explain that I'm on a visit to my...well... fiancé. 'He's been working here for a year now. We've been discussing wedding plans. Actually, we seem to have been discussing them for years. Since I was about seventeen.'

'All of four years, I'm sure,' he says. 'By the way, my name's Dan. What's yours?'

'Cassie.'

'And where is this fiancé of yours?'

I explain, defensively. 'He would have liked to have been with me, but business...'

'Ah well!' Dan says. 'One man's business is another man's opportunity!'

I don't think that's very funny. He's probably the kind of person Richard warned me about. I'm just about to give him a cool good-bye when I hear this drum beat, and the sound of a brass band in the distance.

'What's that?' I ask. 'Listen!'

'A parade.'

'What sort of a parade?'

'Just a parade, I guess. Haven't you seen one before?'

'No.'

'Then you can't have been here long. We have them practically every week.'

Now the band is getting nearer, the drum beat louder. In fact, I think there are two bands, not quite in tune with each other. 'Come and watch it,' he says.

The parade is marvellous. A brass band in front. A company of girls in uniform, led by four, stick-twirling drum majorettes. Several open cars, swathed in tulle, occupied by jolly-faced fat men and women. A decorated float with an entire jazz group on top, just near enough in distance to compete with the brass band at the front, and a truck load of accordionists coming up farther back. A company of dancers ignore all the music and do their own thing. You can see their lips silently moving as they count the beats.

'It's fantastic,' I say. 'Absolutely fantastic! Why didn't I bring my camera?'

The parade has to slow down right in front of us to turn the corner. This plays havoc with the marchers and dancers, who have to impose 'on-the-spot' routines, and then get back into step again. I could have taken some super photographs.

'Don't worry,' Dan says. 'There'll be others. How long are you here for?'

'Three weeks.'

'Is your Richard going to be away much?'

'After he returns tomorrow morning, not at all.' I don't like the tone of Dan's voice. It isn't as if Richard could help being away this weekend. It's just a pity it happened to be my first one.

The parade dwindles. Obviously the best talent is up at the front, and so is most of the music. The stragglers at the back have to keep their own time.

The moment it's over, the crowd starts to split, everybody in different directions, like bees taking wing from a hive. That leaves me and Dan standing on the sidewalk.

'What now?' Dan says.

I give him a look. My plans—not that I have any—don't include him. How to say this without sounding rude?

'The Metropolitan,' he says. 'You know. Museum, art gallery. It's right by here. Everyone should visit the Metropolitan.'

I know that. In fact it's high on my list, but I've planned to do it with Richard. Perhaps I should leave now; go back to the apartment.

'I think...'

'You'll be quite safe,' he says, grinning. 'If I pester you, you can always call an attendant.'

Why not? Why not go with him, I mean? Where's the harm in looking at pictures? Then I'll go straight back to the apartment, wash my hair, boil an egg, have an early night. But right now it's mid-afternnon and the sun is shining all over Manhattan.

The Metropolitan is fabulous. I want to see the French paintings, but get sidetracked by the Chinese ceramics, which Dan raves about. Then somehow we're standing in front of this Goya portrait, with a small boy in it who's just like my nephew, Peter. So I have to buy a postcard of it to send to my sister, and we get lost three times trying to find the sales counter. By the time we've bought it (it is *exactly* like the child) I'm exhausted. My feet are throbbing painfully.

'I'm sorry,' I say. 'I can't take any more. I've got a limit in art galleries. Mental as well as physical. I really must go now.'

'Could you use a cup of coffee?' Dan asks.

I realize I'm dying for one. And it will refresh

me for the walk back to the apartment. So why not?

'Great!' Dan says. 'I know just the place!'

He takes my arm and we walk this way and that, turn corners, cross crossings, looking for this place Dan knows. And at last he finds it. It turns out we're both hungry, so we have these huge hamburgers, which naturally take ages to eat. And then we need more coffee.

While we're eating, Dan tells me he's in advertising 'somewhere near the bottom, right now,' and I tell him I'm with a publisher.

'Have you got a girlfriend?' I ask. Looking at him, I'm sure he must have.

'Sort of,' he says.

'What do you mean, "sort of"?'

'In Wisconsin. Not here.'

'But not serious? I mean, you're not engaged, or married, or anything?'

'None of those,' he affirms.

When we come out of the coffee place the day is brighter than ever. Clear, dry, sunny.

'It's exactly the day for going up the Empire State building.' Dan says, looking up at the sky.

'I'm sorry...'

'You could be here all of three weeks and not get another day like this,' he says. 'I'm warning you.'

So we walk down town, and take the lifts, and here we are on top of the world. Dan is quite right. It would have been a pity to miss this. It's every bit as fabulous as I'd expected. The only thing is, Richard wanted to show it to me. Perhaps I shan't tell him I've even been out. I shall have to think about that, but not right now because Dan is pointing out the ships on the Hudson River and I don't want to miss anything.

It's quite late when we get the lift down to earth again.

'Thank you very much,' I say. 'And now I really must get back.'

'Of course you must,' he agreed. 'There's just one more thing I'd like to show you. The reason is, it's exactly the right time of day for it.'

'What's that?' I shouldn't ask. Once he tells me, that'll be it!

Well, I *did* ask, so here we are, sitting with drinks at a table by the window in the Copter Club, right at the top of the Pan Am building, looking down the length of Park Avenue. Only a minute ago it was daylight, and now it's dusk, with a deep, red fine-weather sky as the sun goes down. Lights are appearing in the windows, making changing patterns in high-rise buildings.

Inside the club it's quite dark. We don't talk much: just sit here. Dan takes my hand, holding it very gently, stroking my fingers. There's a sort of magic around, as if we're suspended high above the world and outside time.

The waiter comes and collects our empty glasses. I return to earth.

'It's no *good!*' I say. 'I've got to go!'

'OK. I'll take you back to your apartment.' He's serious now, not smiling any longer. Is this what it's all been leading up to?

'No need. Just point me the way. I'll be OK.'

He looks annoyed.

'Why are you so suspicious? All I intend is to take you back to the door of your apartment. I'm just not having you wander around New York on your own after dark, that's all.'

I'm rebuked, and glad it's too dark for him to see that my eyes fill with tears. I don't know why I'm so sad.

We take a noisy, rattling subway train, and now we're walking along East Eighty-fourth Street. When we get to the block, beyond Second Avenue, I see that the light's on in Richard's place. At first I think I must be looking at the wrong window, not being used to it, but it's the third floor up, above the entrance, and I recognize the pattern on the blind, which

132

has been pulled down. I feel cold and sick.

'He's come back early,' Dan says. 'Don't look so *worried*, Cassie. I'll come in with you and explain. Good God, he can't eat you!'

Richard, I know, will be very angry.

'I'd rather you didn't come in,' I say.

But there's something else niggling at the back of my mind. Then I remember.

'I don't understand it,' I tell Dan. 'The reason Richard wasn't coming back until tomorrow was because there's no suitable plane from Cincinnati this evening. He made enquiries.'

We look at each other, the same question on both our faces.

'I expect they changed the timetable,' Dan says. 'But I'm coming in with you.'

I fit my key in the lock, and have some difficulty turning it. I give my usual knock to let Richard know it's me, but he doesn't come to the door. In the end, Dan manages to turn the key, and we go in.

What we see is horrible. Richard isn't there, of course, nor is anyone else. All his belongings are scattered on the floor. All the books, some of them with the pages torn out. Records and ornaments smashed into pieces. Cushions slit open and feathers everywhere. The window on to the fire escape at the back is open, the curtain moving in the breeze.

I stand there, transfixed, not knowing what to do; but Dan is already phoning the police and they're round here in no time.

'Kids,' they say. 'Almost certainly kids! Is there much missing?'

I can't tell them, because I don't really know what Richard has. He's always acquiring new things.

'The radio's gone,' I say. 'And I think he kept a collection of small silver spoons on the shelf there.'

They've left now, and I'm shivering with cold and fright and I think I'm going to be sick. Dan wraps a blanket around me, makes me a hot drink, warms my hands.

'Don't worry,' he says. 'I won't leave you. I'll stay until the morning. We'll have to leave the mess until then. Richard ought to see it, find out what's missing.'

Eventually, when I've calmed down a bit, he makes me go to bed. I don't know what *he* does, but when I get up next morning he's in the kitchen, making coffee. We're just drinking it, and I'm feeling a bit better, when Richard walks in.

It's a terrible scene. Richards flares with anger when he sees us together, but when we start to explain, the moment we say the word 'burglary', he rushes in front of us into the living room. At the sight of the mess, he turns chalk white, goes down on his knees, picking up fragments, fingering torn books.

We stand there watching him, though it seems indecent to do so, almost as if he should be left alone with his grief. In fact, he's forgotten that Dan and I are there. He's overcome by the wreck of his possessions. I realize for the first time how much they mean to him.

After a while he looks up, sees me. He is shocked, angry, accusing.

'How could you?' he demands. 'How *could* you?'

I think he means Dan. I start to explain.

'I don't mean that,' he says. He's not worried about me, or where Dan comes into all this. It's his possessions he's thinking about.

'If you hadn't left the apartment, if you'd stayed in as I told you nothing would have happened.'

Everything would be tidy, in its place, immaculate. That's what he means. I'd be in my place, too. Prettily dressed, breakfast table laid, awaiting his return. Or would I? It hasn't occurred to him to wonder what might have happened if I'd been here when the burglars came.

I turn, and look up at Dan. He's already

watching me. We look at each other for what seems a long time.

'He's right,' I say. 'Richard is right. If I'd stayed here, nothing would have happened.' But I know, and Dan knows, that I'm not talking about the burglary.

'I am sorry, Richard,' I say—and now I *do* mean about the burglary. 'I really am. Here, let me help you!'

So the three of us set to work, and between us we start to sort things out. 'Practically everything's replaceable,' I tell Richard, trying to comfort him.

'I know,' he says.

I'm a little bit sad to know that I'm replaceable, too, but one can't have it both ways and I can't be sad for long. Not the way I feel inside.

# Come Home With Me

Coming out of the concert hall, a sharp wind blows up North Street: straight from the sea, and damp with it. I pull my fluffy hat down over my ears. Nicholas turns up the collar of his fake-fur jacket.

'Tea, Genevieve?'

'Yes please.'

There's this little café on the corner where North Street meets the Promenade. From the table in the window we can see the pier; desolate, deserted, the huge waves pounding the iron girders. Two people walking along the sea front lean on the wind. That's the sort of day it is.

'A good concert,' Nicholas says. 'Didn't you think so, Genevieve?'

'Yes. Oh yes!'

'The Torelli now. What about the Torelli?'

At first I think he means something on the menu, but just in time I realize that Torelli's a composer.

'Oh yes, the Torelli! Was that the one with the trumpet?'

He smiles approval at me. 'Of course it was, my love. Did you like it?'

Nicholas is teaching me to like music. We've been to three of these Saturday afternoon concerts now. But not only music: books, painting, everything. He's teaching me all these things. This town is full of culture; some say because of the university, where Nicholas is a student. He's very clever; not like anyone else I've ever met.

You can linger over a cup of tea so long and no longer. I can see they're waiting to close. At the point where the waitress starts piling the chairs on the table and sweeping the floor, we leave.

The wind is like a dagger, piercing the chinks in the armour of my clothes: the spaces between hat and collar, cuff and glove top, boot and skirt hem.

'Where can we go?' Nicholas shouts, his voice carried away on the wind.

'*I* don't know.'

Culture there is, but not after five-thirty p.m, when everything closes. We stand in a shop doorway to shelter from the wind.

'Why do you never ask me to your place?' Nicholas says. 'If my home were here I'd invite you.'

'You wouldn't like it,' I tell him, not for

the first time. 'My family...they're not used to...'

How can I explain my family to someone like Nicholas? He is all BBC2 and the *Sunday Times*. My family—I love them dearly, of course—are permanently on the other channel. Separate worlds.

What would he think of my father, with his mad passion for tomato plants; my mother and her knitting; my grandma? Nicholas meeting my grandma is not to be thought of.

'You're a snob,' he says. 'I've said it before.'

'I'm not. You just wouldn't get on. You and my grandmother, for instance.' Perish the thought! She's my great-grandmother, really. Very old, and thinks that gives her the right to say anything to anyone.

'You'd be bored. I don't want you to be bored.'

'Of course I wouldn't be bored. They're people, aren't they? One can always *study* people.'

People, are they? Well, not like any other people I've ever met. Did I say I loved them dearly? I tell a lie. They are a millstone around my neck. They could ruin my life.

We venture out of the doorway and make for the bus station. There is nowhere else to go.

'There's no concert next Saturday. It would be an ideal opportunity,' Nicholas persists.

'Perhaps it's *me* you're ashamed of? In that case...'

Ashamed of Nicholas? I look up at him—he's head and shoulders above me. I look at his lovely dark hair (we have matching Afros, only mine is blonde), his thin face, now creased into a frown, his eyes like pools of dark water. I'm crazy about him.

'You can't mean it, Nicholas!'

'Well then...?'

It's no use. 'All right,' I say. 'Not today; but you can come to tea next Saturday.'

'Great!' He lifts me from the ground and kisses me, there in the bus station with everyone smiling at us. Then he lifts me on to the bus just as it's about to leave, and waves me goodbye.

It's an unhappy week for me. I spend my time trying to think of a solution to my problem, like sending my whole family on a package trip to Austria, or for a weekend with great-aunt Cissie in Sittingbourne.

'Wouldn't dream of it,' Grandma says. 'Cissie never has the place warm.'

'It's a bad time of the year to leave my tomatoes,' Dad says.

'Besides,' Mum points out, 'you've got Nicholas coming to tea. You wouldn't like us not to be here when he came. It would look so rude, going off for the weekend like that.'

So now it's Saturday, and any minute he'll be ringing the bell. Dad's in the greenhouse, wearing his old trousers and his khaki sweater with the elbow out. Mum's in the kitchen, piping the words 'Welcome Nicholas' in pink icing on the top of a cake. Grandma, who usually spends part of the afternoon in bed, has perversely stayed up and is sitting in front of the television, which is turned on loud because she's deaf.

'I hope we can turn it off when Nicholas comes,' I shout.

'Turn it off? Miss the wrestling?'

'Nicholas doesn't care for that sort of thing, Grandma.'

'Not like wrestling? Nonsense? All red-blooded men like wrestling!'

I go into the kitchen. There's enough food around for a Sunday School party, and of much the same kind. Potted meat sandwiches, raspberry blancmange. Nicholas doesn't eat tea, and for supper he has things like Quiche Lorraine or Spanish omelette, with a glass of dry white wine. On top of all that, Mum's spelt his name wrongly.

'There's an aitch in Nicholas,' I tell her.

'An aitch? Oh dear. Well it's too late now,

141

the icing's all set.'

Ding-dong!

There he is!

'Come in. Give me your jacket. This is my mother. This is my Grandma. Dad's in the greenhouse, he'll be in later.'

'My word, I like your hairdo,' Grandma says. 'Reminds me of those Fuzzy-Wuzzies. Handsome men they were. Big, strong; shining black skin!'

My Grandma is a ninety-year-old sex maniac.

'You're tall enough,' she remarks, scrutinizing him, 'but a bit on the thin side. You wouldn't strip as well as those Fuzzy-Wuzzies.'

'Now Grandma!' Mum says. 'Let's keep it clean, shall we?'

I'm past saying anything. Grandma has good days and bad days. This is going to be one of the worst.

'Come and sit here by me,' she says to Nicholas. 'Wrestling's just starting. Giant Joe Jenkins versus Henry Hammer.'

'I'll serve the tea,' Mum says. 'The kettle's on the boil.'

'Do it quietly, Mildred,' Grandma orders. 'We want to concentrate.'

She leans forward in her chair, her head almost in the box, the sound turned up loud. Dreadful grunts and groans fill the room.

'Give it to him!' Grandma cries. 'Get him by the ears!'

'Grandma!' I plead—a last, desperate plea, which she doesn't hear.

'Pull the hair off his chest!' she yells. 'Get at him!'

'Do you like sugar in your tea?' Mum asks Nicholas. Then she opens the window and shrieks to Dad. 'Albert, I'll not tell you again. Your tea's getting cold. And mind where you tread with those boots!'

'I wouldn't mind,' she says plaintively to Nicholas, handing him a cup of strong, milky tea, 'only none of us really likes tomatoes. Have a potted meat sandwich. Or there's salmon paste, or cheese. Or have a piece of pork pie.' She arranges the plates of food on small tables around him, everything to hand.

'Thank you.'

'Mustard, salt, pickles, sauce?'

'Thank you very much.'

'And don't mind Grandma,' she whispers, 'she's ninety, you know.'

'That's right,' Grandma says—she hears when she wants to. 'And still appreciate a fine man!' She leers at Nicholas and lets out a cackle.

'I'll have a pickled onion with my pie, Mildred,' she says.

'You know they give you wind, Grandma,'
Mum warns. 'I said *they give you wind!*'

I could die. I could simply crawl under the
settee and die.

My father comes in. He's been messing about
with one of his awful gardening sprays, and
reeks of it.

'It's going to be a lovely crop later on,' he
says happily. 'Good afternoon, young man. I'm
glad I chose Ailsa Craig. They have a sharp,
vinegary taste. Are you interested in tomatoes,
lad?'

'Er, yes...that is, I don't know much about
them.'

It's the first time Nicholas has uttered more
than two consecutive words, and now he's said
the wrong ones, because Dad will tell him all
about the subject.

'Ailsa Craig set well. The thing is to take off
the side shoots early on. Planting's important,
too, of course. I use a mixture of three parts
loam and one part...'

'Drink your tea, Albert,' Mum says. 'Have
a coconut bun, Grandma.'

'I don't want a coconut bun,' Grandma says
sharply. 'Gets under my teeth, coconut. I expect you've got all your own teeth, young
man?'

'Yes, I have,' Nicholas says, displaying

them in a smile.

'It's surprising what gets under your teeth,' Grandma continues. 'Coconut, raspberry jam, potato crisps...'

I am frantic. 'Mum, do get her on to something else,' I beg. 'She'll be taking them out if we're not careful!'

'They don't fit as well as they did,' Grandma muses. 'I think my gums have shrunk.'

'Have some blancmange, Grandma,' Mum offers. 'That slips down a treat. Jenny, what about you? You're not eating.'

'Jenny?' Nicholas queries.

'Well, we call her Jenny,' Mum says. 'It's Genevieve really. We called her after that vintage car in the film.'

'Jenny is nice,' Nicholas says.

'Are you having an affair with our Jenny, then?' Grandma asks. 'You look the passionate sort to me.'

'Take no notice. Have a piece of cake,' Mum says.

'Thanks, Mrs Proctor. It looks delicious.'

'You can't beat good horse manure,' Dad says suddenly. 'It gives flavour to the fruit.'

I give up. All children should be separated from their families at birth. Family life is impossible. As soon as I can earn enough, I shall leave. Besides, no man will want to marry me once he's met Grandma. Nicholas is lost to me after today.

I don't see him all the next week because he's away on a course. He doesn't write or even ring me up, and that doesn't surprise me. I know it's all over, and no wonder. Imagine my surprise when, Saturday afternoon, four o'clock precisely, he's on the doorstep. He gives me a big hug and a kiss and he's straight into the living room.

And the next week. And the next. Four weeks now we haven't been to a Saturday afternoon concert. Four weeks in a row he's sat in front of that television, eating Mum's fruit cake, chatting up Grandma. He's even taking an interest in tomatoes. Mum—did I say?—is knitting him a sweater. Last week he stayed on right through *Match of the Day* and missed the last bus back to his digs. I don't think he notices me.

I shan't put up with it today. There they all are, as usual: feeding their faces, feasting their eyes. I've been hours in the bathroom, washing my hair, having a face pack. No one has missed me. I think perhaps I'll walk around the living room starkers, to give them a jolt. But if they noticed at all they'd only ask me to get out of the way of the telly, and I'd catch my death of cold.

I put on my new red jeans and my blue jumper, and a super make-up, and make an entrance, singing. From the reception I get I think I must be quite invisible.

'You're looking better this week, Nick,' Mum says. 'Putting on a bit of weight, I shouldn't wonder.'

Nor should I, the way he guzzles here every Saturday. And I could tell her what he thinks about people who call him Nick. Or used to think.

'It suits him,' Grandma says. 'I like a man with a bit of flesh on him.'

'You like a *man!*' I cry, and I flounce out of the room, out of the house, banging the door behind me. I've heard of girls' mothers pinching their boy friends, but *grandmas....!*

I shall go to the park. It's another miserable day, of course: chilly, and raining in the wind. I daresay *they* are warm enough, stuffed full of food and the heating turned up full.

There's a baker on the corner and I buy the last sliced white to feed the ducks. As soon as I start to unwrap it they come swimming across the pond towards me: mallards, moorhens, and two white ones with broad bands of red down the fronts of their faces, like funny painted clowns. Seagulls, driven inland by the weather, wheel and cry overhead.

I throw the bread, sometimes close to, sometimes vigorously, as far as I can send it across the water. I pretend I'm throwing my mother's potted meat sandwiches, my father's tomatoes, Grandma's false teeth. I put extra strength into that throw. I have these ducks swimming backwards and forwards like mad.

There's a guy standing on the bank, watching me. He's rather dishy: red hair, slim hips. Eventually he comes towards me.

'Excuse me,' he says. 'Will you tell me where I can buy some bread? I'd like to feed the ducks. It looks like fun.'

'I bought the last,' I tell him. 'Here, take some of mine.'

He stands beside me while we throw the bread. Now the seagulls have grown bolder and swoop down, snatching the bread from the water. I start to break off smaller pieces so as to make it last longer. He's really very nice, this fellow.

'Have you noticed how they keep together in families? The ducks, I mean?' he says. 'It's rather pleasant.'

'Stupid, I think.'

'Have you got a family?' he asks.

Have I got a family!

'No. I have not. I'm an orphan. I was left

on the doorstep of a convent. I've got no mother, no father, no aunts, uncles, cousins, brothers. And no grandma!'

'You poor little thing,' he says. 'What a shame! Never mind, we'll soon remedy that. You must come and meet *my* family. My dad breeds pigeons. And you'll love my grandmother. She's a real old character. When can you come?'

'I can't,' I say. 'Thank you very much, but I can't. The nuns are very strict. I'm seldom allowed out. I'll have to go back now.'

I throw what's left of my bread into the water and hurry away. Escape. Life is impossible. The whole world is peopled with families. Parents, grandparents. Where is the man who will care about *me?*

Nicholas is walking towards me. He sees me and starts to run. When he reaches me he lifts me up in the air and swings me around.

'Put me down!' I cry.

He does so, and kisses me three times.

'Why did you go off like that, Jenny?'

'So you actually noticed? Surprise, surprise!'

'Of course I noticed, Jenny, I'm aware of you all the time, whatever else is happening. It's just that, well, when I'm with you and your family, I don't feel I have to talk, or to be anything special. You're all so nice and normal.'

'Normal? My family, normal?'

'Sure. And happy, and undemanding. Your folks are *real*, Jenny. It's a real home. They take me as I am. I can relax. I've had a super time these last few Saturdays, Jenny.'

'I see.' I don't, but I'll take another look.

The warmth greets us as we open the front door.

'Be quick,' Grandma calls. *'Generation Game's* just about to start.'

I sit beside Nicholas on the settee. We hold hands; I lean comfortably against him, warm and happy.

'That Bruce Forsyth is a cheeky one,' Grandma says. 'I like a cheeky man.'

'I'll make a cup of tea,' Mum says. 'You'd like one, Nick?'

# Flight of Fancy

Joe Phillips filled the seed container, clipped it to the side of the cage, then rubbed the small round mirror clean against his trousers and wedged it into position. The millet spray would last a bit longer.

'A palace!' he said. 'A regular little palace! Come on Beauty. Back to bed!'

The bird ignored him.

Putting a hand inside the cage, he rang the little brass bell. 'Come on Beauty,' he coaxed. 'Din-dins!'

The bird flew across the room towards the high window, perching on the bars, staring out at the square of grey sky. She seemed to have this desire to bang her beak against the glass, but the distance between the iron bars and the glass pane was fractionally too much for her to do so.

'Come on girl,' Joe persuaded.

He stretched out his hand, palm upwards. Large, hard, a safe landing place. She turned her back on the daylight and flew down; first, to tease him, on to his head, which was too bald and shiny for her, and then on to his hand.

'That's better,' he said. 'There's my girl.'

He scratched her head, stroked her gently down the line of her back. It had been easy to name her. She was the most beautiful creature in the world. White, except for the sky-blue bars on her wings. Bright-eyed, long-tailed.

Twelve weeks' tobacco she had cost him and now all his earnings went to buy her food and the small luxuries for her cage. It was canteen day tomorrow and he intended to buy one of those bouncy celluloid dolls.

He returned her to the cage and she fluttered around it, battering at the bars, pecking at the door.

'I know how you feel,' he sympathized. 'Feel it myself when that bastard turns the key in the lock. But you know the rules, girl. That's how it is.'

Soothed by his voice she calmed down, perched on the swing and began to chatter.

'That's better. Who's a pretty bird, then? Who's a beauty?'

'Pretty Beauty,' she agreed indistinctly.

She wasn't a good talker. He knew now that he should have had a cock bird but he wouldn't change her. He was trying to teach her his wife's name as a surprise for when he went home.

'Pretty Miriam! Pretty Miriam!' he said.
'Pretty Beauty!'

In spite of her verbal reticence she was his true friend, the light of his life. This last year of his sentence had been lightened and brightened by her presence in his cell. Miriam had brought the cage in on one of her rare visits.

It had not been an easy visit. When you came down to it, they had very little to talk about. No kids. Really, no interests at all in common. Also, Miriam had something of her own going. He knew the sign. Serve him right for marrying a woman so much younger.

He had been almost pleased when the visit had ended. He was eager to take possession of the bird reserved for him.

That was the last time Miriam had visited him, though she still wrote once a month. He wanted so much to see her again.

Ten days more, he thought, only ten days more. But now every day seemed like a month. Same old routine. Same old jokes when he met the others in the workshop.

He didn't know how he would live through the next ten days. He understood Beauty perching on the window bars, trying to bang at the glass. He would like to bang and bang and bang—both fists—as hard as he could. 'Let me out! Let me out!'

But he wouldn't do it. Not with only ten days to go. No-one should know how bad he felt. Sitting on his bed he looked up at the bird, now admiring herself in the mirror. She flung a seed at him, then flew on to her perch and swung wildly across the cage.

The funny thing was, when he had first come in with the whole of his sentence stretching before him, he hadn't felt like this. The loss of liberty he'd accepted as the inevitable consequence of being caught on the job. You took the risk. Of course it wasn't his first stretch so he knew what to expect.

He had settled in well, taken pride in being a good prisoner, earned all the privileges, and his greatest was, of course, Beauty.

And yet, since he'd had Beauty, and though she'd changed the world for him, he'd been less, not more, contented with things. It was as if she had brought him to life, and when you were alive you felt things more.

After Lights Out he would lie on his back, listening to the trains that passed quite close to the prison. He even knew the times of each one of them, though he never knew where they were going.

He pictured them full of passengers, going

to and from work, to meetings, on outings, on holiday. Sometimes he was one of the passengers. He was going to Brighton for the weekend, taking Miriam. They were booked in at the Grand. He'd always fancied that place; sitting outside on the verandah, sipping a scotch. After dinner they'd go on the pier, or see a show, or perhaps they'd just stroll along the beach together, hand in hand.

If he could turn on his side and fall asleep while this was happening, that was good. At one time he'd managed that regularly, but recently it hadn't worked. He would be just about to follow Miriam through the barrier, showing his first-class ticket, when the porter would slam the iron gates and he'd be imprisoned on the platform with Miriam walking away, out of the station. Then he'd be back in his cell, wide awake, the walls closing in.

'Free!' he said. 'In ten days, old girl, we'll be out of here at last; we'll be free!'

The bird jumped onto to the side of the cage, clinging with her strong claws, looking at him through the bars. And suddenly the shocking truth came to Joe. She would never be free. She would always be a prisoner.

He would be allowed to take her home, but when he could come and go as he liked, she would still be behind bars. No escape for

Beauty. True, she'd have a different room to fly around in, different places to perch, but that was no more than him being taken to a different exercise yard. Then, she'd be back behind bars. And he would be the one who would fasten the doors behind her, her jailer always.

'You poor little devil!' he whispered to her.

A few days before Joe was due to leave, Jenkins, who was the warder on duty, brought him a letter. It was from Miriam. It would be about the arrangements for his homecoming.

Not so. She wouldn't be there when he got home. She'd left home. No details. No address. Just the facts. And if he was bringing his budgie with him he should keep an eye open for the cat across the landing.

At first, he had no longer wanted to leave the prison. His cell, which for the last few months had closed in on him so much, became a refuge.

On the morning of his release he left, wearing a new suit, dark grey with a stripe. He'd put on weight in prison and his own clothes no longer fitted him.

He had twelve pounds fifty pence in his pocket—they gave you back what you brought in and a bit extra—and Beauty, in her covered cage, in his left hand. He walked to the station, smelling the forgotten, rain-scented air and then boarded one of the trains he had listened to so often in the past two years in his cell.

The flat was clean, tidy, cold and empty—as if nothing had been used in all this time. He cleared a space on the sideboard for Beauty's cage and uncovered her. She chirped a greeting.

When he had attended to the bird's needs he filled the kettle and made himself a pot of tea. Would Miriam come back? He took the letter from his pocket and re-read it, looking for a sign. There was none. He drank his tea and told his troubles to Beauty.

'Poor old Joe!' she said. 'Poor old Joe!'

He had to laugh. For months he'd been trying to get her to say that but she had never obliged before. He felt a bit better then.

'Tomorrow,' he told her. 'I'll have to go down to the Labour. Get me a job.'

His prison sentence, it appeared, unfitted him for practically any kind of work, in practice if not in theory. He went to an association for ex-prisoners. They were sympathetic, gave him lots of good advice and a cup of tea, but didn't have a job.

When he had reported at the Labour and been for a few abortive interviews, there was little else to do with the days. He let Beauty out of the cage a lot, and for longer periods. He was getting more and more worried by the

157

knowledge that she would never be free.

He found himself apologizing to her as he returned her to the cage after flights. He thought she looked at him reproachfully and he tried to make up for it by buying her new and intricate toys for her small cage.

Then, because there was a spell of fine, warm weather—an Indian summer—he started to take her for walks in the park. He would place the cage on the bench beside him, or on the grass. The fresh air and sunshine were good for both of them.

He wondered if he were to let her out now, in these circumstances, whether she would return to him, hop back on his finger when called. He couldn't risk it. Supposing she claimed her freedom, didn't return?

How would he live without her? She was all he had now. His source of companionship, conversation—he was teaching her new words— and the recipient of his affection. He picked up the cage and hurried home.

He had a bad night; found it impossible to sleep. Beauty, whom he now placed on a chest of drawers in the bedroom each night, was restless too; chattering under the baize cover. At four o'clock he got up, took the cover off her cage, opened the door and let her out.

She flew around and around, crossed from corner to corner; sweeping, diving like a wild creature.

Eventually she came on to his finger and he put her back in the cage and covered her. There was no further sound. She must have fallen asleep. But there was no sleep for him. He got up again, made some tea, watched the pink, morning sky.

It was another fine day and in the afternoon they went to their park seat again. She was at her brightest and best; chattering, strutting up and down, acrobating on the swing. He had never loved her so much.

But if you love people, if you love them enough, you have to let them go. Children—though he had none. Miriam. Now Beauty.

He kneeled on the grass and opened the door of the cage. 'Goodbye, Beauty,' he said.

She hopped on to the ledge, looked around—and flew away. Joe, looking up through his tears, saw a flash of white wings against the top of a tree, and then she was gone. He picked up the empty cage and went home.

Afterwards, even with all the time in the world to think about it, he was never able to piece together the events of the next twenty-four hours. He remembered, vaguely, leaving the flat late at night; wandering around the streets. But some of the time had vanished forever.

Late on the evening of the second day there was a ring at the door. Two policemen stood there.

He brought out the stuff from its hiding place. Nothing much. He didn't know why he wanted it. A radio, binoculars, cheap jewellery and a rather nice painting of a farmyard.

It was only when they had taken him to the station in the police car he found out why they'd called. She was there, in a black iron cage. No frills, no toys. His Beauty. Bedraggled; white feathers damp and soiled.

'Some kids found her in the park,' the sergeant said. 'Knew she was yours. Didn't know where you lived. Lucky she's alive. Budgies can't live outside their cages, you know.'

Three years, he got, because of his former convictions. Well, it wasn't too bad. Soon pass.

The warder closed the door behind him, turning the key in the lock. Joe unfastened the cage door. The bird flew out, circled the room, settled on the iron window bars, trying without success to tap her beak against the glass. A train went by.

'Four-thirty to who-knows-where,' Joe said. 'Dead on time. Think I might have a trip to Brighton tonight.'

'Poor old Joe!' the bird called. 'Pretty Beauty! Poor old Joe! Poor old Joe!'

# Whose Baby Are You, Babe?

Moving stealthily in my crêpe shoes, I entered the Senior Common Room. Today I shall take a peek at one of those glossy monthlies I cannot yet afford to buy. It is practically forbidden to breathe in here; worse than the reading room of the public library. I only come because you should always take up your privileges, and the Senior Common Room is now one of mine. Someone will frown at me for turning the pages too loudly.

Not today they won't, because all is uproar. At the far end of the room, over by the long window, a fair number of the male brains of this university is grouped round something I cannot yet see but which, from the noise, can only be a healthy-lunged, unhappy baby.

I am not all that keen on yelling babies, or any babies for that matter, but I cannot resist the senior faculty. Perhaps that is the real reason why I come in here, I am warmed by the fire of their intellect; I catch, eagerly, every erudite word which falls from their lips.

Professor Edward Root, FRS, Nobel Laureate in Physics, Pro-vice Chancellor, Chairman of a Royal Commission on the Waterworks of the Common Market Countries, is snapping his fingers in front of the baby's face, and making strange clucking sounds, like a constipated hen. Professor Simon Fitzpatrick, Chairman of Arts, author of five thick books on the pre-history of man and of a slim volume on Nordic verse, is flapping his hands behind his ears and mooing like a cow. He does it remarkably well.

The baby lies flat on his back in a blue-lined carrycot. He has kicked off the blanket and his pink-mottled legs are thrashing the air. His face is puce, and his toothless mouth is opened as wide as it will go to let out a continuous, piercing, ear-shattering yell.

Upon seeing the Dean of Asiatic Studies clap his hands and cry: 'Kutchy-koo, then,' his screams become shriller. No wonder. His nappy, ominously stained, is coming adrift.

The entertainment committee is quick to notice me. The hand-waving and finger-clicking stop. Professor Fitzpatrick fades out in the middle of a moo like a bagpipe running out of wind. They are not embarrassed. Oh, dear no! They are just very, very glad to see me.

Twice every week, since I was appointed

junior lecturer in English, I have spent my lunch time in the Senior Common Room, breathing the same rarefied air as them, and they have never noticed me. Now that they are faced with a squalling infant, I have come into my own.

'A woman's touch! That's what's needed,' Professor Root says, smiling benignly at me. 'Here you are, my dear. I'm sure you'll be able to soothe him.'

What he means is, he doesn't fancy changing his nappy. Well, neither do I. I glare at the screaming child, and no doubt petrified by my hostility, combined with my hair, newly-permed into sticking-out corkscrews, he stops crying and glares back at me.

'You see,' Professor Fitzpatrick cries. 'You see! It's extraordinary! The mother figure!'

Seven-stone-ten, and flat-chested with it, I am no mother figure. But I daresay the child knows a sucker when it sees one.

'Who does he belong to?'

'We don't know. We didn't know he was here until we heard him cry. He was hidden behind the curtain. Like Moses in the bulrushes.'

'You mean abandoned? You can't mean abandoned?'

The enormity of it. Also, the folly of it. This

is no place for a baby to be left.

'Perhaps we should inform the police,' Fitzpatrick says.

'I think not,' Professor Root decides. 'I think not. Some unhappy student, no doubt; a moment of panic. No, I think we should look after the child, at any rate for an hour or two. Some young, over-burdened mother. She has, you might say, placed her trust in us. We must give her time to reconsider, to retrace her steps.'

He is quite carried away by his own humanity, and his peers are equally impressed and approving. They don't mean, though, that they will look after it. Oh no! They mean I will. I can tell it by the way they are looking at me.

'Well, I can't stay here,' I tell them. 'I've got a lecture at two.'

With that they all remember that they too have lectures, or tutorials, or committee meetings, just about now. They melt away, making encouraging noises at me before they disappear.

'Let us know what happens!'

'Keep in touch!'

'Bye-si-bye den,' Professor Fitzpatrick booms, lowering his head over the carrycot and poking the child with his large, hairy hand. It utters a piercing scream which, when they have all left, settles down into a steady wail. I fish around in the carrycot. There is a feeding bottle of milk mixture and a clean nappy. Considerate. Well, here goes.

In the cloakroom, with enormous difficulty because the basins are not designed for changing nappies or wriggling infants, I do what has to be done. As there is no chair in the place, I sit on the loo with the door propped open, to give the child its bottle. The milk mixture is thickish, with globules of fat floating on top, but the baby sucks greedily, draining it to the last drop. It then immediately falls asleep.

It is ten minutes to two. I cannot escape my lecture. Must I take the child with me? I return to the Senior Common Room but everyone has vanished. I suppose I should leave a note in case the mother returns.

I would quite like not to, to pay her back for the way she has lumbered me, but the wish to have the child reclaimed is stronger than the desire for revenge. I pin a note to the curtain. *Will the owner of the baby please claim it from Mary Graham, Room 23B Arts.*

At the sight of the carrycot on the platform in front of the blackboard, my students show more interest in me than usual, but since they are first-years and still quite polite, they don't say anything.

Luckily, the baby continues to sleep peacefully, though with strange snuffling sounds from time to time, like a young puppy.

My lecture—the place of Katherine Mansfield in English literature—goes better than I had hoped. I am winding up to a convincing ending when the door at the back of the room opens and a young man bursts in. He is carrying a yellow plastic bag, with a large packet of disposable nappies balanced on top. He is raging about something: flushed, red-haired. There are steps down from the back of the room to the lecture platform and he stamps on every one of them as he descends. He grabs the cot.

'How dare you! How dare you take this child!'

This is a bonus day for my students. Will it popularize my lectures? Will there be queues for next week's discussion on George Meredith?

'Don't speak to me like that! You abandoned your child. Left it to its fate!' A bit dramatic, perhaps?

'Nonsense! I left it in the Senior Common Room. Of which I am a fully paid-up member. Not a place from which one would expect a child to be kidnapped.'

'Kidnapped! Of all the ungrateful ill-mannered...'

The baby wakens, no wonder, and joins in the row. My students have given up all pretence of work and are listening with interest.

'I think that's all for now. Please feel free to leave.'

They are reluctant to go.

'I simply left it there, safe and sound behind the curtain, while I went to the laundrette,' he says.

'Did they come and disturb oo den?' He smiles ingratiatingly at the baby and I am pleased to see that it cries harder than ever.

'If the dryer hadn't broken down I'd have been back long before he wakened. He has very regular habits.'

'I can vouch for that.'

Why does he have to cart a baby around the campus, I enquire.

'I don't. Not usually. It stays in the crèche, but the crèche is closed because of measles.' He seems to think I should know this.

'Where is your wife then?'

'What's that got to do with you?'

'Nothing at all. I was just curious. It's the smallest bit unusual.'

'Typical,' he says, sounding ever so bitter. 'Typical. You go on about Women's Lib: man's role; woman's role. And the first time you see a man carrying a baby round you want to know why it isn't with its mother.'

'No, I don't. Actually I was sympathizing. I thought it might be difficult for you to manage, with your work, I mean. But you are quite right. It's got nothing to do with me. It's up to you and your wife. And I do not go on about Women's Lib.' I am dignified, reasonable, now. Let him do the shouting.

'I haven't got a wife. I don't have to have a wife, do I?'

'Not if you don't want one. I'm glad to see a man taking the responsibility for once, instead of leaving it all to the girl. It's just that...well... most women wouldn't be able to give up a lovely baby like this.'

Lovely baby? What am I saying? It is still yelling, which has caused its nose to run in a disgusting manner. I daresay it is also wet.

'It is a lovely baby, isn't it?' His voice has changed. He is quite maudlin.

'It's like you.'

'Really? Do you mean that?'

'It's got your hair. And your temper, of course.'

Solely to put me in the wrong, it immediately stops crying and beams at each of us in turn. It waves its clenched fists and blows a raspberry or two. He wipes its dirty nose and sopping chin, expertly and with great tenderness. Then he gets down on his hands and knees and deftly changes its nappy.

'There!' he coos. 'That's better isn't it?'

It is obviously the happiest baby in the world.

He looks at me and hesitates. He is going to ask me a favour. It happens all the time and I know the signs.

'I wonder...? I'm sorry I was rude. I was anxious...'

'That's quite all right.'

'Do you think that, as he's quiet now, I might just leave him with you while I pop to the campus shop? They've no facilities for babies.'

'How remiss of them!' What is this place? A seat of learning, or Babyland?

'After that I have a lecture, but I can take him to that...I suppose.' He sounds doubtful.

'Look, if it will help, I don't mind looking after him for a while. While you give your lecture, I mean. He seems to have settled down. But you must collect him at five. I have to go soon after that.'

I have an appointment to see this dishy Professor. We are to discuss Virginia Woolf, but who is to say where that might lead? English Lit, can take you anywhere.

'I promise. His name's Roger.'

'Whose name?'

'The baby's.'

Since I doubt if the child answers to his name, or comes when called, I file that under useless information. Besides, I call him Moses.

'In case of need, what's yours?'

'Sorry! Frank Collins. Applied Sciences.'

'Five o'clock then. Don't be late.'

No sign of him and it's already twenty past five. I am due with my professor in ten minutes exactly and I refuse, absolutely, to take this child with me. Of course he's asleep, and he's an absolute angel, but Virginia Woolf in one hand and a carrycot in the other is not the kind of entrance I had in mind.

I have taken a lot of trouble about this session with the Prof. I am wearing this fantastic rainbow eye stuff and I have brushed my hair into submission. My efforts shall not be in vain.

I have never been in Applied Sciences before. It is really scarey. Notices everywhere. Danger: experiments in progress. Explosives. Keep Out. It is no place for a baby. Dr Collins, I am told, is in the Seminar Room. He is giving a lecture. He is also about to get one.

I march bravely in and deposit the baby on the table in front of him.

'Here is your baby. Take it!'

He looks at his watch, pretending to be surprised. 'Good heavens! But please let me explain. I can explain.'

'I'm sure you can. But don't bother. Just take your baby.'

There is a sigh of disappointment from the students. They would have liked an explanation.

'It is not my baby.' Now he is embarrassed.

'What do you mean, not your baby? Can you deny that you...'

'You will keep on insisting that it's mine.'

We are interrupted by a girl student, beautiful, dark, stormy. She rushes from her seat, pushes herself between us, and gives Dr Frank Collins a ringing slap on the face.

'You dirty skunk!' she cries. Then she bursts into tears and flies from the room.

'Amelia!' he shouts. 'Amelia, come back! You don't understand!'

I understand only too well, and I am not impressed by his behaviour. That was a coward's trick, I tell him. Just because of this girl, this Amelia, to deny your own child. Well, much good it's done you. Poor little unwanted mite!

'He is not an unwanted mite!' Frank Collins shouts. 'He has a perfectly good mother who happens to have been called away for the day.

An emergency. I am looking after the baby in her absence.'

'Who is looking after the baby? And I thought you weren't married or anything.'

'I am not married and I am not anything. The baby's mother is my sister. She lectures, part-time in physics, and while she does so the baby stays in the crèche where it is very well looked after. Today she had to go to London—an emergency. She brought the baby into the crèche as usual. How was she to know it was closed by measels? And why am I telling you all this?'

'I don't know, I'm sure.'

'However, thank you very much for looking after the child. I appreciate it, and I'm sorry to have inconvenienced you. And now I shall take him home. It's time for his bath and bed. My sister might be quite late back.'

He picks up the cot and the child screams blue murder, catching its breath in terrifying gasps, turning brick red. Not displeased, I take the cot from him. The screams cease, the sobs subside.

'I think, purely for the sake of the child,' I say frostily, 'I think I had better come home with you and settle him down. If one of your students could take a note to Professor Potter...'

He is the teeniest bit reluctant to let me accompany him, but I have possession of the baby and it would be undignified to wrest it from me.

'I shall have to take him to my place,' he says. 'In the rush, Elaine forgot to leave a key.'

His flat is one of those done-up Victorian places. High, purple-painted ceilings. Stereo equipment fitted into the marble fireplace. I put the carrycot down on the settee. I am aware that the sooner this child is changed and bathed, the better.

'Have you got a baby's bath?'

'Now why should I have one of those?' he demands—reasonably, I suppose. 'I have a plastic washing-up bowl.'

We compromise on a few inches of water in the big bath. I am allowed to change the baby's nappy, but Frank insists on carrying out the bathing bit himself. He is remarkably good at it, handling the soapy creature with hardly a slip.

Halfway through the operation the telephone rings.

'I'll get it,' I offer.

It's a woman, and she seems surprised to hear me.

'Is Frank there?'

'Who is it, please?'

'Tell him it's Geraldine. Are you his mother?'

'I'm sorry,' I inform her. 'He's bathing the baby.'

There is a pause.

'Excuse me,' she says. 'It's a bad line. I thought for a moment you said he was bathing the baby.' She trills with laughter. Ha ha.

At this moment the baby, happily silent until now, yells to prove his presence.

'I can hear a baby,' Geraldine says. 'It must be a crossed line.'

'No. He doesn't like the water going over his head, that's all.'

There is a click. She is gone.

'Who was that?' Franks asks, over the noise.

'It was a fuzzy line. Didn't get the name. Some woman or other.'

'Oh damn!' he groans. 'Now I shall never know.' Never know which one to explain it to, he means. I've mucked up his love life.

I boil some milk, let it cool. With the expertise of the applied scientist, Frank tests the temperature on the back of his hand and we fight over who will give the baby its bottle. Sweet and clean, deliciously drowsy, the child falls asleep with the teat in its mouth.

Back in the cot it sleeps until Frank's sister returns. As he thought, it is quite late, but we pass the time in testing the stereo equipment, sound turned down.

We take to each other at once, Elaine and I. 'You must come round and see us,' she says. 'If Frank doesn't bring you, come on your own.'

Over the next few days I do just that. I am, you understand, by this time quite fond of the baby. So is Frank Collins. He is a most attentive uncle.

Too attentive, as it turns out.

It is a couple of weeks later. I am in the Senior Common Room.

'It was a beautiful child,' Professor Root says. 'A poppet! What did happen to the man?'

I reply: 'Measles. Running at the eyes and covered in spots.'

But it is a beautiful baby. Adorable. I would like one just like it. And a man who would go to all that trouble for his sister's child would make a wonderful father.

# The World is a Smaller Place

He pushed open the door and came towards her, smiling. Ruth thought how different he looked from most of the academics she met. They tended to be pale, and thin to the point of emaciation, as if trying to identify with their students.

It was a pleasure to see someone who actually had colour in his skin and looked big and solid enough not to be blown over by the strong wind which swept across the campus from the moors. She smiled a welcome.

'Professor Cadman! Did you find anything?'

'I'm afraid not, Miss Peters. Either they'd been taken just before I arrived, or they were really too big; more suitable for a married man with kids.'

His voice was big, too. As if he used it in wide open spaces. But not the strident type; it had a deep, musical quality about it.

'I'm sorry,' Ruth said. 'Accommodation's so difficult. And of course we have to give priority to the students.'

'I understand that. Well, I daresay you'll

let me know when something turns up. Thanks for your help.'

She didn't want him to go. She was tired, and needed to get away on time so she could change and freshen up before the choir rehearsal; even so, she found herself delaying him.

'Just let me have another look through the cards. I've been out seeing prospective landladies this afternoon. It's possible that something's come up in my absence.'

She flicked through the card index while he leaned across the counter.

'Hm! I wonder...' She noticed that Mrs Butcher's flat was empty again. Mrs Butcher didn't keep tenants long because she organized them into doing running repairs on the place. Professor Cadman, however, looked tough enough to hold his own.

'There's one here which is comfortable. But if you're not careful, the landlady will use you.'

'Use me?' He raised his eyebrows. Ruth smiled. 'I mean, you'll find yourself painting the kitchen or mending the fence.'

'Oh well, if that's all...How do I get there?'

She glanced at her watch. Almost half-past five. 'It's a bit awkward by public transport, but it's on my way home. If you can wait five minutes I could give you a lift.'

Twenty minutes later they were standing on Mrs Butcher's doorstep, waiting for her to answer the bell. 'If your face doesn't fit, you've had it!' Ruth warned.

But his face did fit. So did his voice, because it reminded Mrs Butcher of a soldier from New Zealand she'd known during the war.

'You'll be comfortable here,' she said. 'You can move in tomorrow if you want to.'

'Now I really must go,' Ruth said when they'd settled the details. 'I can give you a lift as far as the bus stop if you like.'

'Stay for a cup of tea,' Mrs Butcher suggested. 'The kettle's on the boil.'

'I'm sorry,' Ruth apologized. 'It's choir rehearsal.'

'Always rushing about,' Mrs Butcher grumbled. 'No wonder you're so thin. They work you too hard. How's that young man of yours?'

'Now he *is* overworked,' Ruth said. 'Seventy hours a week more often than not.'

When they were back in the car, Professor Cadman said conversationally: 'What does he do, your young man?'

'Probation officer. Works all the hours that God sends, and simply loves it, too.'

'That beautiful opal ring means something then?'

'It is nice, isn't it? We plan to marry
181

quite soon now.'

They could have been married long ago, if they'd chosen to do it on next to nothing and live in a furnished flat. But neither of them had really wanted that.

They wanted their own things around them and had decided to save, even if it meant waiting for a couple of years.

'What are you singing in the choir?'

'*The Dream of Gerontius*. I'm only in the chorus. I'm not all that good, but I love to sing.'

'Me too. I like *Gerontius*.'

'Have you sung in it?' Ruth asked.

'Yes. Back home—and like you, in the chorus.'

She wasn't surprised. With a speaking voice like his, he'd be a bass. 'You could join us,' she said suddenly. 'We always seem to be short of men. Rehearsals every Wednesday at seven thirty prompt in the campus theatre. Why not do that, Professor Cadman?'

'Why not indeed?' he said.

'Be there early and see Dr Speight. He'll welcome you with open arms. I sit with the altos. My colleague's little boy said that altos were the deep ladies who couldn't hit the right notes. I think he had something there!'

She drew the car into the kerb. 'Here's the

bus stop. There's a bus due about now, I think.'

When she got home, the house was quiet, which meant her father wasn't home yet. When he was there, he was always to be heard, usually in argument. Thank goodness she was sure of Lee—their long engagement had told her that—and her marriage would be different.

I'd have walked out on Dad years ago, she thought. But she understood why her mother stayed. It was because she felt there was no alternative. She hadn't been brought up to be independent. She'd have no idea how to cope on her own.

'You there, Mother?' Ruth called into the kitchen. 'I'm in a rush. Choir night.'

Her mother came out into the hall and smiled at her. 'I'll make you a cup of coffee while you're changing. And a sandwich. You don't eat enough.'

'Thanks! That would be lovely. I must iron a blouse. Father not back?'

'Called at the pub, I expect. I hope he stays there.' Her voice was a mixture of worry and sadness.

Ruth stopped in the act of setting up the ironing board and looked across at her mother, realizing that she hadn't really seen her for months. Not *seen* her; looked at her, noticed how she was. They lived in the same house and they were very close; but Ruth had long ago accepted her mother's unhappiness as something she could only relieve by being there, taking notice.

And lately she'd been so absorbed in herself that she hadn't noticed that her mother was putting on weight, getting thick around the middle. That the roots of her hair were dark where she hadn't troubled to renew her ash blonde tint. That she wore old, fluffy pink bedroom slippers, filthy and greasy where the soles met the uppers.

Ruth was shocked. How could she not have noticed? This isn't my mother, Ruth thought. Not my pretty mother.

Had she been so immersed in her own wedding plans that she hadn't seen what was happening? Was this thing which was happening to her mother, what marriage did to you in the end? Would marriage wear her down imperceptibly until everything seemed pointless, all joy lost in dogged compromise? No—in her case that would never happen.

'Were you happy when you first married, Mother?' she asked.

'What a question! For a year or two, yes. And then I had you, and that kept me happy. You've always made me happy, Ruth.'

And that's why she's changing now, Ruth thought. She's worried about my leaving home —she'll be left to struggle on alone with Father.'

'I shall never be far away, you know. Only ten minutes in the car.'

'I know. I'm thankful. And Lee's a good man. You'll be fine with Lee.'

'Didn't you think you'd be all right with Father, before you married him?' There was a fear at the back of her mind.

'I suppose I did. I must have, mustn't I? But you'll be different. You and Lee will be all right.'

Of course they would! Ruth moved into the bedroom and started to take off her make-up. She was a bit pale, but it was natural with her, and suited her almost black hair. She searched for grey hairs and found two.

Twenty-six. Other girls of her age had got married years ago and had a couple of children by now. She was glad she'd waited until she'd met Lee. He was exactly the man for her. Everyone agreed with that. Kind, clever, hard-working: liking the same things, apart from music, which said nothing to him. And of course, they were in love with each other.

She changed into red linen trousers. Her mother brought the black silk blouse upstairs for her.

'You left this in the kitchen.' She paused. 'I daresay Lee won't want to stay here for ever. He'll change his job and you'll move away. It's only natural. Could be anywhere.'

Ruth's eyes met her mother's in the mirror. Her mother looked away quickly, but not before Ruth had seen the fear. It was all there in that glance. The loneliness, unhappiness, dread of the future.

'Not necessarily,' Ruth said. 'He could get promotion here. Don't worry, Mother. It's going to be all right.'

'Yes. Well, your coffee's ready.'

It's dreadful to be leaving her now, Ruth thought. Every day she needs me more. She wondered if her mother lived at all, apart from the hours when they were together. Really lived, that is.

The music, as always, uplifted, soothed, stimulated: concentrated her strength and her emotions. Nothing mattered when in the end they sang well. While they sang, they were united, unassailable.

She saw Martin Cadman talking to Dr Speight before the rehearsal began. He caught sight of her and waved. Afterwards, when they all went for drinks in the theatre bar, he came across to her.

'Let me buy you a drink.'

'Thank you. A ginger beer shandy.'

'It's a good choir,' Martin said. 'I'm really impressed.'

'It is good, isn't it?' They travel around a lot in the vacations. Music festivals and so on. Of course I don't go because the Accommodation Office keeps open all the time.'

'I'm looking forward to the actual performance,' Martin said. 'Does it take place here?'

'No. In St Matthew's church, in the town. It's huge, and the acoustics are perfect. I must go now. Thanks for the drink. Can I drop you off anywhere?'

'No thank you. We're in opposite directions. at the moment.'

'Well, if you haven't got yourself a car by next Wednesday, I'll give you a lift home to Mrs Butcher's. That's on my route.'

Unexpectedly, Lee was there when she reached home. He looked tired.

'Lee! I thought you had to see someone this evening,' Ruth said.

'I did. But he wasn't in, so I had time to come over.'

'It's a lovely surprise. But you're worn out. It must be a very urgent mission!' She took off her coat, dropping it on a chair. He took hold of her hands and drew her towards him, holding her close, kissing her.

'Seeing you is always an urgent mission, my lovely.'

'You know what I mean. Why would you dash out here as late as this when you're obviously whacked?'

He took a pile of papers from his briefcase and dropped them on the table. 'All right, it is urgent. I got these brochures today, for our honeymoon. Malta, Greece, Austria. The choice is yours but you've got to choose fast.'

'Oh, Lee! They look gorgeous! Shall we go through them now?'

'No. I must go. I still have two reports to write. You look at them and we'll discuss it later.' He took her in his arms again, stroked her gently down the length of her spine.

'Oh, Lee,' Ruth said, 'I don't really care about the honeymoon. I just want to be married to you. To be with you for always.'

'Do you think I don't? But it won't be long now. Goodnight, my lovely. You do look beautiful this evening. Why are your eyes sparkling like that?'

'What about when I'm no longer beautiful?' she said, ignoring his question. 'What then?'

'You'll always be beautiful.'

'What about when I'm fat, and my hair's grey, and I shuffle around in dirty old slippers?'

She was serious, not smiling.

He cupped her face in his hands, looked into her eyes.

'Fat, grey, old, even with dirty slippers, to me you'll be beautiful, my love.'

It was what she wanted to hear. Why was she not comforted?

'Besides, I'll be bald, and have a paunch,' he teased.

'Oh Lee!' Impossible to think of Lee old; his thick blond hair receding, his lean figure spreading. 'You'll be gorgeous when you're a grandfather!'

'Help!' he said. 'What is this? I've got to face being a father first!'

She had meant to tell Lee about Martin Cadman. If ever they met, they'd like each other. Before she remembered to do so, Lee had left.

Martin called in at the office on the following Wednesday afternoon.

'Just to say I still haven't bought a car. A chap in the Department lent me a bicycle. But it looks like the weather's broken, so I'd be glad of that lift if it's still on offer.'

'Of course! I'll pick you up at seven. And deliver you back to Mrs Butcher after the rehearsal.'

'Great! Did I tell you she'd got me replacing the roof tiles? Says she can't get up there herself.'

Ruth laughed. 'Surprise, surprise!'

After Martin had left, Lee phoned. 'Shall I meet you after choir?'

'Better not. Dr Speight might want extra rehearsal time. I'm not sure when we'll finish.'

Putting down the phone, she didn't know why she'd said that. Dr Speight was a fanatic about finishing on the stroke of nine thirty. Rumour said that he'd once stopped the choir halfway through the Hallelujah Chorus in case they should overrun.

Time was racing by, the days flying. On the honeymoon question they were torn between Greece and Malta. Lee said they'd have to decide soon or both places would be booked up, but Ruth couldn't seem to make up her mind.

There were so many things to think about and do. Invitations, wedding present lists, her dress, getting the house ready.

She was touched when her mother threw herself into the preparations with enthusiasm, bravely hiding her fears for the future. At least it took her mind off Ruth's father, who had been rushed into hospital with appendicitis.

'Pity you can't have the wedding while he's out of the way.' Mrs Peters said. 'I'm sure he wouldn't mind, either.'

It saddened them both to realize that this was probably true.

'I might bring a friend back for coffee after the rehearsal tonight,' Ruth said.

'Fine. Do I know her?'

'Him. Martin Cadman. He's a professor from New Zealand over here doing some work at the University. He's taken old Mrs Butcher's flat.'

Her mother, Ruth was pleased to note when she and Martin came back to the house that night, had spruced herself up; done her hair, put on make-up. She looked quite pretty.

'Are you in this country for good?' she asked Martin.

'Oh no. Less than three months. I came to do some experiments at the university, and to look at some of their equipment. I've actually got very little time left here.'

'Then you won't be here for Ruth's wedding?' Mrs Peters said.

'No,' Ruth interrupted. 'He is due to leave about ten days before.'

She paused.

'I'll make more coffee,' Mrs Peters said in the silence.

She picked up the coffee pot and moved into the kitchen. Ruth raised her eyes to Martin, feeling his gaze on her. The kitchen door was half open. Mrs Peters could be seen, standing motionless by the sink, waiting for the kettle to boil. There was no movement anywhere. Ruth felt as though she were carved out of rock, all willpower, all feeling, suspended.

Though she was acutely conscious of every detail of her surroundings, as if seeing them in a painting, all she knew was Martin, and the way he was looking at her.

Her mother returned with the fresh coffee. Ruth supposed, afterwards, that they had drunk it, but she didn't remember doing so. Nor did she have any recollection of Martin leaving the house.

Time had stopped when they'd looked at each other across the room. For Ruth, getting ready for bed, lying straight out under the quilt, staring into the darkness, it had not started again. Nor did she want it to. She wondered how it was with him.

Suddenly for Ruth everything in life was impossible. Her wedding, leaving her lonely mother; staying with her father; Martin; everything. She needed desperately to cry. Inside herself, in every part of her, she was crying. But her eyes were dry; the tears would not come. And above all, over every other feeling, she burned with longing for Martin.

'It's impossible,' Ruth said. They sat in a bar, not eating the sandwiches which Martin had ordered; she not drinking, Martin drinking too much.

'It's difficult,' Martin corrected her. 'But it's not impossible. Awful and heartbreaking and terrible. But not impossible!'

'For me it's impossible.'

'I love you,' Martin said. 'I'm not a child. I'm thirty-three. This is real, and for ever. I love you, Ruth. You love me.'

'I love you,' she said. 'With all my heart and soul I love you. I'm not a child, either, but I didn't know what love was like. I love you, I love you.'

Tears filled her eyes. Since Wednesday—which seemed a lifetime away—she had done all the crying which had evaded her through that sleepless night.

'How can we live without each other now?' Martin demanded. 'Why should we? What we feel for one another will never come again.'

'We can. We must. Even if I could marry you, which I can't, I couldn't leave everything and live in New Zealand.'

'What do you mean by everything?'

'I've told you. My parents. No, not my parents; my mother. She couldn't manage.'

'Why not?'

'I've tried to explain. She needs me.'

'I won't accept that. Your mother is stronger than you think. And I need you; you need me. You have your own life to live...'

'We can't just say that. It isn't true. Would you live permanently in England? If I could marry you, I mean?'

'I couldn't. I've explained that. I have a job to do. I realize it sounds big-headed, but my knowledge is needed on this project. There simply isn't anyone I could hand it over to.'

'I believe you. I'm just trying to show you that we don't only have our own feelings to consider. Other people have claims on us.'

All of a sudden she'd realized her former fears of a lifeless, loveless, marriage had disappeared. Her mother was her main consideration now. 'I understand your feelings, but it's not as simple as that.' Martin persisted.

'We must go,' Ruth said. 'We'll be late for the rehearsal.'

As time went on Ruth began to feel that the only part of her life which was endurable was the time when she was wrapped inside the music—cocooned in sound, protected from the outside world. She wished that at some point before the notes died, she herself could cease to exist, not have to face the world again. One of the lines that they sang echoed and re-echoed in her head. 'Rescue him from endless loss,' they sang, the voices mingling and swelling.

Later, on the way home, Martin said: 'Ruth, please, please think what you're doing! It's our whole lives.'

'I have thought. What else do you think I've been doing?' After that he was silent until she stopped the car at Mrs Butcher's gate.

'Very well,' Martin said. 'I've got to accept it.' He spoke with difficulty. His face was drawn with pain.

Dear God, what am I doing to him, Ruth thought.

'Will you promise me something?' he asked.

'I'll try.'

'The performance is on Friday. Let that be something we remember with happiness. On Monday I catch a plane from Heathrow. Will you come up to London with me on Saturday morning, and will you stay with me every minute—I mean every single minute, day and night, until I have to catch my plane?'

'Yes I will,' Ruth said very softly. Then: 'There are two things...'

'What?'

'Can we pretend, for that space of time, that we're not saying goodbye? I don't think I could bear it otherwise.'

'Nor me,' Martin said. 'We'll just be on holiday. Any holiday. And the other thing...?'

'I want you to promise that you won't ask me, no matter what happens, to change my mind. Promise not to discuss it at all.'

'I promise.'

Monday's grey light was beginning to filter through the net curtains of their hotel room. They were lying on their backs in the wide bed, happy from their lovemaking, unwilling to waste time in sleep, no other world existing.

'It was a wonderful holiday, darling,' Ruth said. 'The best of my life.'

'It's not over yet,' Martin whispered. But it was, almost.

Swiftly, suddenly, pretence gone, she turned to him, clung to him, her tears scalding his body, the bed shaken by her sobs. He buried his face in her hair as his own tears fell.

She thought: I'll never again wake in the night, in the morning, to find you next to me. And all the other nights of my life for the rest of my life...endless loss.

They breakfasted silently. Martin had hired a self-drive car to go to the airport.

'You needn't come with me, my dearest,' he said. 'We can say goodbye here.'

'I am coming with you.'

Waiting, interminably—the plane was delayed

—she wished that she hadn't come. There was nothing left to say. They bought books and magazines, drank coffee, tried to talk. She willed the time either to stand still, or else to pass quickly, please God, not this slow crawl!

Eventually it was over. She watched his tall figure disappear through the departure gate. He didn't look round.

Driving back towards London, she pulled into the side and watched a plane take off and fly out of sight. It might not be his. It didn't matter. Then she accelerated and drove on mechanically, thinking about nothing at all.

Later she had to think.

'I can't marry Lee,' she told her mother. 'I can't marry him, Mother. It's impossible.'

All that, and a great deal more, she said to her mother, and on the next day to Lee.

'It's not you,' she told him. 'I just can't face marriage. It's as well to know it now.'

'But you don't know it, my darling,' he protested. 'It's nerves. It'll pass. We can postpone the wedding if you want to.'

She hated herself. His kindness made it worse. But at least he need never know what it was she couldn't face—sharing a bed with him, waking in the night to find him there, sitting down to meals with him. The wrong man, every day, every night, for the rest of her life. Well, she'd never do that to him.

'Tell me something,' her mother said next day.

'What?'

'You don't need to tell me, really. I know. It's Martin, isn't it? Why didn't you go with him?'

Ruth would have liked to deny it. It was better not to talk any more. But then, she thought, that seemed like denying Martin.

'Because...'

'It wasn't because of Lee. You knew he'd understand, and in time get over it. It was me, wasn't it? You thought you couldn't leave me, my darling. I know you.'

She took Ruth's hands, drew her to the settee, sat down beside her.

'Don't think I don't appreciate it. I'm humbly grateful that you love me so much. I've had you for twenty-six years, Ruth. Every one of them good. And don't think I shan't miss you terribly if you go away, because I shall.'

'Do you think I wouldn't miss you? Wouldn't long to see you?'

'I know you would, my darling. But you'd cope, and so would I. Don't make the mistake of thinking I can't cope. You'd be wrong.' Her mother had a dignity which Ruth had not seen before.

'What I couldn't bear is the thought of your unhappiness,' Mrs Peters said.

'What am I going to do?' Ruth said. 'Mother, tell me what to do.'

'There's the telephone. Use it. I daresay you can dial New Zealand. Did you know that one can dial almost anywhere in the world, now? The world is getting smaller all the time. That's something we should both remember.'

# A Little Light Flirtation

Sunshine invades the dark pavements under the cornices of the Place Gambetta—long, strong shafts penetrating the bar of the Hotel du Centre where I await my breakfast. It is exactly the scene we were promised by the Greenwoods at their Boxing Day party, when we all had horrid sniffling colds and the weather outside was so beastly that all we could think about was next year's holiday.

Monsieur le Patron, no doubt having heard me descend the stairs, emerges from the kitchen. He is wearing his striped apron and there is a small smudge of flour on his face.

'I am sorry, madame, my wife has gone shopping. She will not be long, and she will make you fresh coffee on her return.'

Is there in his voice just the tiniest reproof that I am late down? Would he like an explanation as to why my husband breakfasted, and left the hotel, more than an hour ago? Did he hear us quarrelling in the bedroom? But of course he did. It's a small place. You can hear everything that goes on.

201

I now have nothing to do this morning. That stupid quarrel arose because I dared to say that I was sick of looking at abbeys and refused to inspect another for at least a week.

'It's far too hot to be traipsing around churches,' I said.

'Churches are, without exception, the coolest possible places,' my husband retorted. He is maddeningly logical. It is one of the things I hold against him.

'Anyway,' I told him, 'I want to go to the market in Bergerac.'

He pretended astonishment.

'I can think of nothing hotter than trailing around the market,' he said. (Have you noticed that when men don't want to go somewhere, they use the word 'trailing'?) 'Besides,' he went on, 'I thought we'd come on holiday for a change. Every Saturday morning of our lives we go shopping.'

'Are you really comparing Bergerac market —the colour, the sights, the sounds, the smells —with the supermarket?' I demanded. 'Have you no soul, no eyes, no imagination, no appreciation—unless it's for something that's five hundred years old?'

We went on like that for some time. We've had a lot of practice. I thought when we got around to blaming the Greenwoods—a familiar let-out—we were nearing the end, but the quarrel took a turn and we were off again.

'You are stubborn and unco-operative!' my husband dared to say, ruining this lovely autumnal morning for me.

'And you are a pig-headed bore!' I yelled. I had to yell because he was already halfway down the stairs. And I have not seen him since; nor do I see the car anywhere. Unfortunately it is too late for me to go to Bergerac, since the only bus of the day left some time ago.

And now here comes Madame herself, crossing the Place, laden with cauliflowers, small yellow and green striped melons, ripe red apples.

'Why don't you breakfast outside?' she says. 'It is warm in the sun.'

By now I am more than ready for breakfast. How is it, I wonder, that one can eat to the full in the evening and rise next morning, hungry? It cannot be that the food has no substance. Not that delicious Poulet Rôti Orientale (for which Monsieur has promised to give me the recipe), the apricot-coloured pumpkin soup, the wafer-thin pancake stuffed with creamed asparagus. And that platter of cheeses, that heaped-up basket of fruit.

Of course, quarrelling sharpens the appetite; and then, one is constantly being dragged around sightseeing. I would like to laze the days away, one after another, as if time had no ending. Ah! Here is my coffee and croissants. Madame does not enquire about my husband, but I can be sure she knows.

Eventually when I have finished my breakfast—there is no one to rush me—I walk around the perimeter of the Place, keeping to the shade of the arches; then I turn down the narrow street which leads to the river.

Fish jump in the water; lily leaves scatter the surface; a flock of wild geese fly overhead. Poplars are etched against a cobalt sky and a small red spider spins a web from the book I am holding. I turn right again, passing the church. The doors are open and one can hear the children singing, presumably practising for tomorrow's Mass. I shall make for the château square. There I can sit quietly by the old stone walls and read my own, non-intellectual, non-demanding detective story.

There are two great trees here, a chestnut and a pine, which obligingly cast their shade so that one side of the square is in the hot sun and the other in dense shade. Each side has its own bench seat. I shall choose the latter.

Though only a stone's throw from the village, the square is deserted, except for this man who comes and sits on the opposite side, exposing face and arms to the sun while reading a paperback.

I shall concentrate on my book. I hope he will do likewise. I have no wish to talk to anyone this morning: only to be quiet, and alone. It is heaven to be on one's own. I am savouring the solitude.

As a matter of fact—it is now ten minutes later—he shows no sign of having noticed me. His must be an absorbing book. He has not once lifted his head from it, nor even glanced in my direction. Not that I have kept a constant watch on him, you understand. I am not concerned.

But why does he not notice me? Surely I am still attractive? I am often complimented on my blonde hair and fine English skin. Now if he were a Frenchman...

He could be a Frenchman—with that thick dark hair and slightly aquiline nose. At this distance I cannot see the colour of his eyes, but imagine them to be very dark. That emerald green shirt, opened to the waist to reveal his tanned chest, suits him very well.

Ah! He has at last raised his eyes from his book and I know he has seen me! Will he make a move? But he returns at once to his reading.

I wonder if I should not perhaps move into the sun? It is becoming just a little cool here and there is the slightest draught on the back of my neck. There is nothing to say that he must have the whole seat to himself. I don't want to speak to him, naturally. I definitely desire my own company this morning. I have had quite enough of men, thank you very much. But I am, I really am, almost chilly under these trees.

It amuses me to wonder what my husband would think if his wife were deliberately to scrape an acquaintance with a strange man, say in circumstances like these. Would he rage at me, lock me up, beat the stranger to a pulp? Or would he do everything to win me back? Cosset me; buy me a diamond?

None of these, I am sure. He would probably say: 'How nice to meet you', and buy the man a drink, and in no time at all they would be discussing trade figures and the balance of payments. He is quite impossible. I love him, of course. I love him dearly, but he is quite impossible and should be taught a lesson.

Just as I rise to my feet, this man does likewise; and we both start to move forward. I fractionally more quickly than he. I now realize that I am not chilly after all and almost decide to sit down again, but I cannot make it as easy as that for him. There is such a thing as self-respect.

So, inexorably, we advance towards each other. What will happen when our paths cross in the centre of the square? Will he smile? Will he speak to me?

At the very last moment I do not give him the chance, lowering my eyes before him. I feel sure he looks at me, though. We pass so close that in my nostrils there is his male scent in delicate balance with his expensive cologne, and rays of heat from his body reach out and touch me. The whole combination is extremely attractive, but I must not let him think I am cheap.

So we are now once more at opposite sides of the square: I in the sun, which is too hot for me and I know will burn the skin off my nose most unattractively, he is in the shade, buttoning up his shirt, rolling down his sleeves.

Well, there it is! I have missed my chance, and so has he. I think I shall move away now: walk back to the Place, look at the shops, have an aperitif outside the hotel before lunch.

He is following me! I shall not look round but I am sure I am right because the high walls of the château cause an echo and the footsteps cannot be anyone else's. I have to admit it, I am rather pleased. But I shall definitely not look round. I do not intend to encourage him.

Back in the Place Gambetta I can no longer

hear him behind me because the area is thronged with people, and youths on noisy mopeds are scorching around the war memorial in the centre. But I feel sure he's there. I can sense it. I shall stop and look in the window of the charcuterie and see what happens.

There is the usual dazzling display of pizzas and paella, quiches and pâtés and the window is highly polished so that I shall see his reflection if he passes behind me. But he does not. Puzzled—I am sure he was following—I venture a quick glance to my left and—yes! There he is, gazing in the photographer's window two doors away, pretending to be immersed in all those photographs of happy wedding couples, improbably pious children in Confirmation robes, naked infants on white furry rugs.

So what next? We shall see.

Slowly, I stroll to the corner, admiring a display of straw hats. While I stop to try one on, he looks in the charcuterie window.

I cross the road to the north side of the Place and study the racks of picture postcards outside the stationers. A few more leisurely yards round the next corner and I am back at the hotel.

But he has beaten me to it. While I looked at the postcards he must have crossed the Place diagonally and now he is sitting at a table outside the hotel half in the sun, half in the shade. Did he know I would...? But it is the only hotel. He regards me openly as I walk towards him.

So does my husband, who is seated at our usual table. I join him, shifting my chair to see...

'Well,' my husband says, pouring me a glass of wine, 'what shall we do after lunch, then?' His tone is matter-of-fact, just as if we have not quarrelled, as if he does not owe me an apology.

Madame has placed a carafe of wine before the man in the green shirt, and poured him a glass. With the most discreet of movements he raises the glass in my direction. His eyes are every bit as dark as I imagined.

'We could go for a walk,' my husband says. 'How about that?'

I lift the glass to my lips and the fragrance of the wine comes to meet me: fruity, spicy, ever so slightly sparkling.

'No, darling,' I answer. 'I insist that you go off on your own and see your old abbey. You know you'll enjoy it. It would be selfish of me to stop you.'

'But what about you?'

I sip my wine, and over the rim of my glass

I look towards the table at the back of the terrace.

'I shall be all right,' I assure him. 'I shall find something to occupy myself—in and out of the sunshine.'

# A Question of Choice

'I wonder if Rosemary will have changed?' Kate said. 'Five years is a long time.'

'We all change,' Kate's mother said. 'But perhaps Rosemary less than most. Here you are, a cup of coffee before you go.'

'Do you think I've changed, then?' Kate asked.

'Well, remember I did see you in America two years ago. But...yes, you have a little. You're thinner—it makes you look taller than ever, though at twenty-nine, you can't still be growing!'

'I didn't mean physically.'

'I know. You're quieter, sadder. Perhaps that's temporary, because you've been ill.'

She hadn't really been ill. She was never ill. She'd had a fairly nasty miscarriage and had been slow to recover, in her mind and spirits more than in her body; which was why she was taking a month's special leave from her job in New York.

She *was* sad. That was undeniable. You couldn't be with someone for three years,

211

conceive his child, and then lose both without feeling deep sadness. At least she couldn't. Max hadn't known she was pregnant; he had already gone. If the child had lived, she supposed she would have sought him out and told him. But it hadn't, so that was that.

'I didn't want the baby, Mother,' she said. 'In a way, what happened was a relief.'

Still, she'd often wondered what it would have been like to have borne it to full term. And because in the first three months of its life in her womb she had given it no welcoming thought, she felt guilty that it had left her; as though it was her mental rejection which had caused the physical one. Irrational nonsense, of course.

'Do you mind being done out of a grandchild?' she asked.

'I only mind for you, darling. But I expect there'll be others.'

'I wouldn't be too sure,' Kate said. 'It's not my scene.'

'Perhaps you're right,' Mrs Hampton conceded. 'How fortunate you are that you can do what you want, go where the mood takes you. I was born too soon.'

Kate smiled. 'What would you have done?'

'I don't know. Gone into politics, or explored the world. Who knows? Or maybe I'd still have done the same thing: married early and had you.'

'And, or course, my generation makes excuses. If we'd really wanted to be politicians or doctors or scientists, most of us could have done it somehow. I think the truth is we're a bit envious of your generation. Anyway, you'd better be off or you'll miss your train.'

The Sussex countryside was so fresh, Kate thought, and from the train looked so unspoiled. She recalled the moment the plane had touched down at Gatwick, all the Americans on the flight crying out in wonder at landing in the middle of green fields. It was a journey she had earlier planned to make with Max. Deliberately, she turned her thoughts away from New York and all that it held, and concentrated on Rosemary.

They had been at the University of Sussex together in the early seventies. Rosemary had been the clever one, taking a first-class degree while she herself had only managed an indifferent second. But where had Rosemary's brilliance taken her? Straight into marriage with a fellow student, and a life of domesticity in a Sussex village.

They had corresponded from time to time since she had left for the States five years ago, but Rosemary's letters were usually full of what the children had been up to, or how Derek was coming along in his job. In New York, it had all seemed a world away to Kate, but now here she was, actually arriving at the station.

Derek was waiting.

'Rosemary apologizes for not meeting you. Some crisis with the children. They happen all the time, but you can't ignore them, can you?' He looked and sounded comfortable, and at least ten years older than his thirty years.

Rosemary, on the other hand, when she opened the door to them, looked little different from the student of eight years ago. Her straight, fair hair hung down her back in the same fashion, her blue eyes still sparkled and her face shone like a polished apple. But standing behind her were two children, and underneath the smock-like garment she wore it was plain that another was on its way. She had said nothing about being pregnant.

Kate was totally unprepared for the wave of envy which swept over her. She took a deep breath and forced herself to speak.

'Rosemary! You haven't changed a bit!'

'Heavenly to see you, Kate. Come in. Marcia, take Auntie Kate's bag into her room. Marcia is seven.' Rosemary said. 'And this is Jonathan. He's five. He cut his finger just as

I was on the point of coming to meet you. But he's quite all right now.'

'I'm glad,' Kate said, following Rosemary into the sitting room.

'Collapse into a comfortable chair and I'll give you some sherry,' Rosemary said. 'Derek has got to go back to work. Derek, my love, don't forget to pick up the fish. 'Bye, then!'

Handing Kate a glass of sherry, sitting down opposite to her, Rosemary said, 'I can't say *you* haven't changed. You look terribly elegant and American. I like your hair short.'

'I keep finding the odd grey hair among the dark ones,' Kate said. 'Imagine us both pushing thirty! It doesn't seem possible.'

'It does when I look at Marcia and Jonathan,' Rosemary said. 'I can't believe there was ever another kind of life.' She patted her stomach. 'And now *this* little surprise, due in less than a month!'

'Why didn't you tell me you were pregnant?' Kate asked.

Rosemary's troubled eyes looked into Kate's own.

'Your mother told me about your miscarriage. It seemed cruel to tell you I was pregnant. I hope seeing me wasn't an even worse shock.'

'Good heavens, no!' Kate lied. 'I don't know

215

what ideas Mother gave you, but, you know, I didn't want to have the baby.'

Why then, Kate asked herself, had the first sight of Rosemary so affected her? And now, she thought, Rosemary's looking even more troubled, as if she thinks I'm a completely unnatural woman.

But the moment passed. They changed the subject, settling for memories of the uncontroversial past.

'Do you remember that *awful* little man who used to follow you round the campus?' Rosemary asked.

'You mean the one who was five feet tall and looked like a Yorkshire terrier?'

'That's the one!'

'I remember. Do you remember the sit-in, when we took our sleeping bags into the Admin building and camped there for days?'

In the evening, Kate helped to put the children to bed. On Saturday, they all went down to the seashore. They waded in the rock pools, finding sea anemones and tiny crabs. Marcia presented Kate with a small white shell and Jonathan gave her a grey pebble.

'You must take them home and keep them for ever,' Marcia said solemnly.

'I will,' Kate promised.

That evening she bathed them again, this

time on her own, delighting in the feel of their silky bodies and in the fragrance of their clean skin and newly washed hair. Then she read to them until they fell asleep.

'Do you realize,' she said to Rosemary as the two of them sat in the garden, sipping wine, 'it's the first time I've had anything to do with small children?'

'They're my whole life,' Rosemary said. 'Derek, the children and my home.'

Perhaps it was no more than the complacency in Rosemary's voice which irritated Kate. As if she knew all the answers, Kate thought. She tried to stop herself saying what sprang into her mind, but couldn't.

'But don't you ever feel that you've...well, wasted your education, your gifts? After all, you were easily the most brilliant student of our year. What about all the books you were going to write, the research you were going to do? Would you say, quite dispassionately, that you'd opted out?'

They looked at each other silently. Kate saw the colour deepen in Rosemary's cheeks. I've blundered, she thought—and remembered her friend's quick temper. But Rosemary's reply was quietly said.

'I certainly would not. In fact, I might turn it around and ask you the question. Aren't *you* the one who's opted out?'

'I did what I thought suited me,' Kate said.

'But are you happy?' Rosemary asked. 'Oh, I know you've travelled, read the right books, met interesting people—but does it add up for you? Do you feel satisfied, having turned down marriage and motherhood...?'

'I don't consider...'

But Rosemary would not be interrupted.

'Tell me honestly, Kate, don't you feel a bit superior to me? Admit it!'

'Of course I don't! It's not like that!'

'Because you're not, you know!' Rosemary said. 'I feel completely fulfilled. Can you say as much?'

There was a great deal more, on and on, back and forth. In the old days they'd argued far into the night about almost everything, but this was different: sharper, personal, even a little bitter. And when too much had been said ever to be forgotten, they suddenly flung their arms around each other and wept copious, remorseful tears.

'I didn't mean the half of it,' Kate said. 'Please forgive me!'

'I'm a pig,' Rosemary declared. 'A smug pig!'

The quarrel seemed over, and it was, but Kate was thankful when Sunday came and it was time to leave. At the railway station they embraced each other fondly. But will things ever be the same, Kate wondered?

'We understand each other better,' Rosemary said, reading Kate's thoughts. 'Perhaps it will help us to keep in touch?'

Her mother was away when Kate reached the flat; called, so the note said, to the bedside of a sick uncle. 'Only flu, so I should be back by Thursday. Amuse yourself. Don't mope,' she had written.

Kate did amuse herself. She went to art exhibitions, visited the theatre, viewed the House of Commons, the Tower of London and Westminster Abbey, and shopped extravagantly. In the course of her travels about town, she was spoken to by several personable young men and propositioned by one—and was annoyed with herself, at first, because this gave her a lift. Afterwards she laughed about it.

She didn't mope, but she did think; far into the night, long and hard about many things, mostly to do with herself. It was time to take stock. Her month's leave would soon be up.

'Well, here I am,' her mother said, late on Thursday evening. 'How have you managed? What have you done?'

'All kinds of things,' Kate answered. 'Like making decisions. But let me tell you about my weekend in Sussex.'

They sat comfortably over a cup of tea while Kate talked.

'I think Rosemary seems truly happy,' she said at last. 'Really and truly happy.'

'Does that mean you're going to make me a grandmother?'

'No. Not yet. Perhaps one day, perhaps not. What I *do* know is that what's right for Rosemary, what was right for you—if it was...'

'*You* were.'

'...isn't the answer for me. I'm not Rosemary. I'm not you. I'm me, and my needs are different. My job in New York, my friends there, are my kind of fulfilment. For now, that's where I belong. Later I might go to California, or maybe try to get into university again and do some research.

'Or, my darling mama...I might even meet the right man and marry him!'

Her mother smiled.

'Well,' she said. 'As I told you, your generation has the choice. Good luck to you!'

'Oh yes, we have the choice,' Kate said. 'What we perhaps didn't realize was that the choice could be hard to make. But something tells me I'm making the right one now.'

Back in her New York apartment, she carefully

unpacked the white shell and the grey pebble and placed them on the shelf which held her small treasures. It had been good to see Rosemary again. She must send something for the children, and for the new baby when it arrived. Then she went to answer the phone, already ringing because she was back.

## Wedding Shoes

There it is, on the 'reduced' rack in the shop doorway. It's almost hidden between a thick-soled leather brogue and a red wedgie, as if it's of no importance. Just when I've given up hope of ever finding such a shoe. And I'm in despair because the wedding's on Saturday.

Will it be the right size? Please God, I am praying as I pick it up. Please God let it be a size four and I promise I'll be a good girl for ever.

It's a beautiful shade of green, and just the right colour to complement my bridesmaid's dress. It's real leather, with straps woven around each other. The heel, heaven be prais-ed, is just the right height. Please, please let it be size four!

Alas—is this a punishment for past sins? It's size three-and-a-half.

Nevertheless, I shall try it on. Anyone who has tried on as many shoes as I have this week will testify that sizes vary.

I take it hopefully into the shop in search of its mate.

All is confusion there, as if the whole of Brighton had dedicated this Thursday morning to buying shoes. Hordes of women trailing endlessly from shoe shop to shoe shop in search of perfection.

But not many in search of green leather, I comfort myself.

The assistant, shoe-horn in hand, gives me a frenzied look. I wave the green treasure at her.

'If I could just have the other one please!'

She brings it to me. One on its own was delightful. As a pair they're exquisite.

'I really take a size four,' I explain.

'I'm sorry. This is the only pair. They're a traveller's sample.'

'Perhaps it's a big three-and-a-half,' I say optimistically.

'Could be.'

We agree that sizes vary, so I try them on. Ooh! Aah! They are...well...tight!

No denying it. But they go on. And by using the very last hole I can just fasten the small silvery buckle.

'Of course, you won't ever be wearing them with jeans,' the assistant says persuasively.

Quite right. Nor a leather jacket and a woolly hat. I roll up my jeans to mid-calf level and look at my feet in the long mirror.

Short purple socks are not what these shoes deserve either. But never mind that. They and my bridesmaid's dress were simply made for each other. The real question is, can I walk in them?

Just about. I cover the distance between me and the mirror without too much suffering.

'Of course they'll stretch,' I say.

The assistant agrees. 'Your feet swell, trailing around the shops. They're bound to stretch.'

Yes, everybody knows that shoes stretch. But not between Thursday and Saturday, an inner voice mutters. I ignore it and buy them.

Saturday arrives all too soon. Rush, rush, rush. My instructions from the bride—my best friend Susan—are to go straight to the church and wait for her there.

'I couldn't stand both you and Mummy fussing around,' she said. 'It would be too awful.'

That suits me. I can devote time to myself. I have a long, slow bath. Then I spray on deodorant, smooth on body lotion, sprinkle on toilet water, pull out eyebrows, heat up my hair rollers, try three different shades of nail polish and four of eye make-up...

At last the dress. It slides over my shoulders, the soft, silky material caressing my skin. I zip up the back, adjust the neckline, take a good look at myself in the mirror.

Oh, yes! Definitely! It's me! The way it clings where it should and flows out gently from the hips to the floor. When I get my shoes on, with their lovely high heels, it will be exactly the right length.

I fasten the silver chain with the jade pendant round my neck. The gift of the bridegroom to the only bridesmaid. My mother comes in to inspect me.

'You look lovely, Penny! Really lovely. Your red hair and that shade of green!' She's my number one fan, my mother. She gazes at me in admiration. 'Well, get your shoes on love. I'll tell Dad we're ready.'

The shoes. I had intended to wear them in the house between Thursday and Saturday— get them and my feet used to each other.

In fact, I've hardly been at home. It occurs to me that I could have slept in them but it's too late to start thinking about that now.

They go on. They fasten, just. I do believe they're the tiniest bit bigger than they were; or my feet have shrunk. How will it be when I stand up? The near-agony of Thursday has lessened to mere discomfort.

Everyone says it shows in your face if your shoes hurt, but my face in the mirror looks happy enough—and why not, with this lovely dress and my beautiful, beautiful green shoes peeping out from beneath it?

I put on my hat, chosen by Susan. A nice hat, but on the big side for my size.

I say to my mother as she returns, 'I think I probably look like a bedside lamp!'

'Nonsense,' she says. 'You look lovely! Here, don't forget your muff.'

I don't like the muff. It's pretty enough, with layers and layers of pale yellow cotton primroses, but I'd rather have had a bouquet. The muff was Susan's choice.

I sit in comfort in the back of the car so I don't squash my dress. I put my feet up on the seat to take the strain off them during the ten-mile journey.

Better not tempt Providence by taking off my shoes.

What I have forgotten is that travelling can make your feet swell. Also, you don't realize it's happening.

We drive up to the church and get out of the car.

Oh, anguish! Oh, torture!

I look down at my feet. They have puffed up like batter puddings in a hot oven. Each strap, which I now believe to be reinforced with steel wire, is cutting into a mound of swollen flesh, making a lumpy pattern.

'Look, the Staceys are over there,' says my

mother, and all of a sudden my parents have vanished into the church, oblivious to my agony.

I look up at the church clock. In three hours, perhaps even two, it will be over. Perhaps, once the toasts are finished, I can come over faint and lie down somewhere. The way I feel, there'll be no difficulty in fainting.

But surely, I admonish myself, surely I can stand a few hours of discomfort for the sake of my best friend Susan? Or downright diabolical pain. We were at school together. In the netball team, in the Guides. A Girl Guide sticks it out.

I brace myself and totter up the path to the church. A walking stick would help—something to stop my whole weight being concentrated on those tiny cages of unstretchable leather.

In the porch I lean against the wall, waiting for the bride. Please don't let her be late. Friendship can stand just so much.

A man comes out of the church, looking anxious.

'Hello,' he says. 'You must be Penny. I'm the best man, Martin Fox. The groom's getting frantic in there. He's sent me to spy out the land, see if his beloved is on the horizon. I thought it was the bride who worried about being left at the church.'

He's dreamy! Fair-haired, tanned skin, brown eyes. A bit on the short side, perhaps. Not all that much taller than me in my slender heels.

The thought of my shoes intensifies the pain. The world blurs and swims. He gives me a look.

'Are you all right? You look a bit pale.'

'I'm fine.' A brave lie.

'Then I'll get back to Stuart. See you!'

I am not fine, and it's no use pretending any longer. I cannot stand it another second. They'll have to come off, at least until the ceremony is over. No one will notice. All eyes will be on the bride.

With difficulty, because the buckles are now embedded in delicate flesh, I unfasten the shoes and ease them off.

Oh, the ecstasy! And oh, the wretchedness, as life flows back into my mangled feet! The shooting pains, the stabbing of a thousand pins and needles! I hop from one foot to another to relieve the torment. But it doesn't help.

And here comes the bride. Her car is at the gate. She's looking for me to help her with her dress. The shoes? Where shall I put them?

There's only one place. They will just fit inside my muff, providing I also keep one hand inside it to prevent them falling out. Now there's something I couldn't have done with a bunch of freesias! Thank goodness Susan got her own way about the muff.

I am in no state at present to walk down the long church path to meet the bride. Were it not for the twinging, the twitching, the throbbing, I would think that my feet were dead. I shall have trouble enough following her down the aisle. I wave my free hand to let her know I'm here.

On her father's arm she walks towards me. She looks radiantly happy. But then, no doubt, she is completely pain-free.

We embrace carefully, kissing the air near each other's cheeks, not wishing to disturb our carefully applied make-up.

I'm thankful it's a slow walk up the aisle. The cool stone of the church floor soothes my soles, but my dress now sweeps the floor, collecting the dust the verger has missed.

The bride halts at the appointed place and I take up my stand behind her. With one hand firmly in my muff, I receive her bouquet in the other.

The vicar, already late and with another wedding to follow this one, goes straight into action.

'Dearly beloved, we are gathered here...'

I have not noticed until now, my feet having been only partially alive, that I am standing on one of those iron heating grates let into the floor. Now that life has flowed back into my extremities, I can feel every criss-cross of the grid.

I cannot move away. The grid, as far as my exploring foot beneath my dress can ascertain, is about two feet square. We are at a most solemn part of the ceremony. I would attract attention.

At this moment some devilish device decides that the church is cooling down, and switches on the heat. It rushes up through the grating like a hot desert wind, but it will do nothing to warm up the congregation, since it is all trapped under my wide, floor-length dress. It does not die down until it has thoroughly heated the metal grating. And me.

Surreptitiously, I change from foot to foot—but carefully, so as not to overbalance. All eyes are on the bride. No one will notice that I am sweating freely.

At last it is over. The register is signed. We move outside for the photographs: the bride and groom; the groom and the best man; the parents. The best man and the bridesmaid. We stand close together and wait for the photographer.

'There's something different about you,' the best man says. 'Somehow I thought you were...'

'Taller,' he's going to say, because instead of being eyeball-to-eyeball I am now, deprived of my lovely high heels, obliged to gaze up at him.

'Funny,' he says, 'how one can get the wrong impression!'

He seems happy with the one he's getting right now, and the photographer must think so, too.

'That's perfect!' he calls. 'Hold it there!'

So I look up at the best man and he looks down at me, and I forget all about my feet.

But not for long. The reception is in the village hall, which is only a few minutes' walk away, and except for the bride and groom who have already gone ahead to receive us, we're not bothering with cars. So we set off to walk, me accompanied by this dishy, attentive young man. I will spare you the details. I will only say that in Susan's village they are proud of their ancient, cobbled pavements.

It had rained while we were in the church and the said pavements are now shining wet, with water collecting in the hollows between the stones. Any girl in her right mind would raise her skirt hem, but I am not prepared to let this Martin know what an idiot I've been. He takes me by the hand, which is nice, and with my other hand I hold on firmly to the shoes inside my muff.

The water from the pavement, which has had no difficulty in penetrating my tights, seems unable to escape as easily. It collects in pockets around my toes.

On arrival at the village hall everyone does a vigorous bit of foot-wiping on the course, bristle mat. I smile at Martin, clench my teeth, and do likewise.

Once inside it's not so bad. My feet no longer hurt. They're just icy cold and soaking wet.

The hem of my dress is filthy and I notice Susan's mother looking at it; but it's a busy time for her and there's no opportunity to mention it.

The reception is good. Once I've realized the impossibility of holding on to a glass of champagne, a chicken vol-au-vent, and a pair of shoes inside a muff, and have managed to dump the latter under a chair, things begin to swing. I decide not to leave early.

When the dancing starts I have a bright idea. I go into the ladies, get rid of my tights, wash my feet. When I emerge, Martin is waiting for me.

'I missed you,' he says. 'Let's dance.'

'Great,' I say. 'I always like to dance barefoot. Do you mind?'

It's one of those old-fashioned dances they have at wedding receptions to bring back memories for the oldies. I melt into his arms and we're away. He's a super dancer.

I don't notice much more until someone comes up to Martin and says they're trimming up the car before the happy couple leaves. Toilet rolls, tin cans, the lot. Except, it seems, no one remembered to bring a shoe.

'We've got to have a shoe!' this fellow bleats. 'It's so lucky to have a shoe!'

'Wait a minute!' I say.

Seconds later I am back. I hand over my beautiful green leather shoes. Martin watches me with astonished approval.

'Now there's friendship for you!' he says. 'There's true unselfishness! Such beautiful shoes, too. I don't know how you can bear to part with them. I think it's marvellous of you.'

I look up at him, into his admiring brown eyes. Mine are a bit misty. They were the loveliest shoes.

'I hope they bring her luck,' I say. 'They did me!'

# Night Flight

She lay on her side of the bed, her arm out-flung, exploring the empty space where Eddie ought to be. The luminous hands of the clock showed five past two.

She had come to bed at half past ten, not able to concentrate on anything. Sleep had come quickly enough but she had wakened again after the first hour. Well, there would be no more sleep tonight!

In the darkness she observed how the light from the street lamp penetrated a chink between the curtains, beamed on to a picture on the opposite wall. Wide, white-tipped waves, rolling on to the sandy shore. No ships or seabirds or human figures. Only the sea.

She and Eddie had chosen the painting together, bought it with a wedding-present cheque from an aunt. It was a scene which never palled because it was always changing. Sometimes it appeared calm and sunny, sometimes stormy. Tonight the sea looked cold and grey.

Where was Eddie now? In some downtown

club, as likely as not, consorting with the world's riff-raff. Five years ago, at the beginning of their marriage, she had not thought it would be like this. They'd always been together then; every night wrapped in each other's arms as they slept. But for the last year or two, since he had changed his job, there had been too many nights when she'd tossed and turned in the half-empty, king-sized bed.

She must leave. There was no longer any question of waiting until morning. She reached out and switched on the lamp, swung her feet on to the floor. She dressed warmly and packed a small case. The rest could follow.

Out of habit she made the bed and looked around the room to check that everything was in order. Much of the time, she thought, she'd been happy here. What would the future be like? Everything was changing for both of them.

She found a piece of paper and scribbled a message. There wasn't much to say. Eddie could hardly be surprised by her action since she'd threatened it often enough.

She moved through the silent apartment, gently touching a piece of furniture here, a cared-for object there. Then she went out, leaving the empty rooms to await her husband's return.

The spring night was cold, with a clear sky, blue-black, moonlit and star-filled. She shivered a little, turned up the collar of her coat. Three o'clock in the morning was an impossible time. But there was an excitement in her departure which she knew would carry her through.

At the all-night rank on the corner the driver sat in his cab, studying the sports page, listening to the radio. When she tapped on the door he opened it quickly.

'Hop in, ma'am! Are you OK?' She was aware of his scrutiny.

'Fine, thank you!'

She spoke calmly, as if she was used to leaving home in the middle of the night.

'Well, it's not a good time for a lady like you to be out alone.'

But what did you do when your husband was habitually missing in the small hours? There came a time when action was needed.

The morning sky was pink and mauve and gold as Eddie drove home. A few pale stars defied the daylight, but soon they would be defeated by the sun. He was weary. He wanted nothing so much as to lie out flat between the sheets and let sleep take over. Perhaps Ruth would still be asleep. He was too tired for conversation, let alone argument.

She'd been moody lately: blaming him for everything, not like herself at all. Perhaps a new start was what they both needed. But all he wanted now was rest and sleep. Give him a few hours and he'd be human again.

His key turned quietly in the lock. He tiptoed into the house and went upstairs to the bedroom.

At first, he didn't see that the bed was empty. Perhaps it was because the duvet was drawn up that he thought he saw the shape of Ruth's body beneath it, her dark head on the pillow. It took a second or two to realize that she was not there. The bed was smooth and flat, the pillows plump, as if no one had ever dented them.

Where in heaven's name...? If she'd been downstairs when he came into the house he would have known at once, the way one does when there is life in a place. Quickly, he drew back the curtains, looked up and down the street. Once before, not able to sleep, she had gone out for an early morning walk; got up and left him in bed without him hearing a thing.

There was no sign of her. What should he do? His whole body craved sleep. The sight of the bed drew him like a magnet. If she'd gone for a walk she'd be back soon.

But the bed looked so undisturbed. He turned back the bedclothes, felt the sheet. It was cool. If she had occupied it at all she must have left it before dawn.

Then he saw the note. Relief, apprehension, fear, ran through him simultaneously. As he started to read the telephone rang.

'General Hospital...'

The rhythm of his heartbeats thrummed in his ears. Tears pricked his eyes as he listened to the short message.

'I'll come as quickly as I can,' he said. 'Tell her I'm on my way.'

Luckily there was a cab on the rank.

'General Hospital,' he instructed.

'You're out of breath,' the driver said. 'You don't want to run like that, sir!'

'As quick as you can make it! My wife...'

He didn't want any small talk, only to be left alone.


Eddie waited impatiently in the Reception area while the woman at the desk phoned the ward.

'Won't you take a seat, please?' she said. 'Someone will call back in a minute.'

'Why can't I go up to the ward? They said for me to come right away.' He spoke sharply, his voice unrecognizable in his ears.

'They'll let me know the minute it's all

239

right for you to go up.' She smiled; a calm, professional smile.

He didn't want to take a seat, thank you. He wanted to get to Ruth as quickly as he could. What was happening to her while he was being kept waiting like this?

He lit a cigarette.

'I'm sorry,' the receptionist said. 'No smoking.'

There was no ashtray in which to stub it out. He crushed the cigarette between his fingers and threw it in a garbage can.

The telephone buzzed. The woman picked it up, listened, replaced the receiver.

'You can go on up now, Mr Armstrong. Third floor.'

He waited impatiently for the elevator. He could have run up the stairs in half the time. He got out at the third floor, turned right, saw the entrance to the ward in front of him. Ruth was in a bed near to the door. Not waiting for permission, he walked swiftly towards her. She smiled up at him.

'I'm sorry, Ruth honey,' he said. 'I tried to get here quickly. I came as soon as I got the message.'

There were blue shadows under her eyes. Her face was pale, with a film of sweat still on her forehead. But a smile lit up her eyes.

'It's all right, Eddie. Don't worry! I knew you'd come as soon as you could.'

'Is everything really all right? Is he...?'

'He's just great! You'll see!'

'It's all so sudden. The clinic said another two weeks. Why didn't you call me? I'd have come home.'

'Would you, Eddie? Would you really?'

Her words searched into him, but the tone of her voice, and her smile, were understanding, forgiving.

'If you'd called me,' he said, 'they'd have got me on my radio. The police force doesn't own me.'

She laughed out loud.

'You could have fooled me!' she said.

'You know I wanted to be with you when the baby was born. Our first.'

'I know,' she said. 'And I'm sorry you weren't. Nurse phoned twice before she got through to you. You must have been on your way home. It all happened so quickly. Anyway, next time I'll wait for your day off!'

# Leave it to Mavis

No sooner have I shot down the stairs to answer the telephone, which has been ringing for ever, than the front door bell starts up. Ding, dong, ding, dong. Persistent, both of them; not taking silence for an answer. If I do nothing they will sooner or later stop; but then I shall never know what I missed.

'Hello! Oh Julie! Hang on a minute.'

Telephone in hand, I edge towards the door, but the cord is too short and I cannot, while continuing to hold the instrument, reach the knob.

In the end I abandon Julie face down on the cushion of the hall chair while I answer the door. She is in full flight about what she should wear on the sixteenth and will therefore not notice what I have done to her. Sometimes I read the whole of the previous week's colour supplement or write to my aunt, while listening to Julie on the telephone.

Edith Prosser stands on the doorstep, plum-coloured with agitation, every superflous ounce quivering. Pushing past me, she sinks into

243

the chair, sitting bang on top of Julie whose unfaltering squeak is suddenly muffled. I disentangle Edith, the telephone and the chair and while making signs to Edith to take herself into the living room, I try to tune in again on Julie.

'Don't be long,' Edith calls. 'It's terribly important. And if that's Julie on the phone, ask her if she'll kindly return my secateurs.'

'As I was saying,' Julie trills. Bingo! I am back in the middle. Nothing lost.

'You're not going to believe me,' Edith shouts. 'You're just not going to believe it!'

'If that's Edith Prosser I can hear,' Julie says, 'ask her if she's done with my pinking shears and could I have them back?'

'Perhaps you'd like a brief word with each other.'

I could make the beds, wash up, do the vegetables and sort the laundry while they chat. Normally I could, but they are not at the moment on speaking terms and since I am more eager for Edith's revelations than Julie's speculations, I give a sharp hissing noise... SSsssss...and a slight scream into the telephone.

'The soup!' I cry. 'It's boiling over! I must fly!'

I bang down the receiver. It is the only way with Julie.

'Personally I always stamp hard on the floor

and tell her Grandma's fallen out of bed,' Edith says. 'But never mind that now. My goodness, you're in trouble!'

In trouble? Me? Why, there isn't a cloud in my sky. Apart from the fact that my daughter is getting married on the sixteenth of next month, that I am making her dress, my own and those of the three bridesmaids, icing the cake, arranging the reception, writing my husband's speech and hiring his suit, growing the flowers for the church—apart from all this, all is tranquil. True, the bridegroom has carelessly broken his left leg on the ski slopes, but there is no reason to suppose that it will not be as good as new eventually. So what does she mean trouble?

'There will be no reception! No reception!' she announces.

No reception? What does she mean?

Edith Prosser—did I mention it?—is the mother of the bridegroom. She would be the first to know, after my daughter who never tells me anything, if he has, for instance, changed his mind. He seemed quite cheerful yesterday. His leg! Not...please God! I picture myself with a one-legged son-in-law.

But no; there is a smug look on Edith's face, a tinge of satisfaction in the set of her mouth, and no one can say she is not a devoted mother.

So what is it?

'No reception? What do you mean? Are you telling me the wedding is off and I'm the last to know? I shall have something to say to my daughter.'

'I never mentioned the wedding. No reception, I said. You haven't booked the hall. There's a Darby and Joan party on the sixteenth.'

'Haven't booked the hall? Nonsense! Of course I have. There can't be a Darby and Joan party. Someone is trying to frighten us!' As far as I'm concerned, they've succeeded.

'Well, there is. I looked in the village diary in the post office. I wanted to fix the date for the old age pensioners' keep fit display, and you know we're supposed to look in the diary to see what's going on.'

'I never heard such nonsense!' I protest feebly. 'Darby and Joan party indeed!'

'It's there in black and white. Been booked for ages. The church is down for the wedding on the sixteenth, I'm pleased to say...'

'Well thank you.'

'But no reception.'

'I distinctly remember—'

In fact, disconcertingly, I don't remember any such thing, though of course I shall not admit it. Of course I must have booked it.

Anyone will tell you I am a splendid organizer. Leave it to Mavis, they always say.

If Edith Prosser says it is so, then it is so, is another thing they always say. And it is.

I get rid of Edith by telling her that Julie is due any minute now, and I hurry down to the village, to the post office. Casually, as if I am checking on a jumble sale I do not really care about, I flip through the diary. She is right about the Darby and Joan. She is right about no reception.

Do not panic. Do not panic! Of course there is no other place within thirty miles where you can possibly have the reception and if there is it will be booked up, and it will also be too expensive and not big enough. And the invitations have gone out; ninety-eight, first-class post. But keep calm.

The caretaker of the village hall is sorry he cannot help. He would like to if he could, but the Darby and Joan have this Saturday every year. He would have told me had I tried to book, though it's common knowledge anyway (in fact there was a poster outside the hall). No, I did not telephone, and in any case everybody knows he doesn't take telephone bookings. Only lead to trouble, telephone bookings. He gives me several examples, not one with a happy ending. But he is sorry for me and promises to keep quiet about my dilemma until I have had time to think.

By a combination of bribery and blackmail, the details of which I shall not be able to reveal unless she rats on me, I extract a similar promise from Edith Prosser.

I return home, lock myself in, pour half a tumbler of sherry, and settle down to think. I have several ideas, all of them impossible. It is useless to appeal to the Chairman of the Darby and Joan club to change the date because she hates me since I beat her to the Presidency of the Women's Institute. She would laugh, ha ha, at my downfall. She must never know.

The simplest thing would be a broken engagement. Call the whole thing off. I have said all along they are far too young. But would my daughter agree to this idea?

I realize with horror that my daughter will have to be told. Or will she? Would it be possible...could we have the wedding...'I now pronounce you...' and turn up at the hall? No, I cannot see us sharing celebrations with the Darby and Joan.

How shall I break it to her? In my mind I compose a long letter; abject, remorseful, pleading. But as she will be home from the office by six o'clock it is not really practical to write to her. I calculate whether I can have a nervous breakdown before then. Rush out of the house screaming; see the doctor; be whisked into hospital; and, of course, put under heavy sedation.

'No. No visitors, I'm afraid. Doctor's orders. No, not even family *(especially* not family?) Utterly worn out...overwork...stress...doing things for others...you'll have to postpone the wedding.'

Postpone the wedding! Quickly, I swallow my sherry, put on a head scarf and my dark glasses and make a further quick trip to the post office. I take another nonchalant peek at the diary. The thirtieth is vacant. Two weeks later. But what excuse?

It is useless to plead illness since I am as fit as a flea and everyone knows it.

I break it to my daughter the moment she enters the house. I cannot bear the burden alone one minute longer. At first, thinking I say the wedding is off, she turns chalk white, starts to faint, and has to be given brandy. When I tell her no, it is only the reception, she recovers and has hysterics.

A family meeting is summoned. Edith Prosser, the bridegroom, my daughter, husband, self. The bridegroom offers, the moment he can discard his crutches and plaster, to elope and do away with all the fuss. My husband, bowed down by the expense of it all, shows his first sign of real interest. He straightens his shoulders and agrees with enthusiasm. My daughter bursts into tears and accuses us of conspiring to ruin her life.

'I did it!' I cry. 'I ruined it!' I dissolve into tears along with her. My husband fills his pipe. If I follow my present inclination and throw myself into the river, a quiet wedding with no reception would be in order. Would she still wear white? I sob now without restraint. 'Poor motherless bride,' I hear voices saying. 'Poor motherless bride.' But it is only Edith Prosser and she is saying 'Why not swallow your pride?'

Change the date, she means. Confess. Write to all those people. Tell them what a muck-up you've made of it. Ruin their arrangements and confuse all their hair appointments.

By three am. I have completed the ninety-eighth letter. I am up again early in the morning to post them. My husband has made the arrangements with the vicar and the village hall caretaker. The bridegroom has somehow soothed the bride-to-be. Edith Prosser has contributed nothing but no doubt she will work hard spreading the news in her own inimitable fashion. No matter, all is well again. Apart from a tendency to fall asleep whenever I stand still. I am a new woman.

I am back at home, snug under the continental quilt, having a nice lie-down, when the doorbells rings. If it is Edith Prosser I shall hit her with an umbrella.

It is little Miss Harper, secretary of the Darby and Joan club.

'We heard about the mix-up,' she says. Edith Prosser has been hard at it.

'Poor little girl. We told the Chairman we'd got to change our date. We wouldn't take no for an answer. You'll be pleased to hear that the sixteenth is free for your little daughter's wedding.'

'I'll walk back to the village with you,' I say wearily. 'I think I need more envelopes.'

# Channel Crossing

From where I sit behind the bar counter I can see much of what goes on in the *Place des Oiseaux*. Marcel, who owns the clothing shop, is setting out his array of straw hats on a table under the arcade. He hopes to tempt visitors who know no better than to pay fancy prices. Madame Charente, in the *charcuterie* opposite, is filling the windows with quiches Lorraines, pâtés, salads, cooked meats. She is plump, rosy-faced, smiling, as if she fed well on her own wares. She keeps a good shop.

Did I say 'sit?' There is precious little time for that when one runs an hotel like mine. Always something to do, and usually I'm the one to do it, except in the kitchen, which is Robert's domain. He does the cooking, with a bit of help from Germaine for the washing-up and so on.

I look after the rest. Dining room, bar, six bedrooms. I have slow old Madame Lebrun to help me with the cleaning, and Hortense in the dining room. At weekends Alfonse comes in to help me in the bar. So you see, although it is only a small place, I am kept busy.

Even so, I sometimes stop for a minute and look out through the doorway. Sometimes in the afternoon, when I must iron all the table napkins, I move the ironing board nearer to the door so that I can see what's going on out there.

It amuses me to watch people discover my hotel, stop to read the menu, debate about whether they will or won't come in. Usually they do. My prices are modest, the menu good, and the place looks attractive and clean.

Begonias in pots around the doorway, white muslin curtains at the windows, and no great big dog lying across the doorstep to break your neck over.

There's a couple studying the menu right now. They're English. I can always tell, even without hearing them speak. We get a number of English people here. They buy up the derelict farmhouses and spend good money on restoring them for the sake of spending a month here in the summer.

Our people don't mind. The houses (did I say houses? Some of them are no more than barns or cattle sheds) would fall down anyway. And the money, especially since we have learned their true market value, helps us to buy something better. I wish I had one or two to sell, but all my family have ever owned is this hotel. It wore out my grandparents and my mother and father, and now it's doing the same to me.

They're coming in, this couple. She's a pretty girl. Tall, with long blonde hair tied back from her face. He's just a few years older than she is.

I shall speak to them in French, of course, pretending I know no English.

Well, if it pleases them, and I know it does, why spoil things by telling them that I have an English husband in the kitchen and I can speak and think in their language almost as well as they can?

They sit at a table near the window, not too far from my counter, and order beer. As I serve them the girl smiles at me.

When I move away she takes a large sheaf of papers from her bag. Another one! They've been to the *Agence Immobilière* and that Monsieur Proudet has stuffed them with descriptions of desirable properties for sale.

The young man soon orders more beer and asks if he and his wife can have lunch.

'Why yes, Monsieur, in about half an hour. Nothing elaborate, you understand. My husband's pâté, some fresh trout which he will cook with almonds. And the first strawberries have just been picked.'

They go into raptures. It happens every time and I never understand why. What do the English live on? I ask Robert when I go into the kitchen with the order. What do they eat, that our simplest meal excites them?

'Tinned peas,' he says. 'Fish and chips. Bangers and mash.'

'Fish and chips I would like to try, but I do not think I could possibly live on *saucissons*.'

'Nothing like your *saucissons*,' he says. 'Not the English banger.'

All the same it would be nice to try. All our married life-twenty-five years—Robert has promised to take me to England. To London; to Brighton; to a place called Huddersfield where he was born. But never have we been able to leave the hotel. As well as visitors in spring and summer, we have commercial travellers all the year round—and we're glad of them.

The English couple are ecstatic about their meal. I myself never tire of the smell of butter and trout, mingling together.

'You can't beat a French chef!' they cry. It's a cry I've heard many times, over the years. I keep my secret.

When they come to pay, they ask if they could *possibly* have a room for the night—or two or three nights. I show them the room which overlooks the *Place*, opening the shutters to let the afternoon sunlight into the room.

They fill in their forms. I see that they are Ralph and Helen Mortimer, from Brighton.

'I have always longed to go to Brighton,' I tell them.

'Brighton is all right,' they say, 'but we work in London, which is not so good.'

London! Theatres, shops, cinemas, Madame Tussauds, Battersea Park, London Bridge! Every day it is all theirs!

'Not really,' Madame says. 'I work in a publisher's office. When I'm not imprisoned there I'm dashing to or from Victoria station. It's an exhausting business. At the weekends I'm too tired to live.'

'I'm in computers,' Monsieur Mortimer says. He offers no further information but from his expression I gather that it does not satisfy him.

'So we intend to leave it all,' his wife says. 'Make a fresh start. Do something with our lives!'

'You mean...buy a house in France?' I ask, trying to sound surprised, as if I had not heard it all before.

'Not a house,' Monsieur says. 'A hotel, just a small hotel we can run ourselves.'

257

'Just such a one as this,' Madame adds. 'A few bedrooms, a small bar, good food, friendly people—and five hundred miles away from the rat race.'

Working from early morning until late at night. Shopping, gutting fish, preparing vegetables, chasing dust, mending sheets, polishing floors. And every day washing and ironing those red-checked napkins.

And the accounts. Especially the accounts: to be completed every night, though one is dead with fatigue. What is it like to live a life where one does not have to balance the books every evening?

Naturally, I say nothing of this, at any rate not to Monsieur and Madame Mortimer. But when we go to bed—well past midnight—I speak to Robert about it.

'Think of it! If we were to sell them this hotel we could go to England! We would visit your cousins in Huddersfield; perhaps settle down there.'

'Settle in Huddersfield?' he says, switching off the light. 'Whatever for?'

'Or Brighton if you would prefer it. I do not mind. Both are pretty names.'

'And what would we live on, Marie? Tell me that.' He climbs into bed, makes the nightly inch-by-inch scratching of his chest and stomach, relaxes.

'You could take a job. You are a good chef. You know that chefs are always needed.'

'Exchange one kitchen for another, is that what you mean?'

'You would work shorter hours. Have a day off every week, and two weeks holiday every year. Less responsibility. We could visit the cinema, walk by the sea, go on the pier. Is there a pier in Huddersfield?'

'No. And what would *you* do while I was at work?'

'I have not thought,' I say. This is not true, because I have thought that with the money from the hotel, plus that which we have carefully saved, we could buy a small house. I could sit in an English garden, have coffee with the neighbours, watch colour television and go for leisurely strolls.

'Go to sleep, Marie,' Robert says. 'We must be up early. Remember it's market day.' He turns on his side and is asleep in no time at all.

I cannot sleep; my head is too full of plans. Our hotel is exactly what Monsieur and Madame Mortimer want. Perhaps we could buy their house in Brighton from them in part exchange? When I do fall asleep it is to dream that I am

259

having tea with the Queen Mother, clothed in a dress made from red-checked napkins.

The next day, as they eat their lunch, Monsieur says that they are to visit two new properties which the agent has given them, near to Bergerac. They seem to be just the thing they are looking for, he says. Immediately after lunch they drive off to view them.

I bid them farewell with a smile on my face and anxiety in my heart. As far as I dare, I have warned them off any proposition which Monsieur Proudet might put to them, but there are limits beyond which I dare not go. Besides, they are in cloud cuckoo land and would not believe me.

'If we are to move,' I say to Robert as we eat our lunch, 'we must do so quickly. It is imperative! Any day now they will sign a *promesse!*'

'It is not imperative that we move at all,' he says, refilling his glass. Englishmen are infuriating. No fire in their bellies!

'Do you wish to stay here for the rest of your life?' I demand.

'I wouldn't mind,' he says.

I shall act on my own. There is no other way. Besides, it is my hotel, left to me by my father. Robert cannot prevent me.

The Mortimers return only a few minutes before dinner-time. They rush up to their room, not stopping for their usual *aperitif*. They look flushed with happiness and I fear the worst.

I decide to wait upon them at their table myself, somewhat disappointing Hortense who has fallen for Monsieur Mortimer.

'Good evening,' I say. 'Did you have a good afternoon, then?'

'Marvellous!'

'First-class!'

They offer no details. I am consumed with anxiety. Immediately after dinner—they always go to the bar—I must speak with them.

Alfonse is here helping out this evening and I shall get him to look after the bar and I shall ask if I might sit for a moment at their table.

'I have a proposition to put to you,' I shall say.

They eat their way solidly through salmon, *Coquelets sur Canapés*, some goats' cheese, *Charlotte Chantilly aux Fraises*, complemented by two bottles of our local wine, light and dry. They are very, very happy, and I fear the worst.

What if they do not go into the bar? What if they decide to go for a walk between now and bedtime as sometimes, arm-in-arm, they do?

261

One can hardly run after them saying 'Would you like to buy my hotel?'

If this is what they choose, I shall sit behind my counter until they return and waylay them as they enter the hotel again.

Not to worry! They move directly from the dining room to the bar, choosing, I am pleased to see, a table in the quietest corner. I move towards them, signalling Alfonse to bring the coffee and *Armagnac*. Monsieur rises gradually to his feet while I take my place with them.

'I have a proposition which I think will interest you...'

They listen politely, with interest, even. I point out the many advantages of my hotel. Its position, close to everything. The interesting people who come and go, and return again. The loyalty of our staff who have been with us so long. The small but regular profit. The friends one makes over the years. I almost sell it to myself.

As I talk, I become aware of their discomfort—embarrassment, even. Perhaps I am too late? Perhaps they have already decided on some other place?

And then, because they are not aware that I understand English, I hear the reason for their discomfiture.

'Oh! Lord, Ralph!' Madame says. 'I've warned you before. A holiday enthusiasm's all very well, but you do take things too far!'

'It was fun,' he protests, 'you enjoyed it yourself. Looking over all those nice old places. No harm done!'

'I'm not so sure,' Madame says. Then she turns to me, speaking in French.

'The thing is, Madame Tissot...actually... well, we have changed our minds. We've given the whole matter a great deal of thought...'

Monsieur interrupts. 'You know how it is, one comes away on holiday fed up with the daily grind. You see a new place, think it's what you'd like for the rest of your life. And immediately you want to throw up everything...'

'But we both have secure jobs, which most of the time we enjoy. And when we do have our family, Brighton will be a splendid place for them to grow up in,' Madame says.

'So we must leave tomorrow. It's been wonderful here. We shall come back again and again. And we hope you'll be here to serve us.'

It is not, at first, easy to speak. But of course I do.

'I'm sure I shall,' I say. 'And now, if you will excuse me, I have my accounts.'

In bed, Robert puts his arm around me. 'I've been thinking, Marie,' he says. 'If you're really keen to sell up, we'll consider it. It's a hard life, I know. But I'd thought we were settled fairly happily here.'

'And so we are. My family have been here for two hundred years. What would this place be without a Tissot to keep the hotel? Also there are our good friends: Hortense, Alfonse, Old Madame Lebrun...'

In the dark he does not know that I am crying, just a little.

'That's all right, then,' he says, 'and perhaps next year we can leave them to it for a couple of weeks and take a trip to England.'

'That would be pleasant,' I agree. 'We will go to Huddersfield, will we?'

'Huddersfield? Well if you must.'

'Also I have been thinking,' I say after a while. Robert is on the point of sleep and arouses himself to listen.

'What about, my love?'

'I have made a decision about the hotel.'

'Oh yes?'

'Yes. I have decided that from now on, no matter what you say to me about standards, I shall use only paper napkins in the dining-room. I have finished with that dashed ironing.'

## Festival at Rowdean

'I don't see why I should go to the meeting,' Melanie protested.

'But darling, everyone knows you're back home again. They'll be so disappointed if you don't show up.'

'So they can say "My, how you've grown" and "No young man yet?" '

'They're interested in you,' her mother said. 'After all, they've known you all your life.'

It was precisely that sort of interest which, a year ago, had been just too much for her. So when the opportunity came of travelling abroad for a year with a family, looking after their two small children, she'd jumped at it. Well, that was over now. But as soon as she could she must find another way of escape.

'I think you have grown, darling,' her father teased. 'But in the nicest possible way.' She warmed to the love and approval in his voice.

'Oh, all right, Pop! I'll go for your sake and Mummy's. But this is to be my one and only public appearance. I'm not going to be on show seven days a week for what's left of the summer.'

'I don't think that will be wanted, Poppet,' he said. 'Even when we had the circus in the village we couldn't fill it for more than two nights.'

By the time they arrived, the only empty seats were on the front row. She hated the walk up the length of the hall, conscious that people were looking at her.

'Well, you all know why we've called this meeting,' the vicar said. 'After last year's success as the Best Kept Village it seemed a good idea to have a festival. Tell the world about ourselves. Put ourselves on the map.'

'Begging your pardon, sir, some of us don't want to be on the map. We're all right as we are.'

Melanie recognized the voice of old Henry Richards. He'd done odd jobs around the village ever since she could remember. He kept the village green in perfect condition and suffered every time anyone set foot on it.

'Quite so, Mr Richards. And we shall take a democratic vote. Do we want a festival or don't we? And if we do, what form shall it take?'

'Speaking as a comparative stranger to the village, I think it would be a great shame not to have a festival. Rowdean has so much to offer.'

The voice, deep and resonant, came from the row behind Melanie and was not one she remembered. She turned around to see the owner. Tall, broad-shouldered, dark-haired. A pleasant face.

'Our new schoolteacher,' her father whispered. 'Jon Saunders.'

'What do we want with a lot of strangers tramping all over the place?' Henry Richards demanded. 'Ruining the cricket pitch and all.'

There was a short, sharp free-for-all which buzzed around the room like a swarm of summer bees. Melanie twisted in her seat and found Jon Saunders looking at her. He was older than she was. All of twenty-five, she reckoned.

The vicar banged on the table.

'Well, now that we've discussed the matter,' he said hurriedly, 'we'll have a show of hands. Those in favour of a festival...? Splendid! So we must choose a festival committee.'

Jon Saunders was one of the first to be choosen, and after him the same people who'd been on committees as far back as Melanie could remember. The young man leaned forward and whispered, 'What's your name?'

'Melanie James.'

'I propose Miss Melanie James,' he called out.

'It's the last thing I came for,' Melanie

protested. But no one heard her because she didn't say it very loudly.

Afterwards, over the inevitable cup of tea, the new committee grouped together in a corner. They had all brought their ideas of what form the festival should take.

'Rowdean in History,' Mrs Tompkins said. 'The Women's Institute did it just after the war. Some of us are a little older, of course. I'm not sure that Selina Merry could still ride a horse.'

'Ride a horse?'

'She was Lady Godiva.'

'What's Lady Godiva got to do with Rowdean?' Melanie asked.

Mrs Tompkins looked at her sharply. 'Nothing, I suppose. But we had this splendid horse, and Selina looked quite magnificent. Junoesque in those days.'

'It can go on like this all night,' Melanie whispered to Jon. 'You don't know our village committees.'

'Oh but I do,' he said. 'I'm on several. Parent-Teachers, of course. Preservation Society...'

He had no right, Melanie thought crossly, to look so different from anyone she'd ever met, and be so...conventional. She disliked conventional people. Well, *she* wasn't going

268

to toe the line.

'We have a great deal of talent in the Institute,' Mrs Tompkins was saying. 'Mrs Arkley is coming along very well on the oboe.'

Melanie grinned at Jon. 'Fit that into your scheme,' her eyes said.

They agreed to meet on the following Monday. 'In our house,' Melanie suggested. 'More comfortable than the village hall.'

'A nice idea,' her mother said later. 'Bring you right back into the life of the village. And you'll like Jon Saunders. We've all taken to him.'

If they thought she was going to slide back into a groove, Melanie thought, they had a surprise coming. She was glad, now, to be on the festival committee. Not because Jon Saunders was on it—she had a feeling he might be quite an obstacle—but because it might give her a chance to change a few things.

'How about a pop festival?' she asked her mother. 'We could use the field at the back of the church. Accommodation would be no problem. People would bring tents and sleeping bags.'

'Which reminds me,' her father said. 'I have to be in Germany or somewhere that weekend. Such a pity!'

Melanie looked at him. 'We haven't fixed the

weekend yet, Daddy.'

'Nor have I,' he said. 'Let me know your dates.'

The meeting went on and on.

'It's not so much a lack of ideas as an abundance of them,' the chairman said, trying to make himself heard. 'We really must try for some sort of plan.' He had hoped to be home for the late-night news.

'The children *should* figure in it,' Jon Saunders said. 'It's important. The school choir. Competitions. Wild flowers. A local painting. Scenes from village history.'

'I do so agree with you,' Mrs Tompkins said. 'But I think the scenes from history *must* be the Women's Institute. Don't you all agree? We have the experience, you see. And the costumes, somewhere. King Canute, Eleanor of Aquitaine, the wives of Henry the Eighth...'

'What can King Canute possibly have to do with Rowdean?' Melanie interrupted. 'We're sixty miles from the sea!'

Mrs Tompkins managed a thin smile. 'Melanie dear, I think you're being a teensy bit naughty. It's all part of our British heritage, you know. I hope a year abroad hasn't made you forget *that!*'

'It's made me see that everything's the same

as it always was. Nothing moves forward in Rowdean.'

From the frown on Jon's face she knew she had sounded ruder than she meant to be.

'That's not quite true, dear,' timid Miss Finch ventured. 'Mr Crisp has gone over to self-service. Not nearly as convenient, but *progress!*'

'Perhaps we should decide what the festival is *for*,' the chairman pleaded. 'That might help.'

'*I* thought it was to show Rowdean to the world!' Mrs Tompkins boomed, flinging her arms wide in a welcoming gesture.

'*I* think it's to make the people of Rowdean aware of their own history, and of each other,' Jon said. 'Of their own and each other's contributions to the life of the village.'

'You mean like Mrs Proctor's flower arrangements and Miss Topwell's corn dollies?' the chairman asked.

'If you like,' Jon was enthusiastic. 'Whoever has something to contribute. And if outsiders want to come along and see what we can do, so much the better.'

'Honestly!' Melanie said. 'You can't be serious? That's simply bringing together all the bits of things people do all the time and calling it a festival. And anyone who's lived in this village could tell you the results right now. Mrs Fair-child will win the fruit-cake competition; Mr Carpenter's will be the biggest marrow; Mrs Proctor will get the cup for flower arranging. You can't call *that* a festival.'

'You're forgetting the WI pageant, dear,' Mrs Tompkins said.

'Oh no I'm not!' Melanie retorted.

'Then perhaps, Mr Chairman,' Jon said icily, 'we could have Miss James's bright ideas.'

'With pleasure,' Melanie said. He was insufferable. He'd been in the village less than a year and thought he knew everything about it.

'Above all,' she said, 'it's time we had something different. Not the same old things that we've done forever. A pop group on the green, for instance. The kids would love that.'

'It would kill old Henry Richards,' the chairman said. 'But go on, Melanie.'

'We could invite musicians and artists. Have chamber music in the church, poetry readings in the open air; a company of actors. Flood-lights, fairy lights, and lots of wine! That's my idea of a festival.'

'Don't you think that sort of thing is more suitable for Brighton or Cheltenham, dear?' Miss Finch asked. 'I mean, it doesn't seem quite like Rowdean.'

'I'm not so sure,' Mrs Tompkins said thought-fully. 'A company of actors, or perhaps singers. A joint production with those of us in the village who are interested in the arts. Gilbert and Sullivan. Even Shakespeare!'

She sees herself as Lady Macbeth, Melanie thought. Playing opposite Lawrence Olivier.

*'Couldn't* we arrive at a compromise?' the chairman pleaded. 'So many splendid ideas! May I suggest that Mrs Tompkins, Mr Saunders and Melanie form a sub-committtee and sort it out between them? I'm sure we'd be in capable hands. Those in favour?'

It was an unwritten rule in the village that after midnight no dissenting voice should pro-long the meeting further.

'I'll give you a call tomorrow,' Jon said, tak-ing his leave.

It was after seven when the phone rang. 'I thought perhaps we'd go to the Feathers for a drink,' Jon said. 'I'll pick you up in half an hour.' He rang off, not waiting for agreement. She had a good mind not to go with him when he called. But if she didn't, then he and Mrs Tompkins would get everything their own way.

'I didn't invite Mrs Tompkins,' he said later, when they were sitting in the pub. 'I thought just a friendly drink. We don't even have to mention the festival.'

'That's all I came for,' Melanie said. 'What else?'

'I see. Then if you just wait here with your tomato juice I'll go and fetch Mrs Tompkins.' He drank down his cider and sprang to his feet.

'No use,' Melanie informed him. 'Tuesday night is choir practice. And who but Mrs T, is the first alto? If you knew as much as I know about the village, you'd know what practically anyone was doing any night of the week.'

He sat down again. 'Then since you think we've nothing else to talk about, by all means let's discuss the festival. As long as the WI gets its share of the glory, it'll be OK with Mrs Tompkins.'

Actually, Melanie realized, she would like to have known more about Jon Saunders. Had he a girlfriend? What did *he* do with his evenings when he wasn't sitting on committees?

'If you think I shall come around to your point of view,' she said, 'you're wrong. How about you settling for mine?'

'Not a chance,' he said. 'Because what you suggest is wrong. Your kind of festival is for outsiders. The people who live here would be spectators. They'd prefer to be involved.'

'We shall never agree,' Melanie said. 'It was stupid to put us both on the sub-committee.'

He smiled. He looked no older than one of his schoolchildren when he smiled like that. If it weren't for this stupid festival he might be quite nice.

'Livens it up,' he said. 'You should approve of that. OK then, if we can't agree we must compromise. Have something of yours, something of mine, something of Mrs T's.'

'What a mixture!' Melanie said. He was right, though. It was either that, or she'd bow out of the whole affair. And she didn't feel like doing that.

'Then we'll make a list,' she said.

The list included an essay competition, painting contest, string quartet, roundabouts and stalls and a children's gymnastic display on the green, with poetry readings at intervals throughout the afternoon and the Women's Institute pageant in the evening.

'That leaves flower arrangements, produce competitions, handicraft displays, refreshments, a pop or folk group—as obtainable—plus or minus a madrigal society, all to be fitted in somewhere!' Melanie cried. 'It's ludicrous! Do you *have* to have your gymnastic display, for instance?'

'Yes. It'll be far more popular than your string quartet. Give that up.'

'Certainly not.' She had no idea where she

275

would get one but she wouldn't give it up. 'Besides, they'll be in church. I don't suppose even you will want that cluttered up with vaulting horses, with kids hanging on ropes from the roof beams?'

'Well, thank goodness we agree about Mrs T's pageant,' Jon said. 'She'll be pleased about that. Shall we go and meet her from choir practice and tell her about the rest?'

They took the narrow path which skirted the pond. In the late summer twilight, bats dipped between the trees and swooped over the water.

'It's beautiful,' Jon said softly.

'I know,' Melanie agreed. 'It's seductive, too. It can bind you hand and foot if you let it.'

'And you don't intend to let it?'

'No. I shall go away again.'

'But not yet?' His voice was quietly serious; and then changed. 'Not before the festival, I hope?' he said lightly.

'I wouldn't miss that for the world,' she promised, matching her tone with his.

It was perfect Saturday weather. At six o'clock she drew back the curtains to a flood of sunlight.

'Thank goodness,' she said out loud. She

276

had had this awful dream about a tornado sweeping the folk group into the pond. It was good to waken to a day like this.

She was disappointed not to have managed a pop group, but the folk group from a nearby town would be great, she knew. Jon had arranged his events with maddening efficiency and Mrs Tompkins and her team of lively ladies were raring to go.

'I don't want to give anything away,' she'd said last night when the three of them had met together for a final check-up. 'But do not *fail* to watch the bit where Anne Boleyn goes to the scaffold. Mrs Smithers is *splendid!*'

'Do you think,' Jon said, walking Melanie home from the meeting, 'that Mrs Smithers might actually be sacrificed? For the good of the cause, I mean?'

Melanie laughed. 'Who knows? Mrs T's nothing if not thorough.'

She showered and dressed quickly, choosing a long-skirted, flowered cotton dress. It *would* be a lucky day. She could feel it in her bones.

'You look beautiful, my darling,' Mr James said.

It was already the end of the afternoon. There was no doubt of the festival's success. The children, she had to admit, were enchanting.

The poetry readings were going well, though it was not always easy to catch all the words since the poets' corner had been placed a little too near to the children's roundabout, which did a brisk, unceasing trade.

'Just as well one can't hear it all, dear,' Mrs Tompkins said, on her way to somewhere with a mysterious bundle of props. 'Some of it's not quite...well, you know...'

'All set for the pageant?' Melanie asked.

'Just about. Miss Jennings's bust is giving us trouble. Too big for the costume. But we'll iron it out!'

The string quartet had been installed in the church. The folk group was due to play after the pageant. For the time being Melanie had nothing to do but enjoy herself.

She passed Jon, crossing the green.

'It's swinging!' she said. 'You were right.'

'So were you,' he said. 'Your poetry reading's certainly attracting people at the moment.' She was afraid she knew why.

'Be back here in an hour,' Jon said. 'Watch the pageant with me.'

The pageant was nicely under way when the first clap of thunder sounded. Canute had commanded the waves and now Miss Jennings's Earl of Essex was paying court to Mrs

Tompkins's Queen Elizabeth. History having been rearranged to suit the players, Anne Boleyn was still to come.

'I do see what she meant about the bust,' Jon said gravely.

No one moved at the first clap of thunder, presumably taking it for the approach of the Spanish Armada, but with the second peal the heavens opened and the rain, fervently prayed for throughout the long dry summer, came down in torrents.

The immediate dash was into the church, where the string quartet, busy tuning up their instruments, were astonished at the size of the advancing audience. It seemed that the whole village had turned up to hear them. Without more ado they plunged into their own arrangement of Handel's Water Music at the same moment as the rain began to pour through the roof in various places.

The audience's exit was as swift as decorum would allow. The quartet packed up their dampening instruments and followed to the village hall.

'If we don't push, we can all get in,' the vicar shouted. 'Please enter in an orderly manner! Seats for the elderly, please!'

Shoulder to wet shoulder they stood in the hall while the storm of the century raged outside.

'This is *awful!*' Melanie said. 'Whatever shall we do?'

'Get your folk group,' Jon ordered. 'They're in here somewhere. Get them on to the stage. I'll round up the WI. Be as quick as you can.'

Minutes later he stood on the stage and shouted for silence.

'We're going to have a concert,' he announced. 'Sketches from the Women's Institute. Music. Singing. Everybody join in the choruses, please!'

It was possible that the storm subsided fairly soon. No one really knew because of the singing, led by the folk group, augmented by the madrigal singers and the children's choir and accompanied, whenever they knew the tune, by the string quartet. It was almost midnight before Queen Elizabeth's rendering of 'Rose of England' closed the concert to tumultuous applause.

As they left the hall the air was fresh, and already perfumed with the smell of early autumn.

'A splendid success!' Mrs Tompkins said. 'What wonderful ideas you young people have. Who else would have thought of mixing all this lot together?' She beamed at them both, her red wig askew and still slightly damp. 'We must do exactly the same thing next year!' she cried.

'I'm willing,' Jon said, watching her go. 'But you're leaving, Melanie. You won't be here, will you?'

'I might,' Melanie said. 'I just might.'

They took the path around the far side of the pond. Over the treetops the harvest moon glowed orange in the indigo sky. Lights came on in the houses at the far side of the green. She was filled with a sudden love for Rowdean and everyone in it.

# The Meeting

'I don't know why you always have to meet in such inaccessible places,' my daughter grumbled.

'You forget,' I said. 'We've been brought up to travel. Our parents were always wandering around the world from job to job. That's the reason why we were at the school. It was a place where we could make our own family.'

For most of our childhood the school—in the mountains near Geneva—had been the focal point of our existence. When the term ended we dispersed to places like Djakarta, Tokyo, San Francisco, Copenhagen. Holidays were fun, but when they were over we came home to school.

'Well perhaps I should suggest we have the next meeting in Harrogate? Would that suit you?' I asked.

It had been Mary's idea that she should drive me to Pierre's house in the Auvergne, spend the week of our meeting exploring the region, and collect me to drive me back. Sometimes she treats me as if I'm in my dotage.

283

'Next meeting?' she queried. 'You mean there's going to be another?'

'Of course. You know we have them every ten years,' I reminded her.

'Mother, I know you're marvellous for your age,' she protested, 'but you *are* pushing seventy. So, more or less, are all the others. In ten years' time...'

'So you think we won't make it, even to Harrogate?' I interrupted.

'You must face facts, darling,' she said.

Have you noticed that people only say that when they mean one must face unpleasant facts? My daughter has an elderly outlook. Such a pity!

In the late afternoon, and without too much difficulty in spite of Mary's forebodings about remote mountain retreats, we arrived at Pierre's house.

*'Entrez!'* he said. 'You are the first to arrive.'

We were given a quick drink and then Mary was firmly sent on her way. It had been decided at the very beginning that not even our nearest and dearest were to be allowed at our get-togethers. What we wished chiefly to recapture was our own especial family from all those years ago.

I watched Mary go, and went back into the house. I was home.

'But how odd,' I said, 'to think of oneself at home in a place where one has never before set foot!'

Pierre smiled. He was looking older, I thought. His hair was now white, but as abundant as ever and he was still attractive. I wondered what he was thinking of my appearance, and because he'd always been able to read my mind he at once told me.

'Meg, you look wonderful,' he said. 'Each time I see you, your age becomes you more. Your figure is better than when we were at school. You were fat then, because you ate all those Swiss pastries.'

'You were spotty for the same reason,' I reminded him.

The years fell away. We had always been close, perhaps because we had arrived at school, frightened eight-year-olds, on the same day. He had come from Algeria where his father was stationed; I from my grandmother's home in the north of England because my father had been appointed to Tokyo.

'I was sorry about your wife,' I said. 'I didn't know until the notice came about the meeting.'

'I miss her,' he said. 'But you know what it is like, Meg. It has happened to you.'

We never talk for long about our families. After all, we have only a week in which to make up for the last ten years and to carry us over the next. When I remarked upon this to Pierre his face became grave.

'That is something we must all discuss,' he said. 'It cannot be avoided.'

The others began to arrive. From the cold of Reykjavik, the heat of Jerusalem, the frenzy of New York, the cool green of Ireland, they arrived at Pierre's house in the mountains. It was a good place to be. Pierre had retired rich from the aircraft industry. His house was large —a château, I suppose—and filled with beautiful objects.

We scurried away down long corridors to our allotted rooms to prepare ourselves carefully for the full encounter which would take place before dinner. I changed my dress twice, and then went back to the first choice. With great care I put on my make-up, peering into the mirror to get it exactly right. Perhaps a little more colour on the cheeks? One wished to look healthy.

When we assembled in the salon—a long room with a log fire burning at each end—I thought we looked an attractive bunch. Pretty dresses, beautiful jewellery. The men in velvet jackets. My second thought was how sparsely we filled the salon. We congregated around the fireplace at one end, leaving two-thirds of the room empty.

'But it will fill up,' I said to Pierre, 'when the rest come down.'

'We are all here,' he answered. 'Eleven of us only. No more are expected this year.'

'Only eleven? But last time we were twenty-five!'

'Last time was ten years ago, Meg,' he said.

He signalled to the servant to give me more champagne. I drank it more quickly than usual, feeling the need.

'But Jonathan? Gerda? Manuel?'

'You see, dear Meg, you never would correspond, otherwise you would know these things! Jonathan is well enough, except that he is arthritic and cannot get about. Gerda…well, she is not so good. The journey from Denver would be impossible for her.'

I thought of Jonathan skimming down the ski slope, always ahead of the rest of us: of Gerda reading forbidden romantic novels under the bedclothes. Perhaps I have never grown up. Was this, I wondered, the reason why we met? So that we could be young again? I asked Pierre.

'Not at all,' he replied. 'We meet because all those years ago we were happy together. We loved each other as a family. We still do. But we are not a true family in that we have no continuance. That is what we must face and discuss tomorrow.'

After breakfast next day we congregated in the salon, where screens had been tactfully placed so that the room was reduced to less than its former size and the absence of those who should have been there was less obvious. Pierre informed us about absent members. He had not told me last evening that Manuel had died, and it came as a shock.

Then he said, 'Now, plans for the future!'

There was a stir, felt but not seen, like a cold wind on a summer's picnic. Yet seen a little, the way the wind lifts the corners of the table-cloth or whips away a paper napkin.

'Very well,' Pierre said. 'In your hearts you are aware of what I must say. Last year we were twenty-five. This year we are eleven. This year we are in our seventies. In ten years' time we shall be in our eighties.'

He paused. 'How many of us will be left?' should have been his next words. We caught ourselves looking at each other, then looking away again. 'Will *he* be here?' 'Will *she* still be alive?'

Conchita spoke first.

'If we decide now not to meet,' she said, 'we condemn ourselves to death!'

288

Conchita was always a master of the dramatic. For once it did not seem out of place.

'We say "Farewell, my friends! I shall not see you again!" It is impossible! The heart could not bear it!' She sat back in her chair, closed her eyes against us.

'Better to arrange that we'll meet as usual,' Basil said. 'Then if nearer the time the whole thing fizzles out...'

'That won't work,' Karl interrupted. 'We come from the far corners of the earth, giving up everything to be with each other for a week. As long as any two of us lived we would meet. Who will you condemn to know that he is the last one left?'

'Karl is right,' Helen said. '*That* is the greatest cruelty. We must withdraw while there is dignity left.'

'At the end of the week,' Pierre said, 'we shall put it to the vote. In the meantime, we enjoy ourselves!'

And so we did. But there were reservations such as in all our years together we had never known before.

'But at my back I always hear Time's winged chariot hurrying near,' I said to Pierre. 'How shall I vote?'

'According to your conscience,' he replied. 'You must decide for yourself.'

During the days which followed I found myself looking at my friends. 'Can I bear never to see Karl?' I ask myself. 'What will the world be like without Conchita?'

I was bound to each one of them. But it was when I came to consider Pierre that I realized the impossibility of it all. How could I say goodbye to Pierre for the rest of my life? I could not do it, and I told him so.

'Nor I you,' he said. 'On the other hand, how can I come to a meeting in ten years' time and not find you there? It is not to be thought of.'

'Perhaps I shall outlive you,' I said. 'Women usually do.'

But how terrible if I did, and found myself without him.

In spite of the many diversions laid on for us during that week—a boat on the lake, the cable car up the mountain, drives around the countryside—our spirits flagged as the days went by. On Thursday evening, our traditional gala time, we drank our champagne and looked at each other from tear-bright eyes. No one mentioned the vote. Not one of us, I am sure, thought of anything else.

After breakfast next day our packed bags were

taken down to the hall. Most of us would leave immediately after the final meeting. Pierre had chartered a minibus which would take people to the airport. My daughter was to call for me at noon.

Once again, Pierre took the meeting. Once more the same arguments were put forward.

'We should continue as usual,' Basil said. 'Let things take their course.'

'It will not work,' Karl insisted. 'You have seen how it has been this week. No one has been really happy. Each time it would be worse for those who are left. We have had wonderful times together, but now they are over.' Karl was always one for the cut-and-dried.

'There are eleven of us,' Pierre said. 'If it should be necessary, I have the casting vote.'

How would he use it? While the arguments flew back and forth the issue became a personal one for me. If Pierre used his vote on Karl's side, this would be the end for us.

In the end he did not have to use his casting vote. The verdict was six to four in Karl's favour. So this was to be our final meeting.

I have no intention of describing that last hour. There are things which remain in the heart forever and are not for others to see. The minibus came. They departed. Leave it at that.

By eleven-thirty I was left behind with

Pierre. Because I couldn't bear it, I prayed for the next half-hour to pass quickly.

'We will have a last bottle of champagne,' Pierre said. 'Just the two of us.'

Why not, I thought. And if it made me a little bit drunk, so much the better.

We talked inanities: how long it would take to get back to North Yorkshire; what the weather would be like. Then Pierre said, 'You don't have to go.'

'Not have to go?'

'No. You can stay. You can stay forever. What is there to prevent it? We can be married and live happily ever after. For however long...'

To love, when one is young, is wonderful. I don't forget it. To experience it again when you'd thought everything was over...well, you have to be as old as me to know how that feels.

'I don't know what to say,' I told him.

'You quoted Marvell at me the other day,' Pierre said. 'I give him back to you.'

'Had we but world enough, and time.
This coyness, lady, were no crime...'

I finished it for him:

'But at my back I always hear
Time's winged chariot hurrying near.'

'They also say,' I babbled, 'marry in haste, repent at leisure.'

Pierre laughed out loud at that; threw back his head and roared. I laughed too. I laughed until the tears ran down my cheeks and I was sobbing. I couldn't stop. I think it was the champagne.

'Marry in haste!' he said. 'I've known you sixty—no...sixty-one years. Think of that! So what is it to be?'

'It's to be "yes",' I told him.

We waited until my daughter arrived, then we told her the news over another bottle of champagne.

# Roundabout

Miriam said: 'Anyone would think that it was you getting married instead of me. Why can't you make up in front of your own mirror instead of hogging mine?'

'Because the light's better here, that's why,' Joan replied. 'Do you have any more cotton wool? Anyway, I'm the chief—nay, the only bridesmaid. An important role. You will toss your bouquet to me...which reminds me that the flowers haven't arrived yet. Where can they be? Now if you hadn't spent so long in the bathroom...'

'I don't see the connection,' Miriam said. 'Actually, I reckon the bride is entitled to a long, slow bath on her wedding morning. Not to mention breakfast in bed with a china teapot and an embroidered tray-cloth instead of two fingers of toast while standing at the ironing board. I also think she's entitled to the full use of her own dressing-table.'

She leaned forward and peered anxiously into the mirror. Pulling strands of hair the colour of hazelnut shells over a wide forehead, she made a face.

'Do I look all right? Honestly? Would I look better with a fringe? What do you think?'

Her brown eyes, narrowed in indecision, met Joan's serene blue ones in the mirror. Apart from their eye colouring they really were alike, Miriam thought. The same thick, glossy hair, with a heavy straightness they now valued but which had been a source of grief to both of them in their childhood. Finely shaped noses—perhaps a little thin—with elegantly flaring nostrils. The Pemberton nose, Aunt Catherine called it. Well-arched eyebrows.

'You look great just as you are,' Joan assured her. 'No kidding.'

'I don't know.' Miriam surveyed herself critically. 'Perhaps I should have let my hair grow a bit longer?'

'Well there's not much chance between now and twelve noon! Which reminds me, I must telephone about the bouquet. You have sole use of the mirror for the next two minutes.'

'I really don't think I want a bouquet,' Miriam called out after her retreating form.

'Too late!' Joan shouted, dialling the florist's number.

She came back into the bedroom and stood behind Miriam at the dressing-table. 'They're on their way. Of course you want a bouquet.

It'll be quite small, no yards of trailing greenery.'

'I still think...'

'Do stop fussing! Please, darling! It's not a bit like you.'

'You wait,' Miriam said. 'Just you wait until it's your turn. You'll be far worse than I am. Have you pinched my eye-shadow? My lovely new golden-amber eye-shadow?'

'I have not,' Joan said. 'I may be sharing the teeniest corner of your mirror, in what has always been the best bedroom, but I have supplied all my own make-up.'

'You could have fooled me!'

'Besides,' Joan continued, 'it's not my colour. I shall use just a soupcon of heavenly blue with a suspicion of smoky grey blended in...like so. Yes! Definitely! I'm glad you chose blue for your one and only bridesmaid's dress.'

'I chose blue? As I recall it I had no say in the matter. You went out and bought a dress before the engagement ring was on my finger. When I think how you paraded it in front of Richard...Why are you staring at me like that?'

'I'm not really staring,' Joan said. 'I'm keeping my eyes rigid. This mascara takes hours to dry. Little black specks everywhere is what I do not want. And apart from the fact that my dress was a super bargain in the sales, I thought it might make you two get a move on. What took you so long? It's been nearly three years since you met and fell in love with each other.'

Miriam crossed the room and looked at her dress before taking it off the hanger. 'You know why,' she said slowly. 'And in my book it's a serious step. I had to be sure it was right for both of us.'

But was she sure, not of Richard, but of herself? Now that the time was almost here, suddenly she didn't know. She stepped carefully into the dress, drew it up over her body, tried to fasten the row of tiny buttons down the front with fingers which were trembling.

Joan turned swiftly towards her and spoke gently. 'Here, let me. Look love, everything's going to be all right. I promise you!'

Miriam grasped Joan's wrist; sought the truth in her eyes. 'You do think I'm doing the right thing, don't you? I wouldn't want to...'

Joan smiled. 'Of course I do, silly! I wouldn't have encouraged you otherwise.'

'And you think that Richard...'

'Look...it's you who's marrying him. I don't have to approve. But if you do want my opinion yet again...'

'Yes?'

'I think Richard's gorgeous! Frankly, I'd like him for myself, but you're all he ever sees.'

'He's forty-three...' Miriam reminded her.

'And he's never been married before. I know, I know! You do go on about it. But he'll make a marvellous husband. Everyone says so.'

'I suppose everyone's discussed it,' Miriam said drily. She wasn't upset about that—it was only to be expected.

'There you are then,' Joan said, fastening the last button. 'You look terrific. I'm glad you decided on green in spite of Aunt Catherine's awful warnings. It's such a soft green. Like the first pale leaves in spring.' Miriam smiled at her and thanked her for the compliment.

Aunt Catherine considered green unlucky, along with crossed knives, red and white flowers in the same vase, and the new moon through glass.

'You'll prove her wrong,' Joan said. 'Did you know that if she has to go back to the house for something she always turns round three times and then sits down on the nearest chair before leaving again? Honestly!'

Laughter broke the tension. But Miriam's hands smoothing the folds of her dress were still not quite steady. Across the room she could see her reflection in the mirror. The dress did suit her; she'd made the right choice. The soft crêpe clung to the lines of her body, accentuating her slenderness and the colour was perfect.

Returning to the dressing-table she took the jade and silver necklace which Richard had given her as a wedding present from its cushioned box and fastened it around her neck. It shone softly against her skin. She was stupid to be so nervous. Joan was right; everything would be fine.

'How long before we leave?' she asked. 'Shall I put my hat on yet, do you think?'

'Uncle Jack's due with the car in half an hour. I told you we were in good time. I think he'll make a good job of giving you away. Good practice for when he has to do it for me.'

'Now you,' she continued, 'are going to sit down, have a sherry, and relax. Come along!' She took Miriam by the hand and led her out of the bedroom as the telephone rang. Joan leaped to answer it first.

'It's for you,' she said. 'It's Richard. Aunt Catherine would definitely count that unlucky! Communication with the groom before the wedding is forbidden!'

Miriam took the receiver hesitantly, but didn't speak.

'Don't be silly,' urged Joan. 'Give him my love and tell him he's broken my heart. I always wanted him for myself!'

Miriam put the receiver to her ear. A smile lit her face as she listened. 'No second thoughts,' she said. 'I'll be there. And on time, I promise. 'Bye, my love!' She went into the living room, where Joan had already poured pale golden sherry into crystal glasses.

'They improve the flavour,' Joan said. 'Do you remember how Daddy used to say that? He always insisted on crystal.'

'I remember. He'd be surprised, wouldn't he, to see me marrying before you. Not what he'd have expected at all.'

'He always expected us to make the most of life,' Joan said. 'Never to waste it or run away from it. And he believed in marriage. Anyway, I'll only be a few months behind you.'

'That's right. Shall we drink to him?' Miriam said softly.

They raised their glasses and drank. 'And now we'll drink to you and your future,' Joan said after a little silence. 'And then I'll finish my face.'

'Is there anything I should be doing here, do you think?' Miriam asked. 'Tidying up or something? People might swarm back here after the reception—to look at the presents, I mean.'

'You'll do nothing more,' Joan ordered.

'You will sit right where you are until it's time to put your hat on. No one's going to care about the state of the flat. They'll be floating on champagne and gawping at all those presents.

'I must say, I'd never realized there were so many material rewards for getting married. Anyway, you and Richard won't be here. You'll be off on your honeymoon.' She rushed out of the room to answer the doorbell.

'It's the flowers,' she called out. 'Gorgeous! And here comes another telegram. How is it you know more people than I do?'

Presently Miriam went back into the bedroom. Joan was ready to go.

'You look gorgeous,' Miriam told her. 'Your hat is perfect.'

'So is yours,' Joan smiled, and handed it to her. 'Put it on.' Miriam put on the wide-brimmed, fragile hat; then she turned to Joan for approval. With tear-bright eyes they stood looking at each other.

'I can't give you a big hug,' Joan said, 'because we'd knock our hats off. But I do love you darling. And I'm grateful for everything. And I know you're going to be so very happy with Richard.'

'I love you, too,' Miriam said, 'and I don't know what else I can say.'

'Nothing right now,' replied Joan, 'because here comes Uncle Jack. And remember, no blubbing in church. We haven't spent the best part of a morning trying for a no-make-up effect just to have it ruined by rivers of tears. It'd give the whole game away.' She reached out and, with cool fingertips, touched Miriam gently on the cheek.

But as Miriam stood there in the church, her hand firmly clasped in Richard's as they made their vows, it was impossible to keep back the tears entirely. 'In sickness and in health...To love and to cherish,' she repeated. 'Till death us do part.'

Well, she had done that. With complete confidence, knowing that from now on everything would be all right, she lifted her head and lovingly returned Richard's waiting smile.

Joan and Alan were finishing off the bottle of sherry after the last guest had departed. 'Well, it's certainly been a great day,' said Alan.

'It was a super wedding, darling!' smiled Joan, hugging him. 'But I must say, it's a terrific responsibility seeing one's mother through it all. It's not something I could cope with often. Honestly, she was so nervous you'd think she'd never been married before!'

# A Very Special Painting Class

Lisa, sitting with her spine pressed firmly against the back of the upright chair, hands clasped loosely on her lap and a look of what she hoped was serene sweetness on her face, thought that if she did not move now, this very instant, she would scream.

The muscles across the back of her shoulders were unbearably sore and she was certain they would soon lock solid.

But it would have to be an imperceptible movement.

The slightest visible twitch and someone in the class would protest, however politely.

Clenching her teeth beneath gently smiling lips, she raised her head the tiniest fraction of an inch. Ah, wonderful...!

'You moved!' the lady in the red plastic apron cried, pointing an accusing paintbrush in Lisa's direction.

And if your painting is less than a master-piece—which is more than likely—it will be all my fault, Lisa thought.

She had marked down the red plastic lady

305

from the beginning. There was one in every class and after three years of modelling she could easily pick them out.

On the whole, though, this seemed a reasonable class, which in Lisa's eyes had nothing to do with its general standard of painting.

She had seen too many terrible portraits of herself to worry about *that*.

It was whether they were friendly and realized that she was not a robot that made the difference. That, and not standing with brushes poised at the ready the second they thought she should take up her pose again after the all-too-short breaks, made her job easier.

She liked Mr Saunders, the tutor, and had modelled for his classes before.

'Consider the ear!' he was saying now in his melodious Welsh voice. 'Stop painting for a moment and consider the model's ear!'

'See the crevices and convolutions, the way it joins the head, the shape of the lobe, the delicate hollow where the ear meets the jaw!

'You could spend a lifetime, my friends, in simply painting the ear!'

The ear was his thing and Lisa had heard it all before.

But right now she felt that *she* had been sitting here a lifetime.

The muscles in the small of her back were

contracting again and she doubted whether, when the time came, she would be able to stand upright.

Surely it must be somewhere near to break time!

'Exquisite! It's really exquisite!'

Startled, she just managed not to jerk her head round in the direction of the voice. It must be the young man who was painting her profile from the right, with deliberate care.

He was flanked on both sides by frail-looking elderly ladies, and this had been a strong, masculine, almost vibrant voice.

'Exquisite! he repeated. 'The very perfection of an ear!'

Though she couldn't turn round to look at him now, Lisa had noticed him earlier. He was tall, dark, and if she remembered rightly wore blue jeans and a red-checked shirt.

'I don't know when I've seen a lovelier ear!' the Voice continued.

Really, did he have to go on like this, especially when she was powerless to protest?

He was clearly one of those men who liked to attract attention. It went without saying that he would be no good as a painter. They never were.

So why was he here, at an afternoon painting class largely made up of retired ladies and gentlemen beavering away with varying degrees of skill at their absorbing hobby?

'Break!' Mr Sanders called suddenly.

Lisa relaxed herself slowly, savouring every exquisite moment of relief, and then stood up.

She would not, she decided, turn in the direction of the Voice because that was just what its owner would expect her to do. She knew his type.

'Feel free,' Mr Sanders called out, 'to walk around the class and look at each other's work. It's always a good thing to see what the others are doing!'

This was the time Lisa enjoyed, once she had faced the fact that she was going to see some pretty weird representations of herself.

There was a woman in one of the other classes who always painted her with a mauve face and another who changed her brown hair to black and her blue sweater to green.

Either she was colour blind, Lisa thought without rancour, or she was eternally painting someone who existed in her mind—perhaps herself when young.

Her limbs restored to tingling life, Lisa walked around the room, deliberately starting at the point farthest away from the Voice. With any luck she would not reach him before the short break was over, and that would teach him!

There was the usual motley collection of portraits, some quite awful, others surprisingly good.

The fascinating thing about any class was how every single member of it saw the same object differently from the rest.

She viewed herself with skin ranging from flake white through yellow ochre to burnt sienna, with hair from palest blonde to flaming puce; and was not at all surprised to find as many different noses as there were painters.

Then, she was nearing the Voice. With part of her she wanted to see his work; with another part she preferred to ignore him.

I *could* walk straight past, she thought. But before she'd made up her mind he spoke to her, quietly this time.

'I meant it,' he said. 'You have the most lovely right ear. I can't say anything about the left because I haven't seen it yet. May I?'

Gently, a grave expression on his face, he put a finger against her chin and delicately turned her head.

'As I expected,' he said admiringly. 'A perfect match!'

Lisa looked at him without speaking—mainly because she didn't know what to say. Also, he was good to look at...

He was a head taller than her, and thin. She

quite liked the look of his ears, too, come to think of it.

Of course, I'm only looking at him with a painter's eye, she told herself, ignoring the fact she couldn't paint to save herself!

To her surprise his painting was quite good. He was working in oils, the colours clear, vibrant, their juxtaposition giving form to the portrait.

A touch of class here!

'I like it,' she said with generosity.

'Thank you, ma'am!'

His tone embarrassed her. She had, she thought, sounded condescending—the expert judging the amateur's work.

'But of course I'm no judge,' she said, making it worse. 'I can't paint for toffee!'

He grinned. 'All you have to do is sit there looking beautiful, inspiring the rest of us.'

'Speaking of which,' she said coldly, glaring at him, 'I'd better get back to it.'

She went back to her chair and took up her pose once more.

Several people called out helpful but contrary suggestions.

'A little to the right!'

'Head a little higher please.'

'Further to the left if you don't mind.'

'I have your ear in perfect focus,' she heard

the young man say. 'Stay just as you are.'

She wondered where he came from, what he did when he wasn't painting. He didn't look married, though he was probably approaching 30 like herself.

Do I look married, she asked herself. Can anyone tell by looking at me that I have a daughter of seven, that I'm not married, though I would have been if Julian hadn't disappeared to America before he knew I was pregnant?

She had got over the heartbreak of losing Julian, now, but she loved her daughter dearly.

'Don't just look at the model from a distance,' Mr Sanders was saying. 'Go up to her. Take a closer look.

'Note that the eyes are halfway down the head. Observe the way the eyeball fits into the socket!'

He always did this and she confidently expected the Voice to be in the first rush. She felt slightly disappointed when he wasn't.

But when the others had had their fill and returned to their paint boxes, he came over.

'Has anyone ever told you,' he enquired, in what she had to admit was the most attractive voice she had heard in a long time, 'that you have the most perfect left nostril?'

If I were a ventriloquist, she thought, I could

311

tell him exactly what I thought without moving my lips one fraction of an inch.

'In fact, there's little wrong with your right one,' he continued. 'It's just that the left one is...well...extra special.'

'My name is James Blacker, by the way. May I take you for coffee after class?

'You can't refuse because you're not allowed to speak.'

'Oh yes I can—and I do!' Lisa said through clenched teeth, not moving her lips. 'Go away!'

He smiled, and winked in the most irritating manner before going back to his painting.

When the class was over and they were all packing up their masterpieces until next week, he came across to her.

'I'm sorry,' Lisa said coolly, 'I have to get back. My daughter will be home from school.'

Which was not quite true because Jane went to Lindy's house on class days and stayed there till Lisa called for her.

Lindy was her best friend and Jane enjoyed staying at Lindy's place, so there was never any hurry!

He looked ever so slightly surprised.

'I didn't know you were married.'

'I'm not.'

Now why had she said that? Why not let him think she was and that would be an end of it?

'Then...'

'I'm sorry,' Lisa repeated.

'Will you be here next week?' James asked.

'You know I will,' Lisa said. 'You know you have each model for three weeks, and this is my first.'

'See you then,' James said—and went off to pack his gear.

A typical week followed for Lisa. She had two more painting classes in other parts of the town, her morning job as librarian at the local school, and one afternoon's dog walking on the Downs, which earned a little more money.

All the jobs added together paid just enough to allow her to run her small flat and bring up Jane, independently.

And when Tuesday came around it was Mr Sanders' class again.

She put on her pink blouse, which painters always liked because it allowed them to run riot with colour, and tied back her thick brown hair.

Funny, that in all her life so far, she had never really thought about her ears! Up to now they had just been there; things to listen with, or handy to hang earrings from, like hooks in the kitchen.

I suppose they're all right really, she thought,

peering at them in the brightly lit mirror.

But you look too pale, she decided—and searched in her make-up drawer for blusher and lipstick.

Would he be there this week—James, was it, she asked herself, pretending she didn't quite remember.

He *was* there, standing beside his easel. Mr Sanders was looking at his watch and everyone else was poised, brushes at the ready.

James casually waved a palette knife in her direction, hardly looking at her because he was setting out his colours.

'Sorry!' Lisa said. 'Am I late?'

'Another minute and you would have been,' Mr Sanders said kindly, smiling at her.

She fetched a cushion from the cupboard, found an old box which would have to do as a footstool and settled as quickly as she could into her seat.

Sixty seconds later, with her ankles sedately crossed, hands loosely clasped, head tilted exactly right, she took a deep breath and prayed that she could sustain the position.

There was deep silence as the painters set to work. Lisa always enjoyed these first few minutes. It was good thinking time, before the numbness set in.

Little did anyone know that as she gazed

serenely into space she was planning menus, making out a shopping list, wondering what she would do about that awful beagle's habit of running away the minute she let it off the lead on the Downs—and whether she could afford to let Jane have ballet lessons.

But this afternoon her thoughts entirely refused to be disciplined.

'Now those of you who are doing a three-quarter length,' Mr Sanders called out, 'observe the hands!

'There's character in hands. You could spend another lifetime painting hands.'

Lisa didn't like her hands. They were larger than she would have chosen—practical-looking hands. Her instinct at this moment was to sit on them.

Was *he* painting her three-quarters? She couldn't quite remember, at that exact moment.

Why in the world did she take on a job which meant everyone looking at her, analysing her every flaw and fault?

'Go a little nearer,' Mr Sanders encouraged. 'Study the hands at close quarters!'

Here he came, first in the field this time. Same tight jeans, same checked shirt, lean face, dark hair. He looked every bit as good as she'd visualized him—several times during the last week.

'I'm not painting your hands,' he said quietly. 'Lovely though they are. Nice, capable hands. I just wanted to take a close look at the colour of your eyes.'

He came very close, his dark eyes looking deep into hers.

'Ah yes! Definitely flecked with blue. Now would sapphire be too strong or should I add a touch of yellow?'

Lisa felt a slow flush creep up her neck and sweep over her face as he continued to appraise her.

'Go away!' she muttered, not moving her lips. She was getting quite good at this ventriloquist's stuff. 'Leave me alone!'

'And the skin tones,' he said. 'Definitely a touch of alizarin crimson at this moment!'

'Break!' Mr Sanders cried.

'Come and see my painting,' James invited before Lisa could speak.

She couldn't resist it, and followed him to his easel, standing back from it to get a better view.

It was good, really good. The colour sang out from the canvas, yet was never too strident; the skin tones were pale, yet glowing.

'What do you think?' His voice was anxious, totally unlike his usual manner.

He really cares, Lisa thought, surprised.

'I think it's good,' she repeated. 'But as I told you last week, I'm no judge. Why not ask Mr Sanders?'

'I will,' James said. 'But actually I want you to like it.'

'Well I do,' Lisa assured him.

'And you'll go for a coffee with me afterwards so that we can discuss art and life and the state of the economy?' he asked, the slightly mocking tone back in his voice.

'I told you last week,' Lisa said. 'I have to get home for my daughter.'

'Then let me run you home.'

'I have my bicycle.'

'I know. I can fix it on the roof rack.'

'Look, I'm sorry...' Lisa said.

'Shall we make a start again, Lisa?' Mr Sanders called, saving her.

James did not come near her again that afternoon and when the class ended he left quickly.

Why did I refuse him, Lisa asked herself.

She really rather liked the man. And accepting a cup of coffee was no great deal.

The truth was that she did not want to get involved, and with James she felt instinctively that there might be involvement.

But it's up to you, my girl, she argued at various times during the following week while she walked the beagle, issued the library books, enrolled Jane in the ballet class.

You can be involved as little or as much as you want to. You're an independent lady, after all.

So it would be silly to refuse him again, she told herself as she set off for the third week's class. And if she didn't like the experience she need never see him again.

This was her last week's modelling, after all.

But he wasn't in the class when she arrived, and he didn't come later, as she'd half hoped. She felt surprisingly disappointed by his non-appearance, but of course it served her right.

Now she had lost the chance of what might have been an enjoyable friendship.

There was only one possibility.

During the break she spoke to Mr Sanders.

'I've so enjoyed being here,' she said. 'I wondered, actually...Could I join the class?'

'We'd be delighted to have you,' Mr Sanders said, smiling.

Of course, he might not be there next week, she warned herself, visiting the art shop, spending more than she could afford on paints, brushes, all manner of equipment.

He might be one of those people wo came two or three times to a class and then gave up. But with luck...

Luck was hers, but sooner than she'd expected.

On Thursday afternoon when she returned exhausted from her encounter with the beagle, James was sitting in his car, outside her flat.

'I thought you were never coming,' he said. 'I've got a present for you.'

'How did you know where I lived?' she queried.

'Mr Sanders. I told him I wanted to engage you as a model.'

'And do you?'

'If it's the only way I can get to talk to you,' he said. 'Anyway, don't you want to see your present?'

'You'd better come in,' Lisa said.

He followed her into the house, carrying a brown paper parcel. It was the portrait, of course.

'I've done some more work on it,' James said. 'But not enough. Now if you were to sit for me...After which I think it would look nice over your mantelpiece.'

'I'll consider it,' Lisa promised, trying to keep as calm as possible. 'Would you like some coffee?' She bustled through to the kitchen, then called out, 'By the way, why weren't you at class on Tuesday?'

'I got called away on a job,' he explained.

'I'm a freelance photographer—work most days of the week, sometimes at the weekends, but Tuesday is sacred to painting when I'm at home.'

'I'm serious about painting,' he said much later, sipping his third cup of coffee.

'I'd like to do some more. It's very relaxing, don't you think?' He eyed her anxiously then, and added, 'By the way, Mr Sanders tells me you're joining the class.'

'I might,' Lisa said cautiously.

Was there any need to now? But on the other hand she had spent all that money on equipment—and there was the question of other models who might turn up with even nicer ears and bluer eyes.

'Yes, I think I shall,' she said decisively.

## A Time To Remember

Before she had knitted to the end of this row, she told herself, the telephone *must* ring. It must, it must! Very well then, she thought, starting the next one, she would be very, very patient. Say by the time she reached the armhole. A full inch to go, but she knew that on the small baby garment, not many stitches on the needle, it wouldn't take long. She knitted swiftly and evenly, her needles clicking in rhythm with the swift rocking of her chair.

Her husband looked up from his book.

'Slow down, Kate,' he said. 'Otherwise your chair'll take off.'

'You did put the phone back on the hook?' she asked. 'After that last call?'

'Of course I did! Ease off, Kate. Anyone would think *you* were having the baby. Come to think of it you were a darned sight calmer when Diana was born. Sent me off to the pictures while you got on with it.'

So she had. In those days it wasn't man's work, being there when the baby was born.

'You didn't go though,' she reminded him.

'Sister told me afterwards that you spent all night in the hospital waiting room, drinking cups of tea and asking how things were going. *You* were the worried one then.'

'A first baby at thirty-seven,' he said. 'Of course I was worried.'

'I knew it would be all right.'

'Then why can't you be like that now?' he asked.

'It's easier when you have a job to do,' Kate said. 'Something to get on with. Waiting to be a grandmother is different.'

'You know there's nothing to worry about,' her husband said. 'Diana's young and strong: her husband's right there with her. And they promised to phone you the minute there was any news.'

Kate sighed. 'I know all that.'

She reached out for the knitting pattern, checked the instructions for the armhole shaping. There was no need to do that since it was the fourth jacket of its kind she'd knitted recently. The other three, in blue, pink and lemon, together with pants, vests, leggings, caps—all of which might or might no longer be fashionable babywear, lay neatly folded on the table. On the top of the pile was the web-fine shawl, the crocheting of which had nearly blinded her. Somehow she had wanted to wait until the child was born before presenting the garments.

Grandmother. It was, she could now confirm, a name so special that only those who had achieved it (or nearly so) could appreciate what it meant. Wifehood and motherhood were steps on the way. It was a relationship different from all others; a fulfilment of one's purpose. Yet being a relationship it had to be two way, and surely being the grandchild was the other ingredient of the magic. That was how it had been between her and Grandma Jameson.

'Are you thinking about when Diana was born?' her husband asked.

'Not really. I was thinking about my grandmother. You never knew Grandma Jameson.'

From photographs—there was one of the old lady in the year before she finally took to her bed, standing stiffly upright on a raised dias in the photographer's studio against a backcloth of lakes, mountains, blossom trees, her hand resting lightly on a bamboo table—Grandma Jameson must have been tiny and thin; not much flesh on her fine bones. Yet Kate remembered the feel of her and it had not been like that at all. She was warm, curvy, soft to squeeze against when they shared the same armchair to read *Rainbow*. Her grandmother bought the comic every week, supposedly for

Kate, but they enjoyed it equally.

*Rainbow* came out on a Saturday, but was mysteriously always available on a Friday, and on that day Kate called in at her grandmother's on the way home from school. Before settling down to *Rainbow* they would have a golden mint humbug from the glass jar, and usually afterwards Kate stayed to tea because it was her mother's day for shopping in the town.

In fact, she called in at her grandmother's most days, because her grandmother lived in the next street, in a small house with a side door which opened straight into the kitchen. There was a black iron range, shiny, almost the width of the room, with a bright coal fire in the grate and always something baking in the oven at the side; or loaves of bread and currant teacakes rising under a red and white checked teacloth at the other side.

Grandma Jameson had taught her to bake bread; kneading the strong dough in the yellow-lined earthenware bowl, and if the wind was coming from the east, pushing and pulling at the various dampers to coax the oven to draw properly.

'You need a hot oven for bread,' Grandma said. 'Same as for Yorkshire pudding.'

When Grandma made Yorkshire pudding batter she sat on a stool by the open kitchen door to 'beat the fresh air into it'.

'Yes,' Kate's husband said, 'Diana's all right. We should be pleased about her.'

'I am,' Kate said. She would have liked to have telephoned, enquired how things were progressing, but Robert, choosing to forget his behaviour when his daughter was being born, said there was no sense in that, not while Diana and her husband were both at the hospital.

'Shall I switch on the television?' he asked. 'There's a play. Take your mind off things.'

'No thank you.'

In between her anxious thoughts about her daughter it was comforting to think about Grandma Jameson. She had not thought about her for a long time, though in another way she never forgot her, never would, though it was all so long ago. When you worked it out, Kate thought, she was no older than I am now. Sixty-two. Yet then she had thought of her as being very old. But at the same time, inexplicably, nearer to Kate's own age than anyone else she knew. They always enjoyed the same things, shared secrets, understood each other's needs.

There was the occasion when her grandmother, because she had given some help with the refreshments—baked mountains of scones, great slabs of seed cake—had been given two

complimentary tickets for the Congregational
chapel's annual pantomime, and she had taken
Kate with her to the Friday evening performance. Cinderella, it had been that year, though
the story was curiously altered from the one she
and her grandmother had read together.

'That's to allow for Mr Lacey's poem, Miss
Winterbotham's solo, and the Sunday School
children's flower ballet,' her grandmother explained. 'People expect it. Also there are those
who, mentioning no names, would be cut to
the quick if they weren't asked to perform!'

They sat in the chapel gallery, which had a
totally different feel from its Sunday one, and
shared a quarter-pound, gold-coloured box of
Terry's hard-centred chocolates. At the end of
the children's ballet, as if from heaven itself,
flower petals had descended and covered the
stage around the children. Kate thought she
had never seen anything quite so beautiful.

'If I went every week to Sunday School,' she
said, 'could I dance in the ballet?'

'You might,' Grandma Jameson replied.
'And you'd come to no harm trying.' Well, she
had never achieved it.

It had been arranged that after the pantomine
she should go back and spend the night with
her grandmother. She'd taken to doing that
fairly often about then because her grand-

mother wasn't too well. She had 'turns', and Kate's mother didn't like her to be left alone. At seven years old Kate could be relied upon, her mother said, to use her common sense and run around the corner to fetch help from home if it was needed.

When they got back from the pantomime her grandmother made cocoa and cut squares of sticky gingerbread, and they had taken the tray upstairs and sat up in the big feather bed, eating and drinking until after eleven o'clock. Then, because there was no school next day and it didn't matter if they slept late, they had read the new *Rainbow*—which there hadn't been time to look at before going to the pantomime—from cover to cover. After that, before snuggling down to sleep, her grandmother with one swift movement not unlike the magician in the pantomime had taken from her mouth six white teeth set in a piece of hard, browny-pink stuff and had dropped them into a glass of water on the bedside table. After that they had slept, lying close together, Kate curled into the arc of her grandmother's accommodating body.

That had been the last time she had stayed in her grandmother's house because it was soon afterwards that the old lady had come to live with them for good. She was no longer fit to live alone, Kate's mother said, because she had a bad heart. So the small bedroom at the front, whose window looked into the street, was spring-cleaned and a new flowered wallpaper hung. Grandma brought her own bed, a ewer and basin set, and a rag rug from her living room. After a few weeks she had never left the room again, spending all her time in bed except for the short time every day when she sat in the chair while the bed was being made.

Although Kate missed her grandmother's house, and the bread-making sessions; and although there were no more trips to the pantomime or anywhere else for that matter, there were still lots of things for them to do together. *Rainbow* for instance. From the brown leather purse which she kept under her pillow Grandma would extract fourpence: twopence for the comic and another twopence for the sweets which they would share. Only nothing hard, Grandma said, because her mouth wasn't up to it, and indeed the teeth spent most of their time in the glass. So it was liquorice ribbons or sherbert fountains, both of which Kate and her grandmother liked; or occasionally aniseed balls which could be sucked, not chewed, until they dissolved on the tongue. But three-cornered mint humbugs were a thing of the past.

'I've been checking,' Kate's husband said,

breaking into her thoughts. 'We've got five hundred and forty-two pounds in the building society. With that, and your insurance due, we should manage it nicely.'

'Yes,' Kate agreed. 'That should do it.'

Grandma Jameson, as far as Kate knew, had never been on a real holiday. Once a year she went on the Chapel Women's outing, by charabanc to Morecambe Bay, all of forty miles distant. Once both Kate and her mother had gone along. They had paddled in the shallow water, the women holding up their skirts, Kate tucking her dress into her knickers, and had bought shrimps in a paper poke to eat on the way home.

'I wonder what they'll call the baby,' Kate said. 'They never say. My grandmother's name was Emily.'

'They won't call her Emily, that's for sure,' her husband said. 'Too old-fashioned. Anyway, how do you know it'll be a girl? It could be a boy. They could call him Robert after me.'

'It'll be a girl,' Kate said confidently. 'You'll see.' Both parents, and she also, wanted that. She only saw herself as the grandmother of a little girl. If they still hadn't decided on a name when the telephone call came, she would suggest Emily.

She realized now that she had not known her

grandmother's name until the year in which she died, the year she spent in the little bedroom. Everyone in the family always called her Grandma. Then one day when Kate had been looking out of the bedroom window, describing for her grandmother's interest what was going on down there in the street, the old lady had suddenly said, 'There's no one left now to call me Emily. Well, I never liked the name.'

It had been a long, hot summer that year and sometimes Kate had almost begrudged the hours, especially in the school holidays, which she had spent in the bedroom. Almost, but not quite, because even when her grandmother had said 'Now you must go out to play, love. Get some fresh air,' she hadn't quite wanted to. Towards the end of the summer her grandmother, though still enjoying *Rainbow*, had also taken to something called 'Christian Novels': long, complete stories which came out every week. Since the print was small and her grandmother's steel-rimmed spectacles no longer functioned well enough, Kate read the novels aloud to her. Grandma loved them but to Kate they were boring. No adventure, not much action, loads of soppy love, so that while she read Kate thought of other things and wondered whether she should go out and play hopscotch with the others. She had a lucky hopscotch stone in her pocket with which she was almost certain to win. Then her grandmother would fall asleep before the story was finished, so that it was all right to go out and play.

What sort of games will *my* granddaughter play, Kate wondered? Will they all be new to me?

She cast off loosely, then took the finished knitting into the kitchen to press it before sewing it up. She left the kitchen door open so that there should be no possibility of not hearing the telephone when it rang. It couldn't be much longer now. If the call didn't come before bedtime she wasn't sure that she could go to bed: certainly not to sleep.

She had been wide awake on the night her grandmother had died, lying there in the darkness, listening to the comings and goings: the neighbours, Aunt Cassie and Uncle Jim, her mother and father. They tiptoed up and down the stairs, believing her to be asleep; spoke in low voices in the bedroom.

It had been a long, happy September Sunday. In the afternoon she had dug out a whole pile of *Rainbows*—she never threw any away—and she and her grandmother had gone over their favourite bits. Then Grandma had talked about when *she* was a little girl, and about *her* grandmother who had been born the year before Queen Victoria came to the throne. After that Kate had read the latest Christian Novel and Grandma had fallen asleep after the first few pages. For both of them, Kate thought, it had been a happy day.

She had missed her grandmother very much, especially at first, but the times they'd spent together had been good ones. More than fifty years later the warmth still lived, and was felt. Their relationship had contained all that nine years could encompass. With her own grand-daughter, Kate wondered, would she be able...

The strident ringing of the telephone interrupted her thoughts. She ran into the hall, snatching the receiver before her husband could reach it.

'Yes! Yes, that's right!'

As she listened the pent-up tears ran freely down her face, but her eyes were shining bright pools and her mouth trembled with joy. She reached out to her husband, took his hand and held it tightly.

'Well?' he said. 'Well?'

'It's a little girl. Seven and a half pounds. They're both well and send all their love.'

Presently she replaced the telephone receiver and her husband held her in his arms.

'Oh Robert!' she said. 'I can't believe it!

Robert, I'm a grandma!'

'And I'm married to a grandmother,' he chivved her. 'Makes me feel ancient!'

She smiled at him, and wiped her eyes with the handkerchief he proffered. They went back into the living room.

'They're going to call her Kiyomi,' Kate said. 'Kiyomi.'

'Well...it's uncommon at any rate.'

'Not in Japan, I daresay,' Kate said. 'It's probably quite an ordinary name in Japan. I think it's rather pretty.'

'Yes,' Robert said. 'Did they say what time it was in Tokyo?'

'Seven o'clock tomorrow morning,' Kate said. 'Doesn't it seem strange that we don't live in the same time?'

Robert shook his head, shrugged his shoulders.

'If it had been a little boy,' Kate said, 'they were going to call him Takashi, after his father. It's best, I suppose, that they have Japanese names, because of when they go to school. Emily wouldn't have done.'

Standing by the table she picked up a pile of baby clothes and gripped them tightly, holding them for a moment against her breast.

'I'll parcel these up,' she said steadily. 'Then tomorrow we can post them. And they're going to send us lots of photographs, Takashi said. You know what the Japanese are like for taking photographs. I daresay there'll even be some of her wearing the things I've knitted.'

'We'll buy a nice album,' Robert said. 'And then, don't forget, there's the visit. We've got the money for the visit.'

'I know,' Kate said. 'There's always the visit.'

# A New Beginning

Primrose came out of the house, mounted her bicycle and rode through the farmyard towards the road. Her father emerged from the barn and called to her.

'Tell our Kathleen I might not make it tonight. I don't like the look of Truby. And you can drop in on Mr Harris and ask him if he'll call.'

Truby was a sick cow. Mr Harris was the vet. There was always something to keep you tied to the farm.

'Kath'll be disappointed,' Primrose said; her words carried on the air as she rode away.

Every Saturday afternoon she cycled the three miles down the dale to the village. Her sister and brother-in-law kept the inn: the Black Swan, known locally as the Mucky Duck. Kathleen had had to look after everything in the war years and on Saturday evenings she'd been grateful for Primrose's help in the bar. Now that her husband was home again it wasn't strictly necessary, but for Primrose it made a welcome break from the routine of the farm.

'Not for much longer,' she said out loud, startling a snipe which perched on the dry-stone wall. That was what solitude did to you: made you talk to yourself. Or to sheep or hens or birds. Human beings were seldom handy in this remote place, and the thoughts which occupied her mind for most of the time now were not easy to discuss with her parents. They knew she wanted to get away, appreciated that after helping on their small, difficult farm all through the war years she had earned her freedom. And since her brother was back again they could manage without her. It was the *kind* of distance which she wanted to put between herself and her home which worried, almost frightened them. London, they insisted was no place for their Primrose.

'All the same, that's where I'm going,' she informed a sheep which was nibbling the short grass at the side of the road.

She would miss Starsdale: she didn't doubt that. It had been her world for twenty-four years. But for the last year or two the green fells which rose up so steeply on either side of the narrow valley, and which she had once thought of as shielding and protective, now seemed to imprison her. Starsdale was one of the wildest and most remote of all the Yorkshire dales; too stony to grow crops and with not even enough level ground, except at the lower end of the dale towards the village, for grazing more than a few cattle. And Top Farm was the highest in the dale. Beyond it the road petered out into a single track, and in the hills there the river had its source.

She would miss the river. She had paddled in it, dammed it, fished it, ever since she could remember. But in London there would be so many compensations. Shops, cinemas, buses. Bright lights again now. In the country the blackout was always with you.

Just before the village she stopped on the bridge to speak to a friend of her father's. They leaned over the parapet, gazing into the water. You could catch trout here, under the bridge, with your bare hands.

'I heard tell you're going down to London,' the man said. 'Is that right?'

'Yes.'

'I were there once,' he said. 'Just for the day. Went up on the night train from Harrogate. Didn't think much on it.'

Kathleen was pleased to see her, as always. In spite of rationing she always managed a spread for Saturday tea. Primrose looked at the contented faces of her sister and brother-in-law and their two children as they sat down

337

to eat. Perhaps if she'd been the eldest, like Kathleen, had already been married when the war came, she wouldn't feel so restless now.

'Toby Metcalfe mentioned about me going to London,' Primrose said. 'I swear that the birds of the air carry messages down this dale. You only have to breathe something...'

'Still talking about it, are you?' her brother-in-law said.

'It's not talk,' Primrose assured him. 'I'm going. I've had enough of Starsdale. *I've* never been away from it.'

'Nor have I,' Kathleen said. 'Nor ever wanted to. But why London? You could take a job in Skipton, or Harrogate. Live there; come home at weekends. Or Leeds, even!'

Primrose laughed. 'You make Leeds sound like Babylon! No, I want a real new beginning. If I'd joined the ATS, not had to stay on the farm, I'd have seen the world by now.' Her brother had beaten her to it, joining the Air Force as soon as the war started, so that when she was old enough she couldn't be spared.

After tea they got everything ready in the bar. It would be a busy evening. Beer was in short supply but that wouldn't prevent most of the men in the village from spending the evening there, making their drinks last, having a game

338

of darts. Nowadays they even brought their wives to sip at a gin and orange.

Halfway through the evening a stranger came into the bar. He was tall enough to have to stoop as he came through the doorway, and thin as a lathe, his demob suit hanging on him.

'I'd like a half-pint of bitter,' he said. By his voice—soft, with the vowels slightly flattened—he wasn't a stranger. Kathleen gave him a warm smile of welcome as she pushed his beer across the bar counter.

'Our Primrose doesn't remember you,' she said. 'She was just home from school when you joined up.'

He held out his hand to Primrose, looked at her with appreciation. 'I'm William Kellet. Pleased to know you now, anyway. Before the war I lived over at Paston with my grandmother. I live there alone now.'

'William was in Burma, with the Fourteenth Army,' Kathleen said. 'You couldn't pop home for seven days' leave from there. *And* they had a longer war.'

'That's all behind us,' William said. 'It's nineteen forty-seven. There's a new life ahead. Here's to it!' He raised his glass and drank. When he smiled, Primrose thought, it lit up his whole face, shone in his brown eyes.

'You're right,' she agreed. 'A new beginning, that's the thing.' She was going to like William Kellet: they saw things the same way.

He continued to stand by the bar, chatting to the two sisters, but in the end Primrose had to leave him. There were tables to clear, glasses to wash, customers to serve.

At nine o'clock Jim Fletcher came in with his accordion and the usual Saturday night singsong started. It grew hot in the bar and a few people took their drinks outside, standing around the doorway or sitting at the tables in front of the inn. Out there the warm July day was cooling as the sun went down.

When Primrose came back to the bar William Kellet was no longer there. She looked around and saw his tall figure leaning against the door frame.

'I'll collect from outside,' she said to Kathleen. 'We're short of glasses.'

She thought, as she went past him, her shoulder brushing his sleeve, that William hadn't even seen her. His gaze was fixed on the scene in front of him. The high fell silhouetted against the sky; the square-towered church across the green and the lights coming on in the cottages around it. But as she returned he stepped out in front of her, barring her way.

'Can I see you again? Tomorrow?'
'I'd like that,' Primrose said.

William had arranged to walk up the dale and call for her at the farm, but well before the agreed time Primrose set off to meet him. Somehow she didn't want him in the bosom of her family just yet. They thought alike, she and William: she was sure of that. For a little while she wanted him to herself so that they could discuss important things like freedom and progress and which way the world was going, instead of the trivialities which were talked about in her own home. She was sick of hearing about the price of sheep, and the shortage of feeding stuffs.

She wore her navy and white spotted dress, square-shouldered, wide-belted at the waist. In London, if she could acquire the material, she'd have something in the New Look which had just come in. She wouldn't dare wear it in Starsdale. She had arranged her hair, bleached by the sun, in wide rolls away from her face and cheekbones, and brushed it full and loose below the nape of her neck. Her arms and legs were bare and suntanned.

She saw William in the distance. They waved, and she sat on a limestone boulder and watched him walk—almost march—towards her. In spite of his leanness he looked brown and fit.

'I feel like climbing up the fellside,' he said as he reached her. 'How about you?'

Sure-footed, strong, every inch of the way familiar to her, she reached the top ahead of him. When he caught up they sat down together on the springy grass. The breeze teased at her carefully arranged hair and William laughed as she tried to prevent her skirt blowing around her thighs.

'The talk is that you're leaving Starsdale,' he said eventually.

'That's true.'

'London, isn't it? What are you going to do there?'

'To start with I'm hoping to work in one of the big stores. I haven't definitely got a job, but they sounded interested, said I could call in and see them. And they have a hostel where I could live. Of course that would only be a job to start with. I don't know what I might do in the end, I'm not afraid of hard work, you know, or strange circumstances.'

'Are you ever afraid of anything?' William asked.

She thought about it. There had been nothing in her life—she felt almost ashamed—of which to be afraid. The dangers of war had not come near to Starsdale, though there had been physical discomforts in plenty. Shortages; restrictions; and then this last terrible winter which had cut them off from the world for several weeks on end. That imprisonment, after years of war, was what had finally decided her that she must go somewhere where life was freer, more civilized.

'I'm afraid of being trapped,' she said. 'Caged. Of not being able to get away. That's what frightens me.'

'You're only trapped if you want to get out of the cage and can't,' William said. 'If you're happy in it, there's no problem. It can be a refuge.'

'Kath is like that,' Primrose said. 'Happy where she is. But I don't want a refuge. I'm twenty-four and I haven't begun to live. I want to strike out.'

'A pioneering woman,' William said, smiling at her.

'Perhaps. Tell me what you're afraid of.'

He didn't answer at once. He looked at the countryside, down the length of the dale. 'I was afraid of a lot of things in the war,' he said at last. 'Boredom, pain; the enemy, death. Most of all I was afraid of never seeing this place again. Sometimes it was only the determination to do so which kept me going. It was like that

343

for a lot of the chaps.'

'I can understand that,' Primrose said. 'But now that you're back, now that Starsdale is safe, what are you going to do? What's your new beginning to be?'

He was probably clever, she thought. He'd be able to go anywhere, do anything. 'You could go to university,' she said. 'There are places for people like you who missed it because of the war.'

'Oh I know what I'm going to do,' he interrupted. 'I worked all that out when I was in the jungle. I'm going to farm. Not necessarily in Starsdale itself, but in one of the Dales. I've got my gratuity, and a lot of pay saved up. You couldn't spend much where I was. I'll have to start small, but there'll be lots of encouragement for farmers. We've got to produce more...'

He went on, but she stopped listening, closed her ears. She was conscious of bitter disappointment. A farmer! To know freedom, to be emancipated, have the world in front of you and then hop tamely back into the cage! Why had she thought he was different? He was exactly like the rest. He would end up like her father, her brother, half the men she had known all her life. No enterprise, and an ambition contained in a few acres of land. Familiar land, at that.

'I think women are the pioneers,' she said.

He turned and looked at her, his face a question mark.

'You don't approve of my ideas?'

'It hardly matters whether I do or not,' Primrose said. 'I'm not going to be here. Shall we go back?'

Her parents had asked her to bring him back to tea, and she did so, but the brightness had gone out of the day. Before the meal was over her father was discussing sheep with him. What else, Primrose thought? Men in this place would always talk about sheep.

William touched on his plans. 'I thought I'd look for a place over in Wensleydale,' he said. 'It's a broader dale. I think there's more scope for growing things, certainly more land for grazing.'

'Easier than this side of the hill,' her father said. 'I'll grant you that. And the cheese will be starting up again. Did you know Stilton was coming back?'

'I did!' William sounded as excited as her father. Imagine getting excited about cheese, Primrose thought.

It was long past dark when William rose to go. Primrose walked with him to where the farm gate opened to the road.

'Lucky for you there's a moon,' she said. 'In the pitch dark it's a difficult road, keeping so close to the river.'

They leaned against the gate, watching where the moon caught the fast-running water, lit up the limestone walls which crisscrossed the hills. Primrose wished she liked him less, as little as she liked his ideas. With absolute certainty she knew she had never been as attracted to anyone in her whole life. He put his arm around her shoulders, then turned her so that they faced each other. In his eyes she saw the love she had waited for. There was hunger in his kisses. Response leapt in her as she returned them.

Each day after that they met. Sometimes she would cycle to the village; sometimes he came to Top Farm. Each time he talked about his plans and she about hers. Fields, crops, sheep, cattle; shops, people, theatres, streets. Sometimes they spoke rationally, trying to see each other's point of view; at other times they shouted at each other in anger, unable to communicate. But every day, sooner of later, they ended high on the fellside, or on the grass bank by the river's edge, wrapped in each other's arms. Then their worlds were not divided, but entirely contained within that space.

On the last Saturday in July Starsdale was

to hold its first summer show since nineteen thirty-nine. Nothing grand, everyone said, but a gesture to show that things were getting back to normal. There would be classes for flowers and vegetables. The home-baking section would be for eggless cakes and fatless sponges, but no shortages would affect the children's wild-flower collections. There would be sheep, and some cattle, and in the flat meadows by the bridge sheepdog trials would be held.

William was there from the start, with Primrose, a shade less enthusiastic, by his side. The sun shone and the ground was still hard and dry underfoot.

'It's fantastic!' William said. 'There was a time when I thought none of this would ever happen again. Now it's all here! Business as usual!'

He held her more closely to his side as they went into the hot, steamy tent where most of the exhibits were.

'Oh William!' Primrose said. 'You are hopeless! All everyone's been through and you want to return to business as usual!'

'But it's a return to the *good* things,' William said. 'To show that they endure. Surely you can feel the excitement in that?'

'Well, perhaps,' Primrose said uncertainly.

347

'Look over there,' William said. 'If we want a bit more excitement it seems as though they've finished judging the cakes. Let's see.'

Ten golden sponges stood in a row on the white-clothed table; in the middle the first prize, flanked on either side by the second and third. Primrose, hardly stopping to read the cards, grabbed William's arm, then jumped up and down in the air.

'I've won!' she cried. 'It's mine! First prize!'

William stared at her. 'You mean to tell me that *you*...the sophisticated, can't-get-away-from-here-fast-enough Primrose Tatham, has entered a fatless sponge cake in a village show?'

'Of course,' Primrose said. 'Anyone will tell you that the eldest unmarried Tatham daughter has always won the sponge cake prize. Kath did it last in nineteen thirty-nine. I couldn't not try. Oh, I'm so pleased!'

William threw back his head and laughed. 'So am I,' he said.

It was later in the day, when they were watching the sheepdog trials, that Kath's husband came up to them.

'I've just heard of the very place for you,' he told William. 'A farm over in Wensleydale. Likely to be reasonable because it's run-down. Owned by an old couple who are moving out to live with a daughter in Harrogate. Why don't

348

you go over and look at it?' He moved away.

'Will you come with me to see it?' William asked Primrose. 'Tomorrow?' He spoke quietly.

'Oh William!' It was impossible, she found, to keep the dismay out of her voice. The time had really come. She knew that when William finally found his farm it would be the parting of the ways for them. He would settle down there; she would go, as planned, to London. They both knew this was to happen. Foolishly, she hadn't expected it so soon.

Next day her father lent them the old Vauxhall and some of his petrol ration to go over to Wensleydale. They took the road over the head of the fell, climbing higher and higher until, at the top, Wensleydale was spread out before them on the other side. A broad, hospitable dale: villages; cattle looking like farmyard toys in the great meadows.

But nothing she had imagined had prepared Primrose for the neglect they found on the farm, and she could tell by the look he gave her that the same thought was in William's mind. The outbuildings had had no upkeep, it seemed, since long before the war. The fences were down, the walls broken. The old man now only kept a house cow and a few hens and ducks.

His wife took Primrose into the farmhouse. It was shabby and neglected here, too, but in spite of the outward appearance there was a happy, lived-in atmosphere to it that was almost tangible.

'You'll like it here, love,' the old woman said.

'I'm not...'

'It's a house for young people, for families growing up. We've been happy here.'

'I can tell,' Primrose said.

'There's a lot to be done,' the woman continued. 'I'm not saying there isn't, both in the house and on the farm. It's a challenge right enough. It needs somebody young and strong, who isn't afraid to make a new beginning.'

The men came into the house.

'Now we'll leave you to discuss it, while I make a cup of tea,' the woman said. 'Come along, love!' She took her husband's arm and led him out of the room. Primrose joined William where he stood, looking out of the window.

'Look!' He pointed to the wide meadow which sloped away from the house.

'It's an empty field,' Primrose said. 'Though I don't doubt you see it filled with grazing cattle, or piled high with hay!'

'I'm going to take it, Primrose,' William said. 'The land is fertile. I can really do things here. It's what I want.' He turned away from the window and faced her, took her hands in his.

'Primrose...Please...?'

She disengaged herself, walked around the big room, looking at it as though she, too, saw something which was not yet there. Then she came back to William, stood on tiptoe and put her arms around his neck.

'Do you know,' she said, 'that newly-married couples can get dockets to buy furniture?'

## A Matter Of Time

She lay in bed in the still, early morning, the light beginning to creep into the room down the sides of the blind. The new day seemed reluctant to appear, as if it was being dragged unwillingly from the dark night and would prefer to return, as would she, to a few more hours of oblivion. But she knew she had come to the end of her sleep, in this country which was strange to her, where the clock on the bedside table showed a time which did not accord with her body.

The room was small, the bed pushed close to the window. She put out an arm and reached for the blind. At first it resisted her unfamiliar tugging, refusing to cooperate with this stranger who did not know its little ways and then, perversely, and with a noise like the stutter of machine-gun fire, it shot away from her and rolled itself up, revealing the outside world. For a moment she was afraid that the sudden noise, the influx of light, would awaken Martin, and that his impatient mood might still be upon him; but he did not stir in his sleep and the

regular rhythm of his breathing remained un-
broken. But then America was his country.
Even after so long in England he had, from the
very first day, settled back into it.

She wondered, fully awake now—though
with the feeling that no one else in the world
was—how far the trouble between them was ac-
centuated by the fact that they seemed to be
inhabiting two separate areas of time. When her
body clock had adjusted to his, for it was she,
the stranger in a strange land, who would have
to make the adjustment (and why was it taking
so long?) would the rest of their lives then come
together? The differences between them which
in England had seemed not to matter now
whittled away at their marriage like a chisel
carving into wood. How long before what had
seemed a strong tree would be as fragile as a
twig which would snap when a storm came?

Yet she loved him, else why would she so
willingly have come so far, leaving behind a
life—a large family, friends, places—in which
she had been so firmly and happily rooted? But
it seemed not so firmly rooted since a little
disturbing of the soil, a sharp tug (by Martin,
who was strong) and she had been taken from
the ground with no trouble at all.

They had arrived at the house late last night.
It was part of Martin's inheritance from his

354

aunt, this white-painted, weatherboard house and the filling station in the small town four miles away, and it was difficult to tell which of the two had most strongly lured him back here. Perhaps neither. Perhaps only the place itself, for Edburton was his home. He had been born and raised here, only to break away in a moment of discontented independence from everything that was familiar. At that time even New York City was too near, and he took the plane for England. But when his aunt, who was the last of the Manstons, died, he knew he had to come back. There had always been Manstons in Edburton.

Driving from Manhattan, where they had stayed only long enough to buy a second-hand car, she had been surprised by how quickly the noise and dirt had given way to the green, tree-covered hills of New York State, the road high and curving above the Hudson River so that the boats below looked like toys. But darkness had fallen with a swiftness which still surprised her and, when they had turned off the express-way, the narrow rutted road leading to the house was illuminated only by the car head-lights which picked out the slender trunks of trees, crowding against the side of the road, and an occasional startled animal.

Now that the daylight had come, and was

all the time growing brighter, she observed that the trees came almost up to the house, only a stretch of lawn having been cleared to separate it from a dense wood. The trees were so tall that from where she lay they blotted out the sky and seemed to stretch away forever: impenetrable. The silence, too, was complete, not broken by so much as the sound of a bird, though it was not to be believed that all those trees did not provide a habitat for them. Back home she was often annoyed at being awakened by the too-early whine of the milk float, the clanking of milk bottles on the step, the rattle of the letter box when the postman called. She would have been glad to have heard those sounds now. But no one called here. That was for sure. She was utterly alone in an alien world.

But how could she be alone when Martin lay beside her? He was asleep, but surely he must soon waken? Time was passing, and now a pale sun filtered through the tops of the trees, sparkling the dew on the grass around the house. She turned to her husband and lay close against his back, her arms around him, seeking company. But he slept on, oblivious of her body against his, and after a while she got up and went along to the kitchen to make coffee. Struggling with the intricacies of the unfamiliar coffee machine, with its variety of knobs, dials, switches, plugs, she all but gave up, deciding to settle for a glass of milk; but after an alarming emission of steam, gurgles and slow drips the strong dark liquid emerged. She took a cup into Martin.

He was still asleep but she touched his shoulder and he wakened instantly.

'Just look at the time, will you?' he said. 'I have to get going. Lots to do. The filling station first—find out what sort of a mess that's gotten into. Then I have to see the lawyer.'

He sounded happy, energetic, his irritability gone. She would try to match his mood and all would be well.

'I can be ready in no time at all,' she said.

He frowned. 'I hadn't counted on you coming with me. Not today, honey. These things all take up time. You'd have to hang around.'

'I could explore...' she began.

'The supermarket, real estate agent, half a dozen little shops. You'd be through in an hour flat. Depending on what's happening at the garage, I might have to put in a full day there. You'll be OK here, Linda. Find out where things are. Get organized. We brought up enough food from the city, but if there's anything you want, make me a list and I'll pick it up.

It was not things she wanted. It was his presence. Surely he could understand that.

'It's our first day here!' she protested.

'Sure,' he said, his voice sharp. 'And I have a hundred things to do that can't wait. Don't tell me you can't be left alone for a few hours! It's something you're going to have to get used to. But as soon as things are a bit more settled I promise you it'll be different. Until then, you'll just have to stay put. For God's sake, Linda, don't fuss! Not now!'

He drank another cup of coffee, grabbed a bowl of cereal and, with a swift kiss, and a wave of the hand, was away. From the porch she watched him drive down the track, the car quickly disappearing into the trees. The sun had gone and there was a mist; or perhaps it was vestiges of low cloud, since the house was set so high.

Inside the house she went from room to room, opening drawers, peering into closets. Aunt Thomasina had obviously been a lady of methodical habits. Everything was orderly. In the linen chests and the drawers blankets, quilts, tablecloths were neatly folded and stacked. The contents of the store cupboard and larder were logically arranged. Throughout the house all was as clean as a new pin; nothing to be done except perhaps, here and there, a little light dusting.

There was a photograph of Aunt Thomasina on the sideboard. How like Martin she was! Strong chin, dark eyes which looked directly out of the picture into Linda's own. If Martin and I had children, Linda thought, what sort of a mixture would they be? Her own looks, small-featured, grey-eyed, fair, were the opposite of his. But Martin did not want children, at least not yet, not until they had settled into a home.

In England she had been content to wait. She had her job as physiotherapist, often working with children, but in Edburton it was doubtful that she could be employed. Perhaps, she had suggested earlier, she could help in the filling station: serve petrol, anything. But it seemed that old Mr Vincent, who had looked after the place for Aunt Thomasina, had been there for years. One could not take his job away from him. Besides, he could do minor repairs on cars, which was a side of the business Martin thought he would want to build up.

By mid-morning there was nothing left to be done. She sat on the porch, trying to read, watching the blue jays fly from tree to tree, glad of the sight and sound of them for company. Perhaps she and Martin might get a dog;

a large, shaggy dog. She thought a little about what she would name it.

Early in the afternoon the sound of the telephone shrilled through the house. It was Martin.

'There's a lot to do down here,' he said. 'Don't expect me back until six at the earliest.'

Four hours more.

She went out into the garden, though it was not so much a garden as an undulating area of grass with a few shrubs which she imagined had strayed in from the forest. Then the sun came out again and she decided she would go for a walk, though whichever direction she took it must be into the trees. She would not, she thought, gritting her teeth, simply walk down the road and back. She would walk in the woods. From where she stood there were no discernible paths, so she plunged into the woodland at the back of the house, and there found what might, at a stretch, be described as a trail. She kept to it though, scrambling down steep banks, crossing narrow streams; sometimes she lost it for a while.

The forest, she had to admit, was beautiful. Pink and grey lichens grew on rocky outcrops, deep green moss carpeted areas of forest floor; a fungus, bright red as a tomato, sprouted on a fallen tree trunk. In a clearing by a dried-up pond there were many fallen trees, each stump inexplicably sharpened to a point. They were like giant pencils. She thought some primitive tribe must have been at work with tools. It was spooky. She shivered, and decided to turn back, and at first when she turned she lost her sense of direction and set out the wrong way. Then, realizing that she was still climbing when she should be going downhill, she righted herself and in the end, walking quickly, sometimes running—though common sense told her that she was not being pursued—she at last sighted the house through the trees.

'I saw the strangest sight,' she told Martin later in the evening. She had cooked her first meal in the house and now they were sitting by the wood fire which Martin had lit in the wide fireplace. Outside it was growing dark and the tree frogs were croaking. 'All the tree stumps sharpened to points. Pointed branches strewn about, too. Were there Indians there, once?'

Martin laughed. He seemed relaxed, rather than tired, after his day's work.

'Not Indians. Beavers! You must have been to Beaver Dam. They've moved on now. We don't see them any more. If you'd climbed another half-mile you'd have reached O'Hara's pond. It's a fair-sized lake, actually. We can swim there, and watch kingfishers. You *will* get to like it here, Linda, I promise you!'

He put an arm around her and she leaned her head against his shoulder. She wanted to like it. It was Martin's country and she wanted to make it hers also. But could she ever bear the solitude? Beautiful it certainly was, but she needed people.

'Come Sunday,' Martin said, 'I'll take you around a bit.'

Five more days. What would she do with them?

'By the way,' Martin said casually, 'watch out for snakes when you walk in the woods.'

'Snakes?' She felt faint with horror.

'They're mostly harmless and not all that big,' he assured her. 'Also they prefer to move away from you as fast as they can. But keep an eye open.'

She wouldn't need to. Nothing would get her back into the woods again, not without Martin. But next day, having written to her mother, to each of her three sisters, and to two friends, there was nothing else to do except go for a walk. She took her courage, and a stout stick, and went. This time the way seemed easier. The old beaver dam was a familiar landmark and when she decided to turn back to the house she did not lose her way.

Each morning that week she did whatever housework she could find, and wrote letters (in the end to people who were no more than mere acquaintances). Each afternoon she walked. She did not meet any snakes but once she saw, in the distance, what she thought to be a skunk, and felt glad to find the still forest inhabited by more than herself and a few birds. But skunks were not people. They were not even approachable!

Sunday came.

'We'll walk up to Independence Rock,' Martin said. 'You can get the lie of the land from there, see where you fit in.'

If at all, Linda thought, but did not say because she wanted this to be a good day.

They set off down the road, turned into the trees and began to climb. A few hundred yards from the road they passed a house, low and white, similar to their own.

'Do we actually have neighbours?' Linda asked eagerly.

'The house was vacant when I was here last,' Martin said. 'We'll drop by on the way back and find out. Somehow it looks inhabited.'

'It's got to be,' Linda pointed out. 'There's a pair of roller skates on the grass and washing hanging on a line.'

They continued to climb until, at the summit, the hill gave way to a large rock plateau, and the tall trees to low bushes. Below the plateau the ground fell away sharply and ahead and around them the country spread out, mile upon mile, to hills so distant that they were no more than a smudged purple line against the sky.

Linda held up her hand.

'Listen!' she commanded.

'It's a wren,' Martin said.

'Not that, silly! I mean the other sound. It's traffic!'

'Oh sure! It's the expressway,' Martin answered. 'It's actually not all that far from here. But the sound won't disturb us in our house.'

But, Linda thought, when I want to remind myself that civilization still exists, I can come up here.

They sat for a while, Martin pointing out the landmarks, and then he said, 'We'll go back now. It's not much more than fifteen minutes downhill. Then we'll get the car out and maybe go somewhere for lunch.'

As they neared the white house a young woman came out on to the lawn and greeted them.

'Hi!' she said, 'I'm Marge Potter. I saw you going up to the rock. Do you live in the neigh-

'bourhood? Not many people know the rock otherwise.'

'We live at White Barn,' Martin said. 'We just moved in. It was my aunt's house.'

'You mean you're Aunt Thomasina's nephew? I've heard about you. And I guess this is your wife.'

'Linda,' Martin answered. 'You knew my aunt?'

'Sure,' Madge said. 'We've lived here more than a year. I got to know her from the start. She helped me settle in. Look, why not come in for a cup of coffee, meet my husband, Don, and the kids.'

They followed her into the house.

'It'll be great having someone at White Barn again,' Marge said. 'How's everything going?' The question was to Linda.

Linda hesitated.

'Linda hasn't had much of a chance,' Martin said. 'I've got the filling station down at Edburton, as I expect you know. It's taken every minute of my time this week. And so far she hasn't got her own car, though I'm actively looking for one. Then she'll be able to get around.'

'You're looking for a car for *me?*' Linda said.

'Sure! You didn't think I would leave you marooned forever, did you? I meant it to be a surprise, but perhaps that wasn't a good idea.'

'Well in the meantime, Linda, you must let me ferry you around,' Madge said. 'I take the kids to school in Edburton every day. Why not come down with me tomorrow? I could show you the shops—what there are—and we'd be back before midday. Sylvie usually collects the kids in the afternoon.'

'Sylvie?'

'Sylvie Booker. She lives at Oak End House. It's about half a mile away, only you can never see these places for the trees. You'll like Sylvie. I've got friends in Edburton too. I'll introduce you. Look, why don't you two stay for lunch? I've got a pot roast in the oven. There's plenty.'

Linda looked at Martin.

'We'd like that,' he said. 'But some other time. I'm taking Linda out to lunch today, driving around the countryside a bit, looking up a few old friends of mine. You know.'

'I know,' Madge said. 'Well, maybe next weekend. I'll fix it with Linda later on.'

They left soon afterwards, walking back arm-in-arm to the house. The sun was hot overhead but the trees protected them, casting a cool shade.

'Race you!' Martin said suddenly.

They ran up the lane, sprinted across the

grass, jumped the porch steps and flung themselves into the living room, Martin slightly ahead. Linda sat down on the sofa, took off her shoes, put her feet up.

'It was a nice walk,' she said. 'I liked Marge and Don. It's good to be home, though.'

Martin sat down beside her, put his arms around her and turned her to face him.

'Did you mean that?' he asked. 'Did you mean exactly what you said?'

'What exactly *did* I say?'

'You said "home". You used that word. Did you mean it, Linda?'

'Yes,' Linda said. 'Yes, I meant it.'

## Model Of Beauty

It's always like this on a Monday at half-past five. Rush rush. Four tiddly mistakes discovered by Sir in his rotten letter, but must catch tonight's post even though it's taken him three weeks to write it. Correcting fluid dried to a white goo; typewriter ribbon playing up.

If Ms P had a spark of humanity—which no one could accuse her of—she'd let me off early on Mondays. 'I would, Jilly dear,' says she, 'if you were going for a few more typing lessons. Or even 'O' level English. But portrait painting is non-vocational. Nothing to do with your job.'

Which is precisely why I'm doing it. It's the reason why I'm now battling on the bus with my shoulder bag, box of paints, bundle of brushes, packet of sandwiches and a piece of hardboard measuring ninety by forty centimetres. Walking up the hill from the bus stop the board—according to the way I hold it—either obscures my vision or bangs me cruelly on the ankles. Either way it catches every breath of wind and threatens to take off. It will be worse on the way home when the paint is wet.

The sandwiches are because there's no time for a meal. You have to get there early to grab an easel, also to claim a place in the crowded room. Some of the people in my class have squatters' rights on bits of floor. They've been occupying the same spot for about a hundred years and you're in dead trouble if you forget it. There's one man they say has only ever painted right-side profiles in all the years he's been coming here.

But here I am. I've got the easel which is too stiff to adjust in any direction until it decides to give in and falls apart, casting your wet painting on the floor. And I've got my square yard of floor. If the two women in front of me keep still instead of darting backwards and forwards like spiders in a mating dance, I'll occasionally catch sight of the model between their raised arms. If she turns up, which models don't always.

This one does. She's new this week and for my money she could have stayed at home. Fat, fifty, florid and fussy. Fussy? Well, first of all the platform's at the wrong angle. After it's taken four strong men to move that, the chair isn't comfortable. She needs more support for her poor old back. After that the light's in her eyes; no, not that light dear, the other one. Next the chair is too high (she means her legs are too short) so Teacher has to find a box, not too big, not too small, but exactly the right size for a footstool. It's damned cold in here, she says. (She should worry. She *could* have been posing in the nude, which looking at her, God forbid. I haven't got that much flesh-coloured paint.) But to be fair, she doesn't ask Teacher to find a heater, she goes off herself in search of it and comes back twenty minutes later with not only a heater, but a cup of hot Bovril.

'She's a real professional!' the young man next to me says, admiringly. Which turns out to be true, since once she's settled—which means when she's repinned her hair, blown her nose, not-so-surreptitiously undone her bra, draped herself in a woolly shawl and drained the last of the Bovril—she suddenly relaxes and takes up the post.

Relaxes, but remains immobile, not an eyelash moving. So you know you can paint with confidence; that if her nose is full frontal right now, that's where it'll be at the end of the session. Not like the student models we usually have who, without seeming to stir, do a turn through one hundred and eighty degrees in the course of the evening. Which is all right for the two-right-eyes-in-the-middle-of-the-forehead school, but I am more your Renoir or Manet. Sort of.

This young man standing next to me is painting like a fiend: juggling a handful of brushes, squeezing out great blobs of flake white, burnt sienna, costly cadmium red; wielding his palette knife like a chef at the Savoy. When it's time for the break he's white with exhaustion and I offer him a crab paste sandwich.

'Isn't she *marvellous!*' he enthuses. 'The model, I mean.'

'She keeps still,' I admit. 'She's not much to look at.'

'But she's superb!' he cries. 'Absolutely splendid! That huge, drooping bust, the rolls of fat around her stomach, the pouches under her eyes, all those sagging muscles. She's exactly what I like to paint. Oh yes, you can keep your pretty young things!'

Which is a pity, and I hope he's only talking in terms of painting, because already I quite fancy him. He is in every way the reverse of old, fat and flabby, with a drooping bust. About twenty-four and as thin as a park railing.

'Can I look at what you've done?' I ask. He's thrown a cloth over the easel.

'Sorry,' he says sternly. 'I can't bear anyone to see my paintings until they're finished.'

Some of the people in the class are like that:

others prefer the teacher to stand right behind them all the time, admiring every brush stroke.

On the first stroke of nine from the town hall clock, old saggy-boobs stretches, sneezes, starts to scratch the vast area around her middle. She's like someone awakening from a spell. If Teacher kisses her, will she turn into a fairy princess? Before he can try it she has packed her string bag and gone, crying 'See you next week if I'm spared,' as she vanishes through the doorway.

By chance—well almost by chance—the young man and I leave together, and because there's so much to be said about Art we go and have a coffee in the Wimpy. Art doesn't get much of an airing but I learn that he's called Pete, that until he makes his fortune as a painter he's slaving away in insurance, that he doesn't have a steady girlfriend. Also that he lives alone in a flat; well, a flatlet; well, actually, a bedsitter with a kitchen in a cupboard.

Next week the model doesn't arrive. What did I tell you? She has sent a note which Teacher reads out to us. 'I have caught my death from that wicked down draught. All being well I'll see you next week.'

'So I'm going to suggest that we paint each other,' Teacher says brightly. 'Choose your subject! Paint away!'

Everybody starts twisting around like they were doing a square dance, squealing, 'What, *me?*' 'Not old *me?*'

'*You*, Jilly. I shall paint you,' Pete says at once. 'No question!'

What, *me?* Since he is a self-confessed admirer of floppy busts, double chins, piggy eyes, I am more shattered than flattered.

'As you wish,' I say, very cool. 'I won't paint, then. I'll just sit.' That way I can hold in my stomach, present my best profile.

After ten minutes I know why those other models moved. I have a sharp pain in my back and my Mona Lisa smile is slipping. By the end of the evening I need that coffee in the Wimpy.

'Have another,' Pete says. 'I want to ask you a favour.'

What he desires is that every Wednesday I should go round to his place so that he can continue with the portrait. When it's finished he wants to enter it for the end-of-term exhibition. Apart from the sheer physical hell of sitting it sounds like a good idea to me.

Not so to my mother, whose ideas of painters derive from old films about Paris. Women with black hair and low necklines leaning out of upstairs windows.

'A daughter of mine,' she cries, 'flaunting

her body for the public gaze!'

'I shall *not* be flaunting my body,' I assure her. 'It is not to be a nude painting. I shall be wearing my green polo-neck.'

So on Wednesday I sit for two excruciating hours while Pete paints me against a background of cupboard doors and a peony-patterned curtain. Then we relax on the settee. We talk about life: about my deep hatred of Ms P and the tribulations of typing; about Pete's promotion to the Claims department which will enable him to afford a real flat with a bedroom.

Wednesdays prove not to be enough for all Pete has to do on the portrait, so I go on Tuesdays and Thursdays also. Sometimes on Saturdays. Mondays we still go to class. Floppy Flo has been restored to life and actually I'm enjoying painting her. I've grown to love every fatty ounce and her super-droopers are dear to me.

Posing so often for Pete, twenty minutes is about as much as I can sit at a time. For the painting, that is. But it's coming on, Pete says, though he won't let me see it, keeps it covered. I don't insist because I'm not a masochist. Also, I know it could be the end of a beautiful friendship. He's still raving every Monday evening, by the way, about our model's curving contours. With the best will in the world, and breathing out like a pouter pigeon, I can't achieve more than a size thirty-four, A cup. As for my bottom: like two fourpenny teacakes, my mother says.

This idyll can't last, because tomorrow is sending-in day for the exhibition. Teacher has persuaded me to submit my portrait of Gladys the Great and Pete is sending his of me—carefully wrapped in an old bath towel. All I've seen is a square inch of green jumper, knit two purl two, through a hole in the towel.

'I want you to see it hung,' he says, as if we were talking about the Summer Exhibition at the Royal Academy.

Surprise, surprise! They're both accepted; which if you could see mine would convince you that our art school does not threaten the Nation Portrait Gallery.

'Number twenty-seven,' the typed list says. 'Portrait of Jilly. Pete Fenton. Number four, Model with shawl. Jilly Raynes.' There is a little red star on mine which means I've sold it. Thirty-five pounds! It can't be true, I say; but it is. In which case it must be my Auntie Edith.

'Now come along and see mine,' Pete says.

He takes my hand and I can feel that his is trembling as we walk to the other end of the room.

'I hope you'll like it,' he says nervously.

'I shall,' I reply bravely. And if I don't he will never know. I shall fall back on admiring the technique; go on about tonal values, linear composition, all that crap they talk in class. In any case I know it doesn't matter any more. However Pete sees me, if he likes it I like it. We've got more than a few tubes of paint going for us.

The painting hangs in the middle of the end wall, just above eye level. From halfway down the room I catch sight of it and grab Pete's arm. It's quite, quite stunning! I float towards it on a pink cloud. Who is this lovely, slim, raven-haired creature wearing my green polo-neck?

'It's beautiful!' I whisper. 'Oh Pete, it's fantastic!'

'It's you,' he says. 'It's exactly like you!'

'Can I buy it?' I've got thirty-five pounds if Auntie Edith doesn't rat.

He says it's definitely not for sale, not at any price, but adds that he'd be all for an arrangement whereby we could share it. So we've painted the walls of our new flat white, and it hangs over the fireplace.

'To think that we owe it all to Ample Annie,' I say. 'If she hadn't caught her death you'd never have studied me so closely!'

# View From Beacon Hill

She stood on the very edge of the cliff, motionless, her head bent forward as she watched the sea boiling and foaming around the rocks far below. But for the fact that her dark hair streamed out behind her, and her long skirt flapped against her legs in the wind which always blew around the headland, she might have been carved out of the rock.

She stood there a long time. Once or twice, when a giant wave thudded against the rocks, the spray came up and enveloped her, but she made no backward movement to escape it. At one point she unclasped her hands, which so far had been held close against her ribs, and moved them slowly up and down over her abdomen, as if she were stroking the child in her body. Against the noise of the wind and the sea she didn't hear the man who approached her over the springy turf. He moved quietly, not speaking until he had her arm in his firm grasp.

'Please stand back from the edge,' he said. 'The cliff is dangerous here. It ought to be fenced off, and perhaps it will be after it's given way under someone's feet.' He spoke quietly, but with authority. The woman turned her head towards him, but hardly seeing him, as if there was a sea mist between them. Then she resumed her study of the sea.

He kept hold of her arm—she made no attempt to break free—as he followed her gaze. Pink sea thrift grew precariously on the rock face; grey-headed jackdaws, which had always nested in the cliffs at this point, wove erratic patterns through the air. Further out twenty or thirty herring gulls hovered over what must be a shoal of fishes.

She turned again and this time focused on the man: on his sand-coloured hair, blowing untidily in the wind, his dark blue eyes, his finely-chiselled features. The great, the clever, the romantic Gregory Spence.

'I remember you going up to university,' she said. 'I was still at school. It's light years away.'

His going had put her, along with most of her fifth-form mates, off her food for at least three days. They'd presumably recovered. She never had.

'I enjoyed university,' he said. 'Shall I enjoy working for Pembertons?'

'You'll rise to great heights,' she said.

'You're that kind of man. Nothing will stand in your way.'

'*We* will,' he corrected her. 'We'll be together, you and me.'

A great wave broke against the cliff and sent the salt spray drenching over them. Salt water dripped from their hair and skin.

'Look,' he said, 'can't we move back a bit? It's just on high tide. We'll get soaked.'

She shrugged. 'I enjoy watching the sea breaking against the rocks. Each time it's like a battle in a long war. The sea retreats then it gathers strength and comes back fighting.'

'And the rocks withstand it,' Gregory said. 'Come and sit down, Alison. The grass is dry a yard or two back. Tell me what's been happening while I've been away this last term. Sometimes I think I shouldn't have stayed on at university after I'd got my degree. I'm a late starter in a real job.'

She walked away from the edge of the cliff and joined him on the turf, sitting down clumsily because of the weight of her body.

'What *does* happen in Little Fairford? There's a new one-way system around the village since you were home at Easter. Little boys fall in the pond. Marriages go wrong. Respectable, well brought-up young ladies conceive illegitimate babies. All life is here.'

'Stop blaming yourself,' Gregory said gently. 'You're not the first.'

'And I won't be the last. Now where have I heard those comforting words before? From just about everyone. But I'm all of twenty-four and I have heard of the Pill. I wasn't the innocent village maiden betrayed by the Squire's wicked son. So why am I about to produce in ten days' time?' She spoke sharply, pulling blades of grass from the turf, throwing them aside.

'I know it's tough,' Gregory said.

'Tough? Is that how you'd describe it?'

'What's happening about the shop?' he asked.

'My Olde Worlde Aladdin's cave? My necklaces, bracelets, earrings? My coral, amber, jade? It's being looked after by Judith. It being tiny and me being the size I am, I sweep everything off the shelves every time I turn around.'

They sat for a time without speaking. Then she said, 'Did you know that people come up here on to Beacon Hill to make decisions? Did you know that?'

'Not precisely,' he said. 'I know it's always been an important place in the neighbourhood. They lit a beacon here at the time of the Spanish Armada. They've always lit them,

382

haven't they, for times of celebration and rejoicing?'

'They had one for the Coronation,' Alison said. 'I was born that night.'

'I beat you to it,' Gregory said. 'I was carried up here by my parents to see it. I'm sorry to say I don't remember a thing.'

'This place has always been special to me,' Alison said. 'I used to come up here all the time when I was a kid. Every time I had a world-shaking decision to make. Should I have my hair cut short? Should I make it up with Peggy Foster or never speak to her again? Did Tim Barrett really love me? I was always consulting the oracle.'

'Is that what you were doing when I arrived this afternoon?' Gregory asked.

'No,' she said. 'There's nothing left to decide. They await me in the County hospital and *it* is going to be adopted. I shan't see it after it's born. They say it's better that way. It will go to a good home, to people who really want a baby and can give it everything it needs. Oh no, the decisions are all made.'

'You know it's for the best,' Gregory said quietly. 'Afterwards there'll be you and me...a whole new life. We'll be married as soon as you're up and about. That counts, doesn't it?'

'Oh yes, that counts. I just wish...'

'Please don't,' Gregory said. 'Not now. You made your own decision. You gave it a lot of thought.'

Her eyes were on the sea again, watching a coaster passing down the channel. 'Yes,' she said softly. 'I did that.'

When Gregory had heard that she was pregnant he'd wanted her to have an abortion. He hadn't felt able to take on a new career, a marriage and a child. But much as she loved him, wanted to please him, that hadn't been possible for her. For those who wanted it she had nothing against abortion. For herself, to see it through, to have the baby, was something deeply instinctive that she had to do. And the baby—she tried always to think of it impersonally, never as *her* baby—would bring love and happiness to some other family. When it was over, she thought, she would be at peace again. She loved Gregory very much, wanted to marry him.

'Yes,' she repeated. 'I gave it a lot of thought.'

The next day Gregory was on Beacon Hill before her. As she came in sight of the top she saw him sitting there and was pleased. He spotted her and came down to meet her. She was breathless, and glad of his helping hand.

'I hadn't realized the rabbits were back up here. I've been watching them. Did you know?'

'I knew. I haven't been away,' she reminded him. 'Life came to me right here in Little Fairford!' She sighed, wishing she could stop herself making bitchy remarks. It happened all the time now. Were all pregnant women tetchy towards the end? She wished with all her heart that the next few weeks were over; normal service resumed.

On the third day she was at the top of the hill before Gregory. She was really too tired and too heavy to climb the steep hill now, but doing so had become an obsession with her. As long as she was able to make the ascent, stand on the cliff, watch the sea, she was not conquered. She was still in charge. She could withstand whatever beat against her.

It was no longer high tide at this time in the afternoon and the rock pools were visible below the cliff. When she was small she used to explore them with her father: looking for crabs, poking with sticks at sea anemones to make them close up. It was a lifetime ago. Could she really be only twenty-four?

Gregory came, as she had known he would. He'd bought a slab of milk chocolate from the kiosk at the foot of the hill and they sat down to eat it.

'I've been wondering if I'll live to be very old,' she said. 'Seventy or eighty. It'll seem centuries.'

He took her hand, stroked each finger. 'No it won't,' he said. 'We'll be together. We'll have so much to live for that you'll never know where the time went. And you *are* doing the right thing, Alison. I'm sure of that.'

'You mean—since I wouldn't get rid of it—having it adopted?'

'Yes.'

She felt the anger well up in her, drew her hand away from his, rose awkwardly to her feet.

'And what the hell do *you* know about it?' she shouted. 'When have *your* feelings been involved? I don't want your stinking approval! You haven't the faintest idea what you're talking about.'

She was humiliated that she couldn't run away quickly down the hill and leave him there. Tears filled her eyes but she was determined that he shouldn't see them. She walked to the edge of the cliff and looked over, seeing the beach below through a haze of tears. Gregory came after her and put his arm around her shoulders.

'I'm sorry, Alison,' he said. 'And you're

386

wrong about one thing. I *am* involved. I love you. We can do marvellous things together, you and I. You know that.'

'Right now I don't know,' Alison said. 'I don't know how I'm going to feel about anything when this is over.'

That was their last afternoon together before Gregory had to go off on a ten-day training course in the Midlands. He was unlikely to be back before the birth. By the time he returned, she thought, maybe she would be her old self again. Slim, shapely; perhaps more cheerful.

Twice more she climbed up the beacon, and the second time she knew it must be the last. It was too much for her now. She sat there, remembering all the other occasions when she'd brought her troubles to this spot, offered them to the healing of the wind and the sea. She put her hand on her abdomen and felt the baby kick against it: strong, vigorous. She wished Greg were here. She missed him badly. It was almost dark, and turning chilly, when she left.

The next day was clinic day. They were pleased with her at the hospital. 'You won't last until next week's clinic,' the doctor said. Before she left she saw the welfare officer and went over all the arrangements with her.

In fact, she thought some hours later, she might as well have stayed there. It would have saved Judith turning out in the early hours to take her to the hospital. Before morning her baby was born.

Afternoon visiting hours were from two to four, which Judith couldn't manage because of the shop. Alison opened a book and prepared to shut her ears to the conversation of the other women's visitors. There were two other new mothers in the small ward.

Gregory was right beside her before she saw him, bending over to kiss her. His face was a question mark as he pointed to the crib on the far side of her bed.

'I thought...?'

'That I wasn't going to see her,' Alison said. 'I had to make a decision, Greg. Last time I climbed up the hill I thought about everything. The baby...you...I thought about the lot.'

'And?'

'It was when the baby kicked against my hand. Oh, she'd done it a thousand times, but that once was different. I knew I couldn't let her go, Greg. Adoption's a splendid thing. I know that. But that's not for me either. I cancelled all the arrangements next day at the hospital. I'm going to keep my baby.'

Gregory moved around to the other side of the bed, peered into the cot, touched the child's face.

'I knew I was choosing between you and her,' Alison said. 'I'm sorry, Greg. I chose my baby.'

The child waved its hands around in the air and when Gregory uncurled its fingers it clung to him. He looked up and saw the woman in the next bed watching him.

'She's going to be a daddy's girl,' she said. He heard Alison's quick intake of breath.

'You haven't asked me what I'm doing here,' he said.

'So I haven't! Why aren't you in Stoke-on-Trent? Did Judith...?'

'No one told me. I didn't know until I arrived back. I ditched the course because I had to see you, and it was important for me to see you before you had the baby.'

'Why?'

'I wanted to ask you to keep it. For both of us. You see, I realized I wasn't only involved with you, I was involved with her. I couldn't let her go. After all, I am her father.'

'Do you think,' Alison said after a while, 'that they'd let us light a bonfire on Beacon Hill?'

The publishers hope that this book has given you enjoyable reading. Large Print Books are especially designed to be as easy to see and hold as possible. If you wish a complete list of our books, please ask at your local library or write directly to: Magna Print Books, Long Preston, North Yorkshire, BD23 4ND England.

$R$

LT R476su     c.1

Rhodes. Elvi.

Summer promise

TC13,551     $20.95

DEC 3 0 1998